"With the bittersweet but gritty *Railroad Schemes,* Holland returns to the rough-and-ready days of California, when fortunes were lost as casually as they were made. . . . Engrossing and atmospheric, it's an intriguing look at a bygone age."

—*San Francisco Examiner & Chronicle*

"*Railroad Schemes* is a marvelous page-turner involving the coming-of-age of Lily Viner and grand and petty thieves on both sides of the Southern Pacific Railroad's advancing tracks."

—*Minneapolis Star Tribune*

"The only disappointing element of Holland's new historical novel is its pedestrian title. In every other respect—fully realized characters, suspenseful plot, well-integrated historical details, and vibrant local color—it is, as usual, an outstanding example of the genre. . . . Impetuous, unsophisticated Lily is a wonderful creation; her typically adolescent confusion and her love of reading are endearing characteristics. Plenty of rough-and-tumble action, a fine evocation of the various ethnic and social classes who settled the West, and the punch of an ironic ending add up to irresistible storytelling."

—*Publishers Weekly*

"Readers will take great delight in Holland's story of pain, love, and death, featuring train robbers and would-be railroad barons as well as gangs of ordinary men who follow orders if they are not too complicated. . . . There is mystery and suspense here, and even a bit of lovemaking."

—*Library Journal*

Previous Books by Cecelia Holland

Lily Nevada*
An Ordinary Woman
Valley of the Kings
Jerusalem
Pacific Street
The Bear Flag
The Lords of Vaumartin
Pillar of the Sky
The Belt of Gold
The Sea Beggars
Home Ground
City of God
Two Ravens
Floating Worlds
Great Maria
The Death of Attila
The Earl
Antichrist
Until the Sun Falls
The Kings in Winter
Rakossy
The Firedrake

For Children

The King's Road
Ghost on the Steppe

*forthcoming

RAILROAD
SCHEMES

♦ Cecelia Holland ♦

A TOM DOHERTY ASSOCIATES BOOK
NEW YORK

This is a work of fiction. All the characters and events portrayed in this book are either products of the author's imagination or are used fictitiously.

RAILROAD SCHEMES

Copyright © 1997 by Cecelia Holland

A Forge Book
Published by Tom Doherty Associates, LLC
175 Fifth Avenue
New York, NY 10010

Forge® is a registered trademark of Tom Doherty Associates, LLC.

ISBN: 0-812-57900-3
Library of Congress Catalog Card Number: 97-19555

First edition: November 1997
First mass market edition: December 1999

Printed in the United States of America

0 9 8 7 6 5 4 3 2 1

To Vernell, and all the wandering sufis wherever
they may be

◆ Chapter ◆

I

Lily looked through the open door; in there she could see people moving around, she heard them talking. They seemed to be doing something interesting, but before she could see what it was her father grabbed her arm and towed her off along the boardwalk.

"Don't gawk. Carry this." He thrust the black valise at her. "Make yourself useful. Don't hang back, keep up with me."

She clutched the sack full of her books in one arm and held the valise with the other. Her father strode away ahead of her, his saddle slung over his shoulder. Jewell Viner was skinny as a fish bone; the saddle made his shape monstrous. He would yell if she did not follow. She went after him along C Street, the main street of Virginia City, looking eagerly all around her.

Plastered up against the side of Sun Mountain, the city was long and narrow, laid along a steeply sloping ledge that faced east over the Washoe Desert. The sun was just coming up. The fresh young daylight was spilling across the street, shooting up through the alleys; the glass windows on the upper story of the hotel up ahead of them glared back at the rising sun. The wind had died down for a little while and the air was filmy with dust. Across the roofs of the next street down, B Street, she could see a dozen rising wraiths of smoke from the mouths of the mines.

She thought she felt the ground trembling under her feet like a drum. Over all of Virginia City lay a blanket of sound, the clatter and boom and bang of the engines of the mines, an interminable rhythmless crash. Her father had told her that Sun Mountain was made of silver; Virginia City was steadily gobbling it up, bringing out the ore through miles of tunnels and drafts that ran directly under the streets and buildings. Lily imagined the ground beneath her to be holey as old cheese; she wondered why the city didn't just collapse down into the center of the earth.

She went on along C Street, trying to keep up with her father. The buildings she passed were crammed into the narrow space; where on either side of the street the boardwalks ended, the front walls of the buildings began, as if the boardwalk took a right turn upward.

The city was stirring alive. Down below, where the mills were, a horn tooted, and then several. In the building behind Lily a door slammed, and someone called out. A cat stood up on the sill of a window and stretched. The boardwalk filled up with people, mostly men in workpants and boots, carrying picks and shovels and the pails with their lunch. One went by her still buttoning his shirt.

"Keep up, will you?" Jewell shouted over his shoulder.

Lily was looking all around her at the steady tide of people rushing by her. Across the way, a man leaned out a window and emptied a pot into the street. An Indian struggled up the street past her, bent double under a bundle of wood. In the street an empty ore wagon rumbled by. A whistle shrieked almost overhead; out of a doorway rushed half a dozen men, pulling on hats and coats, who hurried off down the street and disappeared into the steady tramp and rush of the crowd.

She trotted a few steps to catch up with her father. Up ahead, in among the general clatter and clang of the city, she caught the sound of hammers banging. "What are they building?"

"Stupid fools," her father said. "It burns down, they build it up again. You'd think they'd give up, leave it the way Nature wants it." He gripped her arm and hustled her along. They passed a gap in the wall of buildings, laced across with a framework of raw lumber. Already the yellow lumber was flecked with grainy black soot. As they went by she watched two men raise a piece of the wall up into place and nail it fast. Through the empty frame she could see the steeply tilting hillside behind. The smell reached her of pitchy green wood.

Her father hurried her around a man sweeping off a section of sidewalk, another opening the door of a barbershop, the red and white pole slowly turning. She was looking around again and not paying attention and when her father stopped abruptly she nearly collided with him.

He was reading a sheet of newsprint stuck up on the barbershop wall. Lily stood on her toes, trying to see over his shoulder. All she could make out were the words SOUTHERN PACIFIC in fat black type. That was the Railroad. Her gaze strayed; beside the newsprint was a poster, illuminated with two dramatic masks.

She lunged toward that, just as her father wheeled away, banging into her so she staggered back. Without seeming to notice he caught hold of her and piloted her on up the boardwalk.

"Damn the Railroad!" he said. "They're wrecking the country. First they done in California and now they're after Washoe."

Lily pushed at his hands, twisting to look back at the poster. "Dad," she said. "Hamlet. Look. There's a play. Shakespeare."

Paying no attention, he crowded her on ahead of him, fuming against the Railroad. "Everything's money, money, money. Used to be a beautiful country. Now it's just money all the time. Damn the Railroad. They'll strangle this country in a steel noose." One hand on her arm, he steered her past several men lying neatly up against the wall of a saloon. "Here's the hotel. Do you remember what to do?" He pulled her to a stop in front of a double door. There had been glass panes once in each wing of the door, but one glass was cracked across and the other boarded over.

"Yes, Dad," she said. She had done it often enough before. Her father was poking around in his pockets, and she turned to look out into the street. "There!" she cried. "There's a woman riding a horse. I don't see why I—"

"No daughter of mine is going to fork a horse. The whole idea disgusts me. I don't even want to think about it." He held out a ten-dollar piece. "Remember, don't say anything about me at all. Don't give our right name, where we're from, nothing."

"No, Dad." She put down the valise to take the money from him. He turned and went into the narrow slit of the alley between this building and the next.

Lily pushed her hair back under her hat; she squared her shoulders, so she would look older, and went in through the double doors.

That took her into the lobby, with its unpainted walls and plank floor seeming as if it had been built yesterday. So early in the morning, the lobby was empty. The walls muted the racket of the mines to a distant thrum. Beyond the wide doorway on her left the barroom was nearly empty, the swamper dozing over his broom, somebody in the back tunelessly singing. She went on to the hotel desk, on her right, and rang the bell.

Through the open door behind the desk, she could see the clerk in the back room playing cards. The bell brought him out. She said, "I want a room. Two beds. In the back, by the stairs." She looked him in the eyes, to show she meant business, and slapped the ten-dollar piece loudly on the desk.

He scratched his nose, his eyes sharp with curiosity. "You're just a child. You alone?"

"Do you have a room or not?"

He studied her a moment longer, and turned the ledger book around toward her. "Can't give you the room by the stairs. You can have the back corner."

"That's all right," she said. She took the steel pen out of the inkwell and wrote "John Smith" on the last line of the book. The clerk gave her a key and three dollars change.

"No parties, card games, or animals in the rooms, no fires in the rooms, out by noon or you pay another day."

She nodded. She knew all that already. "Thank you." He was already going back to his card game. She took the key, stooped for her sack full of books and the little black valise, and went to the stairs. Before she reached the top step her father caught up with her. He had sneaked in the back door.

"Any trouble?"

"No. It was seven dollars." She gave him the change and the key.

"Seven dollars. Last time it was five." He frowned at her, suspicious. "You palming money on me, Lily?"

"No, Dad. Last time was another hotel." She climbed the stairs, her father close behind her.

"He cheated you," Jewell said. "He took advantage of a girl."

"Dad," she said. "It said seven dollars on the sign behind him." She went down the corridor. "I got the corner room."

"I like the room by the stair," he said, on her heels. "You forgot that, didn't you?"

"No, Dad," she said. She stopped by the door and waited while he put the key into the lock. He pushed the door in, and now, before they went inside, before he closed the door on her, she said, "Dad, I want to go downstairs for a while."

Jewell wheeled around toward her. "You're not going anywhere. Get in here and shut that door."

"Oh, Dad, come on." She hung back; if he even hesitated, she could slip away and be gone. "We haven't been in Virginia City for such a long time, I just want to go down and walk around and see the people. Can't I?"

"No," he said. He grabbed her wrist and hauled her into the room. Two iron frame beds with blue plaid covers stood against either side wall, taking up most of the space. Jewell gripped her arm tight. "You're lying to me, Lily. What do you really want to do?" He moved up past her and put his palm against the door and shut it, hard.

"I told you," she said, defeated. "I just want to look at the people." But she knew he wouldn't let her go. She had walked in the front door, rented the room, signed the register, done everything right, and still he would not reward her. She went to the bed by the wall and sat heavily down. She threw her hat onto the floor. "What are we doing here, anyway? Why didn't we just stay in the mountains?"

"Is there somebody you were gonna meet?" He moved up toward her, menacing, his head jutting forward. "Don't lie to me, Lily. I can always tell."

He couldn't. She lied to him all the time and he believed it. She said, "Leave me alone, Dad."

"You're an ungrateful worthless little slut," he said, and whacked her, backhanded, open-handed, across the side of the head. She yielded to the slap so that it didn't hurt. She turned her gaze toward the wall, her throat tightening. Everything in her yearned toward the city out there; she willed herself that way, through the solid wall, into the real world.

"Don't you sulk on me, or I'll really hit you."

"I'm not sulking," she said between her teeth. "I just want to go outside."

He was leaning over her, talking into her ear. "Listen. I'm your father. I'm the most important person in the world to you. I gave you life. I'm always working, getting by, keeping you alive, buying you everything you want and need. All I ask is you be faithful, obey me, and you won't even do that."

"Sure, Dad," she said to the wall. Her cheeks and throat felt hot.

They had been up in the hills for three months, she had seen no one but him, for three months, and now here they were in the city, people all around, houses and stores and theaters, and she couldn't even go for a walk. She foresaw the entire day, maybe their whole time here, spent sitting in this little room, washing out their dirty clothes in a pail.

She had her book, at least. She turned, reaching for the sugarsack on the floor by the bed. Her father slapped at her hand.

"Don't get into that, there's no time for that."

"Time?" she said, surprised. "What's going to happen?"

Jewell leaned down and got her by the arm, pulling her up onto her feet. "You got to keep your mouth shut, right? And stay away from these hardcases."

"Hardcases," she said. Then someone was coming here. Her father made her stand up. He looked her up and down, gave a little fretful shake of his head, and plucked at her shirt, making it hang loosely around her.

"What are you, trying to look like a whore?"

She pulled away from his grip. When he got like this there was nothing to do but stay clear and wait. Maybe he was planning something big, some scheme, some plot; a lot of complicated things going on at once always made him nervy.

"Damn it, stand still." He reached out and pulled her hair down over her face, like a disguise. "Don't say anything, remember? And stay out of the way." Somebody knocked on the door.

Jewell backed off, looking at the door, and then pointed imperatively from her to the bed. She sat down on the bed again. He went to the door and opened it, and two men came in from the hall.

"Well, well. Got here right on time," her father said, suddenly hearty and loud, his face red. "Come on in. Shut the door."

"I'm always on time," said one of the men. "You know Pigeye, here. Who's the girl?"

"My daughter."

The other man was smiling at her, his head bobbing. "Nice to meet ya, miss. I heard Jewell had a daughter."

Jewell said, "Let's keep this between us, understand?"

The first stranger went to the bed by the window, pushed the valise off, and sat down in the shaft of strong sunlight. He threw his hat down. He had shaggy dark red hair, but no beard. He was smiling, as if Jewell amused him, and he said, "Then just between us, whyn't you send her out while we talk business?"

"No." Jewell swung around, his arms out, fencing her into the corner. "She stays here, where I can watch her."

The redheaded man, still smiling, looked past her father at Lily. "You know how to keep your mouth shut, darlin'?"

Jewell swelled, furious, but said nothing. Lily realized he was afraid of this man, who wasn't even very tall or heavy, just an ordinary man in muddy boots and a long coat. Under the coat, she saw, he had a gun on his hip. The other newcomer had gone over by the window; he was pale, balding, what hair he did have pale and limp, his brows and eyelashes too, so that his tiny eyes looked insignificant against the broad pink expanse of his face. Pigeye, his name was. She looked at the redheaded man again.

"I'll be quiet," she said. "I'll read." She cast a quick look at her father and leaned down from the bed for her sack of books. She worked her way back into the corner and opened her new book.

The redheaded man said, "All right, Jewell. This is the deal. You know Cantrell, the silver boss in Pioche? He had a bargain with the Southern Pacific went sour and the Railroad put the arm on him and he had to pay them twenty thousand dollars in silver bullion. The Railroad sent Brand out to Pioche to pick it up—you know Brand?"

"The railroad agent," her father said. Lily turned a page, to keep up appearances. "The crip."

"Yeah," said the redheaded man. "You call him a crip to his face. Anyway, he's bringing the silver on the stage here to Virginia City. Cantrell's offered me six thousand in gold to get it back for him."

Jewell grunted. He sat down on the foot of her bed; the mattress sighed. "Whyn't just take the silver?"

"You want to drag around seventy-five pounds of silver? We can carry six thousand in gold in our pockets. The trouble is Brand."

"Kill him," Jewell said.

Lily licked her lips. She turned another page.

"Trouble is," said the redheaded man, sounding amused again, "is how easy it would be for the wrong people to get killed, him inside the stage, us outside it coming at him all in the open, you know. You know?" The other mattress crunched now. The redheaded man had some kind of accent, some sounds drawled, almost lilting. Now his voice dropped to a purr. "Only, seeing your girl here, I'm thinkin' there's a nice way to manage that."

"What?" Jewell said. Lily put down the book and looked up.

"Can she use a gun?" the redheaded man asked.

"No," Lily said. "I won't hurt anybody. I won't do anything where anybody gets hurt."

The redheaded man turned his attention to her. His mouth still curled, but his eyes were hard and not smiling; the intensity of his look made her uneasy. She realized she didn't like him. She wondered what he wanted her to do. She wouldn't do anything to hurt anybody, but she knew her father needed money.

If they had money, they would stay in town longer.

He said, "The whole point in this is, nobody's goin'

to get hurt. Except the Railroad, and they deserve it. Very likely you won't even have to fire a shot, just look like you're about to. Can you do that?"

"She's in," Jewell said harshly. "She's a good girl, she'll do whatever I tell her."

The redheaded man ignored him, only watched Lily so hard she shifted her weight a little on the bed, getting her feet under her. He said, "If we don't do it this way I'll have to shoot everybody on the stage. You want that on your conscience? Do it my way, nobody gets hurt, we each make two thousand dollars."

Jewell said, "I told you—"

"Shut up," said the redheaded man, watching Lily. "Well?"

She gathered herself, her arms around her knees. Now her father was staring at her, and when he caught her looking at him he nodded twice, hard, a command.

She looked back to the redheaded man. "You have to promise not to kill anybody, even if it goes wrong."

He said nothing for a moment, and she straightened, ready to argue. But his smile widened a little and he nodded. "I promise."

"Then I'll do it. I can shoot."

"Good," said the redheaded man. He turned toward the other two men, drawing them toward him. "Now, pay attention, this needs some timing."

◆ Chapter ◆

II

At midafternoon, the stage from Pioche stopped at the foot of Six Mile Canyon to change teams for the last hard haul up into Virginia City. So far everything had gone without a hitch. Brand got out to stretch his legs, the while keeping an eye on the only other passenger, a drummer in a bowler hat, who bounded off as soon as the wheels stopped rolling and headed for the tent saloon.

Powell, the shotgun guard, climbed stiffly down from the box; he took off his hat and beat the road dust out of it. "We made it. Ain't nobody gonna take us on this close." He glanced at Brand beside him. "Buy y'a drink."

"In Virginia City," Brand said.

"Suit y'self." One shoulder kinked, Powell hobbled painfully away after the drummer. Maybe he had piles.

Brand circled around the coach to walk his stiff legs loose again. In the distance he could hear the roar of Virginia City, like the thunder of storm that never broke. Being this close was no guarantee of anything. Still, he thought Powell might be right, for once: they had moved quickly, and few people even knew about the silver. He came around the front of the coach, where the driver had unhooked the team and led the horses away, and stepped across the whiffletree and leaned up against the wheel.

He looked out over a collection of shacks and tents tucked down in an angle of the hillside, out of the constant vicious wind. Once a stand of cottonwoods had grown here, now nothing was left but a few chewed stumps. Mining claims pocked the bars and side canyons all around, but a lot of the miners seemed to be going after easier loot than silver: the tent where they sold liquor was packed. The side walls rolled up in the midday heat. The solid block of shadow under the peaked roof churned and waved arms and shouted. The roof itself sucked and bellied in the wind.

The stage office was an unpainted wooden cube glorified by a high warped false front. A web of ropes held the false front upright against the whims of the Washoe zephyrs. Everything was covered with a grime of yellow dust. Half a dozen men clogged the roofless porch of the stage office, gawking and chewing and spitting and calling out to the driver as he brought out the fresh wheelers and settled them to their harness. Brand shifted his weight against the side of the coach, wanting to get going.

A tall slender girl came out of the stage office, clutching a ticket and a lumpy sugarsack. At her appearance all the men stopped talking and stared at her. In the harsh dusty sunlight she stopped a moment to draw her sack up onto her shoulder and look around her. She wore a long ruffled dress that looked way too large for her; a gaudy tasseled shawl was wrapped around her shoulders. On her feet, like some kind of joke, were heavy muddy man's boots. She had no hat; she put her hand up to shade her eyes from the sun.

She was tanned like a boy, and her eyes were large and dark. She looked around her with a burning eagerness, as if she expected to find her life's desire somewhere in this desert. Brand could not take his eyes from her. Tall and slim, she was beautiful, he thought, as a young birch tree, an idea that startled him. It was not her looks that fascinated him, but the passionate eagerness in her eyes.

He was working, he reminded himself. He looked elsewhere. The driver came up beside him.

"Ain't that pretty, now? And she's all ours."

Brand's attention snapped back to the girl. "She's coming on this coach? Not if I can stop her."

"Hey," the driver said.

The girl was looking around; she saw the driver and held out her ticket uncertainly. "Is this the stage to Virginia City?" Her voice was high and light. Brand tried to guess how old she was: sixteen, seventeen, maybe even younger. He wondered what kind of family she had, who let her travel around by herself. The other men were eyeing her in ways that made Brand want to knock a few of them in the face.

"Yes, miss," the driver was saying. He reached for her ticket. Brand barged up in between them.

"Look, miss, you can't take this coach."

"Come on, Brand," the driver said. The girl stepped back, startled, and frowned at him.

"I have a ticket. I have to go to Virginia City, I have a sick uncle there."

"You're going to have to wait," Brand said.

"Why?" she said.

The driver said, "Come on, Brand, the next coach is tomorrah. You're gonna leave her here alone overnight?"

Brand shook his head; he knew there was no place for her to stay here. "How'd she get here?"

The girl stepped forward, all the fire of her look fixed on Brand. "I have to go to Virginia City. I have a ticket. I'm taking this coach." Pushing the ticket into the driver's hand, she went to the coach door.

Brand reached out his right arm and put his hand on the door latch, barring her way; he glanced past her, saw everybody watching, and lowered his voice to just over a whisper. "You don't understand. I can't tell you why, but you could be in danger."

She said, "Let me on the coach."

He gave up. Stubborn bitch. "Just don't get in the way." He pulled open the door for her.

"Thank you," she said with enormous dignity. She climbed on board, and her foot slipped on the iron step. Brand, holding the door with his right hand, put out his left arm to catch her.

"Thank you," she said again, nicer, and then she caught sight of the stump that ended his arm. She blushed and jerked her gaze away, and scrambled the rest of the way into the stage. The drummer had come out of the saloon and now hustled along after her, with Brand still standing there holding the door with his right hand and feeling stupid. The driver climbed up onto the box.

Brand stepped back, looking toward the saloon. "Where's Powell?"

Mac, the driver, was settling himself on the box. "Oh, he'll be out in a minute."

They waited. The shotgun guard did not come out of the saloon. Brand said something under his breath and strode across the yard to the tent. Pushing and shoving his way through the press of bodies, he found Powell in the back, slumped against the side of the ore wagon that served as a bar.

"Come on," Brand said. "We're going."

"Go without me." Powell raised a chipped cup full of whiskey. "I'm done for the day."

"The hell you are," Brand said. He reached out and took the cup out of Powell's hand and tossed it over the ore wagon. "You're getting on up on that coach and riding shotgun all the way to Virginia City."

Powell wheeled toward him, swaying a little; he was taller than Brand by some inches. Their eyes met. After a moment Powell's gaze wavered. He turned away and walked toward the nearest open wall of the saloon. Brand followed just behind him.

"They ain't paid me in a month," Powell said over his shoulder.

"You do your job or they won't pay you at all." Brand herded him to the coach and watched him scale the side up to the box. Mac the driver grinned down at him and unwrapped the leather ribbons of the reins from the brake handle sticking up beside his knee.

Brand got into the passenger seat, next to the girl, and pulled the door closed. Almost at once the coach rolled off. Glad to be moving again at last, he tried to loosen himself up. Before sundown they would be rolling down C Street. The job was nearly over.

Not over yet. He paid attention to the other people in the coach. The girl had pressed herself into the angle of the seat, with her sugarsack between her and Brand, and was reading a book. Brand tipped his head a little, trying to make out what was on the spine; the only word he could see looked like *brunt*.

The drummer sat opposite her; Brand had hoped he would be staying back at the mining camp and was annoyed to find him here again, jouncing along in the stage. Brand braced himself on the flat hard bench. There was no comfortable way to sit. He turned his face toward the window and watched the country roll by.

They rattled down out of the wash and forded the river. The land here was hilly and the road did a lot of twist and turn. The winter rains had ended and the sage had bloomed and died back; the whole country seemed to be fading away, dull as dust. Brand caught himself rubbing the palm of his hand over his stump. He could not settle himself on the seat. He noticed how the drummer, round and red-faced, was watching the girl; the drummer's mouth curved into a grin like a Toby jug. Suddenly he leaned toward her.

"You hear me? You the prettiest thing I seen all year." He reached out to pat her knee.

The girl recoiled from his touch. She gave the drummer a hard look and went back to reading. Brand hoped she remembered what he had said to her. She needed a lesson and he decided against helping her out right off. If it got bad he'd stop it.

"Now, that's not friendly," the drummer said. "Seems to me, a man gives you a compliment, you should at least say thank you."

"Thank you," the girl said, her nose in her book. She rummaged in the bulky bulging sugarsack, found a pocket watch, and looked at it. When she turned back to her book, she kept the little round watch in her hand.

The drummer craned his neck. "What time is it?"

"One-fifteen," the girl said, without looking up from the book.

Brand gave a snort of amusement. The watch was off by hours, or she was deviling the drummer.

"Well, thank you," the drummer said. "Thank you kindly, little miss, and you don't mind me saying so, you're pretty as a prairie rose." His hand stole slyly toward her knee.

The girl swiped at him. "Stop touching me." She glanced at Brand, who did nothing; he had warned her. He could see she was terrified, pressing herself as far back into the corner as she could get.

"Now, now," the drummer said, drawing his hand back. "I didn't mean no offense, miss. No offense at all." She was reading again, or pretending to, but Brand could see the sheen of her eyes. Under the brim of the bowler the drummer sneaked a look at Brand, sizing him up, and when he made no move, turned back to the girl.

"When we get to Virginia City, I know some real fancy places." He put out his hand again toward her. "I'd surely like to take you places, little miss."

The girl lifted her book and hammered at his hand with it. With a squeal he jerked back his arm, glanced quickly at Brand, and grabbed hold of the book and wrenched it out of her grip.

"Let me have that! What's so—"

Brand reached out and snatched the book away. "All

right, pin-peddler. I've had enough of you. You say one more word to her, I'll throw you clean off this stage while it's still moving."

The drummer let out a yelp; with a whine of indignation he scrambled along the seat out of Brand's reach. "Whyn't you mind your own business?"

"Miss." Brand twisted around toward her, saying, or beginning to say, "Do you want me to throw him off the coach?" but he only got half the words out. The gun in her hand stopped him. It was a big Remington .46, looking in her slender light-boned hand like a cannon.

He said, "Now, come on, miss, he won't hurt you," and the gun moved to point at him.

The girl said, "Give me my book." Her voice was tight as a strung wire.

Brand's jaw dropped open. He still had the book in his hand; the gun was aimed at his wishbone. Her voice was light and high like music, but under the wings of her brows her eyes blazed.

He said, "Now, come on, miss, you know you aren't going to shoot that thing," putting his hand out slowly to take the gun away from her.

She shot; in the confines of the stage the report stunned his ears. He never saw where the bullet went. The drummer whined and wrung his hands together, cowering down on the opposite bench.

"Give me my book!" The girl reached past the leveled gun and plucked the book out of Brand's grasp.

From outside and above the front of the compartment there was a quick hammering, and Powell called, "Hey, Brand! What's going on?"

Brand said, "Now, look, girl, whatever you think you're doing—"

The drummer whimpered. "Sweet Mother of God. How did I ever get into this?"

Powell pounded on the compartment again. "Hey, Brand?"

The girl said, "Don't move, or I'll blow your brains

out." She glanced at her watch again. She was crazy, Brand thought. There was a high shrill note in her voice, and her eyes shone. His back tingled. No telling what a lunatic might do.

He shouted, "Keep going, Mac, Powell, I'll handle this!" He leaned toward the girl, keeping his voice even and hard. "Put the gun down. You're getting yourself a whole lot of trouble."

"Shut up," she said, "and sit still."

The coach slowed, leaning around a bend, then suddenly jerked to a stop with a lurch that threw him off balance. He grabbed the window frame to catch himself. The fist thundered on the compartment above his head. "Hey, Brand, the road's blocked."

He froze, staring at the girl, putting all this together now. The drummer twitched, and the girl shot his bowler off, without even seeming to look. She said, "Get out. Now. You first." With the octagonal muzzle of the Remington she jabbed at Brand. "Keep your hands up!"

"Hey, Brand," Powell called.

Brand slid back across the seat, until he could see out the window, and looked. They had been rolling up Six Mile Canyon; here the gorge narrowed, the banks high and stony on either side. Craning his neck, he could see a long jumbled pile of rock blocking the road in front of the stage. He faced the girl again, her level, implacable gaze; the drummer was sobbing on the other seat.

"You can't get away with this," he said. He began inching his hand along his thigh, toward the gun on his hip. "There's a man with a scattergun on the box." He realized Powell was probably worthless. He wondered if he himself would shoot a girl.

He had to. It was his job.

Outside, from the top of the bank, a voice yelled, "You with the shotgun! Throw it down or I'll blast you!"

"Please," the drummer whimpered. "Please."

Brand heard something hit the ground, just outside the window, and looked; Powell's shotgun was lying in the dust. Over his head, abruptly, there was the loud thud of somebody jumping onto the roof. He wondered how many robbers there were.

"Get!" the girl said. "Now!"

Brand gave up; they had him cold, this time. He pushed the coach door open and got out. As he stepped away from the coach the drummer rushed out behind him and sat down abruptly in the dust. "Holy Mary Mother of God," he said.

Brand glanced at the top of the stage, but all he could see was the back of the man who was going through the baggage. Mac sat slumped in the box, the reins slack in his hands. Beside him Powell had both hands up in the air. Brand swung around to look at the top of the bank of the gorge.

There, half sheltered behind a rock, was a man in a long duster, a bandanna over his face and a shotgun aimed down into the road. He said, "Keep your hands up. You, One-Hand, throw your gun down." Brand squinted at him, trying to pick up something to recognize him by; slowly he took the pistol from inside his coat, stooped, and laid it on the ground.

"Kick it."

Brand put his foot to the gun and moved it a little way down the road. The girl got out of the coach beside him and his eyes switched toward her. His temples throbbed. She looked so small, so harmless. He was going to catch hell for this.

"It's not here," said the man on the coach roof.

"It's there." A third man, this one on horseback, rode around the rear end of the coach. Like the man with the shotgun, he had a bandanna covering his face. "Keep looking," he said to the man on the top of the stage.

"There's nothin'! And no more place to look."

The rider went up beside the girl, who turned and held the Remington six-gun up to him. Brand lifted his head an inch, his gaze hard on the rider. He knew this man, masked or not. His temper flared. He said, "I might have guessed this was your game, King. Using a girl."

The horseman swung around; the Remington in his hand lined up straight at Brand's chest. Brand sucked in his gut. Above the edge of the bandanna the robber's pale eyes glittered, and Brand saw that he was going to kill him.

The girl launched herself across the space between them. "No!" She spread out her arms, shielding Brand from the man with the gun. "You promised me. No killing."

Behind the screen she gave him, Brand dove for his pistol in the dirt. The rider bounded down out of the saddle and knocked the girl out of the way. The muzzle of his gun thrust into Brand's face. Brand knelt in the dirt, his hand outstretched, the pistol just beyond his reach. An inch from his nose, the bore of the Remington looked big enough to crawl into. He lifted both arms up and slowly straightened, and the muzzle of the other man's gun stayed level with his nose the whole way.

"Good," said King Callahan. He pulled down the rag of his mask. His eyes were snake's eyes, hard and cold even though he was smiling. He said, "I know I'm going to regret this, but I did promise her. Sit down by the wheel there and put your hand on your head, and the other arm let hang."

Brand went to the rear wheel of the coach and sat down. The drummer came over and sat next to him. The man on top of the coach was looking over the edge and whistled.

"You ain't gonna kill him?"

King said, "Find that silver."

"It ain't here, I'm telling you."

King did not take his gaze from Brand. "You think he's along for the air? Break up the coach." He turned and spoke to the man on the bank above him. "Come on, help him. Get inside, break up the seats."

Brand's stump tingled and throbbed. He wished King had killed him. He would never live down being taken by a girl; he'd have to hear all the old jokes all over again.

The outlaw on the roof swung down into the coach. A moment later, wood broke with a splintering crunch. The horses spooked forward a few steps and the wheels rolled. The driver lifted his hands; on the bank, the man with the shotgun stopped on his slow way down and wagged his gun in a warning.

Inside the coach came a yell. "Here it is!"

Brand threw his head back. He gave an oblique, angry look at King Callahan. "That silver belongs to the Railroad. You take it, we'll get you, if it takes the rest of the century."

"Well, hell, Brand," the outlaw said, "I'm pleased to give you something to do." His faint brogue curled the edges of the words. The strongbox sailed out the door and hit the dust; it was so heavy it dug a hole into the hard-packed road.

"That's the elephant," said King. "Come on out, let's get out of here."

The other man jumped out of the coach; the man carrying the shotgun came down the bank with some speed now and helped drag the chest away up the road, behind the stage. King spoke to the girl, who was standing beside his horse holding the reins. "You leave anything inside?"

She gasped. "My books." She dropped the reins and dashed into the coach, reappearing at once with her sugar sack. King swung up into his saddle and holstered his pistol. Brand twitched; but the man in the duster had reappeared by the back of the coach and stood watching him. The girl handed her sugarsack up to King and he hung it by the string loops from his saddlehorn and leaned down, reaching for her. She gripped his arm and he drew her smoothly up to sit demurely sidewise behind him: a joke, like the muddy boots. A joke on Brand.

Brand stared past her at the outlaw. "You're dirt, King. Using a girl like this."

The rider swung his horse around; the girl clung to his belt. "You keep talking," he said. "I'll just spend the money." His horse bounded away up the road.

Brand darted across the dirt to his gun. The driver said, "Hell's bells, Brand, don't get yourself killed." Brand ran back past the rear of the coach, out into the broad and empty road.

There was the long fresh dent the strongbox had made as it was dragged over the ground, a carpet of fresh hoofprints, nothing else. He ran up the road a hundred yards, looking up at the high bank on either side, and then stopped and held his breath. All he heard was the wind keening off the rocks.

The strongbox. That was heavy: they wouldn't travel far before they did something about that box. That gave him somewhere to start, anyway. He put the pistol into its holster under his coat and jogged back toward the stagecoach.

Powell was standing by the coach. He said, "They got the drop on us. Wasn't anything we could of done."

"You could try staying sober," Brand said to him. He went to help Mac the driver haul the jumble of rocks and boulders off the road. "And I'm not done yet."

◆ Chapter ◆

III

Lily Springbreeze Viner was fifteen years old, and she had never had a home.

She could not remember her mother. When she asked her father about her, Jewell got angry and sad and wouldn't tell her anything, and she had begun to think maybe she had never had a mother, but only Jewell.

All her life, she and her father had drifted from place to place, putting up sometimes alone in the wild, sometimes in the tents and shacks of mining camps, sometimes in cities, in hotel rooms, in the backrooms of saloons and brothels, once in a graveyard. Her father was a gambler and a robber. He had taught her to shoot, but he would not let her ride a horse. He made her do robberies, but he wouldn't let her go to school.

She knew that most people did not live like this. She saw ordinary people often enough, but only from the outside; she never got to know them. She knew the other way of life best from her books. She liked novels: the girls in those stories lived in houses and visited other people in their houses, large and beautiful houses with furniture, that had belonged to the family forever. They danced. They gave plays in their living rooms. They rode in carriages and walked in gardens. They played cards, like her father, but nobody ever got shot. There were no fistfights. Nobody got drunk. The girls worried mostly about getting married, and they always did, although that outcome seemed doubtful for most of the book. None of them ever carried a gun. None of them washed pots, or cooked bannock, or wrung out her own underwear. Much less her father's underwear. She longed with all her heart to be a girl in one of Jane Austen's books.

Right now she was changing her clothes in a storage shed tacked onto the back wall of the same hotel in Virginia City where she and Jewell had met King and Pigeye. The books were in their sack beside her on the storeroom floor. Once she got dressed she could read a little. Here the light was bad, but it was better out in the middle of the storeroom, where the men were. Standing on one foot, she stuck the other into the leg of her pants. She had hated the loose, sloppy feel of the long dress; she was glad to get back into her own clothes.

She could hear the men's voices out there in the middle of the storeroom, but the crates and barrels piled up around her gave her a little privacy. Near the sloping ceiling a tiny window showed, nearly blocked behind the boxes. The daylight was fading. In a few minutes, with lots of money, they would go off and find something good to eat. For a while, her father would be in a wonderful mood.

The man from Pioche, whose silver they had recovered, had finally come in. She went around the stacked crates toward the middle of the storeroom; she had never seen a silver boss before, although of course she had heard stories.

The light came from a single lamp suspended from the rafter. The men were standing directly under it, the strongbox in their midst.

"Pretty good deal," said the man from Pioche. He was short and fat and had a big belly. She was disappointed; she had expected someone more imposing. "Six thousand dollars in gold for twenty thousand dollars in silver."

"I'm content with it," said King Callahan.

"Yeah, well." Jewell Viner leaned forward over the strongbox. "I'm not. I say we should get more."

King's head snapped up. Lily watched him narrowly. King scared her. After promising her he would kill no one, he had nearly killed the one-handed man. Now his voice grated, the drawling accent stronger. "I told you we'd each make two thousand. You didn't complain then." He nodded at Lily. "There's your girl. Let's go. We got to move out of here, this is taking too long."

Jewell said, "I'm going to get what's due me."

Lily gritted her teeth. She thought: Come on, Dad. Let's get the money and just go. She cast a glance at the nearby door, which led into the hotel. He had said they might stay in another hotel tonight, a fancy one, with carpets and mirrors and people who brought you things. Her father tramped toward her, his eyebrows kinked over his nose. He was breathing hard, as if he had been fighting.

"Come on," he said to her. "You ready?"

She said, "I have to get my shoes on."

She went back into the little hollow among the crates where she had changed her clothes. Her father followed her. She lowered her voice to a whisper.

"I hate them, Dad. We don't need them, let's go."

"Damn him," Jewell said. "Damn him!"

Lily stuffed her dress-up clothes into the space between two crates and sat down to put her boots back on. Her father's jumpiness worried her; he did bad things when he was like this. Even in this tiny space he was pacing back and forth, and now he bolted out to the middle of the storeroom again. She gathered up her coat and her sack of books and followed him.

The shed was slapped up against the hotel; besides the door going inside, there was another opening out to the alley, through which the man from Pioche was now leaving. He had a helper with him, to haul the strongbox full of silver. When he was out, Pigeye shut the door behind him. Under the hanging lantern in the middle of the room, on an overturned crate, King was dividing gold money into stacks. He was in a hurry, every move spare, compact; he didn't even count the coins, but just leveled the stacks.

Jewell said, "Should be four, given as Lily did most of the work."

King said, "We agreed on three."

"Yeah, well, I changed my mind."

King straightened. He had lost his smile. "We agreed on all this beforehand. Don't front up on me, Jewell, I'll make you sorry."

"Dad," Lily said. "It's all right." She went up behind her father and put one hand on his arm. He flung her violently off.

"I don't agree to anything that's losing me that kind of money!"

King glanced at Lily. His face was expressionless. He reached for his coat, which was slung over a box behind him, and put it on; he carried a gun in a holster slung under his left armpit and he reached inside to adjust it. His gaze flicked toward Lily again and back to Jewell. "This way we're out quick and easy. Or we would be if you'd shut up. Take your money, let's go."

Jewell shouted, "Not until I get what's due me!" With a wild swing of his arm he swept the stacks of money off the table into the dirt.

"You stupid son of a bitch!" King dropped to one knee and grabbed with both hands for the money in the dust. "Get it yourself, then, you bastard!" He crammed money into his pockets; Pigeye started forward from beside the back door to gather up the fallen coins. Lily moved away, her breath short. Her father was standing back from the scramble, his eyes glaring and his lips drawn back from his teeth. His hand was on his gun. She held her breath, afraid of what he would do next.

"Dad, come on, let's go."

Then, behind her, so loud she jumped, came a thunderous banging on the hotel door.

"You in there. Come out with your hands up!"

All the men whirled around. Jewell gawked at the hotel door; his eyes looked all white. Without a word, he spun around and plunged toward the opposite door, which led into the alley. Lily started after him. King yelled, "No!" but Jewell threw the door open.

In from the outside darkness like dragon tongues licked two streaks of red flame; the double blast packed Lily's ears and set them ringing. Jewell staggered back. His eyes were wide and popping, and his mouth gaped. Lily screamed, "Dad!" Between her and Jewell, King reached up overhead to the lamp; suddenly the room was thrown into darkness.

"Dad!"

Lily started blindly forward, toward where she had seen her father fall. In front of her guns crashed, the red muzzle flashes licking through the dark. Then somebody ran into her and spun her around.

"Come on! Climb! Get to the window, quick!"

The hand on her back propelled her around toward the wall. Still clutching her coat and the sack of books, she scrambled up the irregular stack of the crates toward the window. Below them a swath of light leaped into the room. The hotel door was opening. The man climbing after her wheeled, sticking out his gun, and shot into the light-filled opening. Another shotgun blast bellowed in the dark beyond the crates. Lily's foot slipped on something loose and it tumbled toward the floor. At the top of the wall she reached the little window, covered with oiled paper; she had to duck her head because of the ceiling.

King slid past her. With one hand he smashed out the paper window, pushed himself headfirst into the opening, and eeled through. "Come on!" he shouted. She stuck her head and shoulders through the window, out into the cold clear air, ten feet above the alley.

Below her men milled around in the alley; as she came out, one was pointing up, and the others were turning to see.

"Lily!" King shouted, above her. "Up here!" From the roof above her a gun roared, twice, three times. The men below her scattered, yelling. Half in and half out of the window frame, she twisted to sit up, reaching up toward the eave above her. With his free hand King gripped her wrist and hauled her onto the roof. Pigeye came after her, his harsh breath panting loud in her ears.

Lily got her feet under her. "My father," she said, looking back.

King grabbed her arm. "Run!" He towed her across the sloping roof.

She clutched her books and her coat; her feet slipped and slid along the shingles of the roof, and only his grip on her arm kept her from falling. Her father. Where was Jewell? She turned her head to look back, half thinking he would be coming after them. To her left, down below the edge of the roof, the haze of streetlamps glowed, and she heard someone shouting, "Up there! Up there!"

A cold fear rushed over her. She turned forward. King was still towing her along by the arm and he pulled her to a stop at the edge of the roof. Just beyond her toes a chasm yawned, a gap of five or six feet between her and the flat expanse of the next roof, behind a square false front. The wind thrust into her face. The monotonous thundering of the city machine banged in her ears. Pigeye was pounding after them. In the street the excited uproar sounded louder and harsher.

King yelled, "Jump!" and pushed her.

She leaped toward the next roof; he gave her an extra boost as she went, and she lost her balance and landed flat on the roof, the books under her. A moment later he was landing next to her. She got up, looking back again.

"My father."

"He's dead, girl. Believe me." King got up, stooping, bent-legged, and took off across the roof.

Pigeye rushed past her after him and she got up and followed them to the far side of the top of the building. Across a narrow space another building loomed, a story higher than this one, a wooden stair going zigzag up the side. King flew across the narrow crevice of the alley and landed sprawled across the railing of the stairs.

Lily leaped after him and landed on him. All the breath popped out of her. They were hanging across the railing, their legs dangling over the alley: they would slip and fall; they would die. She dove forward, over his head, onto the safety of the stair landing.

He rolled himself over the rail and got up, gasping for breath. "Thanks," he said to her. "Next time, don't lead with the goddamn books." He bolted up the stairs. Pigeye came hurtling through the air and slammed into the railing just beside Lily, and she ran away from him up the stairs after King.

As she went, she fought one arm through a sleeve of her coat. Behind them, people shouted. A gun barked. Halfway to the top of the stair King was diving in through an open window.

Inside a woman screamed. Lily paused long enough to get her other arm into the coat, bent her head, and stuffed herself into the square space of the window frame.

The room beyond was dark, but inside it a strange man's voice was shouting, "What is this? What is this?" She scrambled in through the window. A far door opened and she dashed toward the faint glowing wedge of light.

She stopped. Her father. She turned to go back, and somebody grabbed her arm and dragged her along through the door. Outside was only a stair landing, dimly lit from below, and piled up with old wooden chairs; King let go of her and ran straight across to another door and threw that open.

Pigeye was coming after her. Lily followed King into a darkened room. Somebody yelled, "Hey! Hey!" Ahead of Lily a piece of the dark peeled away from a square of faint light, which King's head and shoulders immediately filled. Lily scrambled up onto something in her way. She wobbled over something soft, which twisted under her feet and shrieked, and knew she was walking on people. She scrambled headfirst out the next window.

There was nowhere to go, no stair, no landing, a three-story drop to the ground. She climbed out onto the narrow sill, clinging to the frame. In the dark she could not see King. Pigeye, behind her, shouted, "Go on, damn it!" She saw the next roof, lower than this one, and leaped.

This roof tilted; she hit the slope and rolled; King caught her. He grabbed for the sack of books. "Drop 'em, damn it! Come on!"

"No!" She bundled the sack of books to her chest. He turned and ran, and she struggled after him, her breath like a fiery liquor in her lungs. He ran down the roof to the back edge and jumped. Lily, sliding after him, simply fell.

She sank to her knees into a pile of garbage and dead leaves. The back of the building came up nearly flush against the mountainside; the space she stood up in was no wider than she was. She leaned on the wooden wall, gasping for breath. Pigeye crashed down next to her. At her feet, barely visible in the dark, King was stooping, pulling trash and leaves out of the way with both hands, and suddenly he began to disappear, feet first, under the building.

Pigeye shoved her. "Get going."

She crouched, saw the gap under the building, and went through it after King.

The dark beneath the building was complete. She could see nothing. The great mass of the building above her muted the racket of the city to a hum. The dry air smelled bitter. She banged her head against the building above her and after that crawled along on her belly, her head down. She pushed the sack of books ahead of her.

Her father. Her father was back there somewhere all bloody. Her chest hurt. She realized she was crying. King had stopped crawling. She reached out in front of her and touched a rough wooden slat; in front of her a little skirt of split slats filled the space between the bottom of the building and the ground.

Behind her Pigeye said, "Can't stay here." He was panting.

"How far you think we'll get on foot?" King said. Under his voice she could hear an intermittent clicking: he was reloading his guns. Lily pulled her coat closed around her and did up the horn buttons in the front. Suddenly a clatter sounded, just beyond the skirting, growing louder and louder and then passing by and fading away into the general roar.

That was the boardwalk, out there; those were people running by, people hunting for her. She lowered her head to the ground, thankful for the dark.

Pigeye said, "We should have left her up there. They wouldn't hurt her, a girl, and she'll just slow us down."

King said, "She made a fool out of Brand. He won't forget that. I'd say she's in considerable trouble."

"We shouldn'ta come right into town. Why'd we come back here, anyway?"

"Everything would have gone slick as fresh cow shit if Cantrell hadn't been late and Jewell hadn't started to argue," King said. "If everybody had done what I told 'em, we'd all be rich."

They were just voices in the dark. She lifted her head. She could not sit up; she could only lie there and think of her father while the tears dripped down her face. Then abruptly a hand fell on her arm.

"I'm sorry about Jewell," King said.

She said, "You can leave me if you want. I'll take care of myself." The tears spashed on her hands. All she wanted was to climb back up into the open air and go find her father.

The hand stayed on her arm. King said, "We got to

get some horses." They had left their horses at a livery stable corral down on D Street.

Pigeye growled, "Yeah, well, too bad we came back here, isn't it? You shoulda shot him out there on the road."

"Told her I wouldn't."

"Yeah! Her again, see. This girl is trouble big, I'm tellin' ya. She's the reason they caught us. They prolly recognized us afore we even stepped out of the saddle. I say leave her."

On her arm the hand tightened; she moved, trying to shake loose, but he held on to her. He said, "I want that sorrel horse of mine, that's the best horse I've had in a year."

"Well," Pigeye said, "Brand will be all over the place waiting for you to come claim it."

"Maybe."

"Damn, King, don't take it for a dare!"

"Sshh. Here." King let go of her. In front of her wood ripped and broke. He was pulling out some of the slats. Her eyes had adjusted somewhat to the dark, and she could see movement. He squirmed away from her, forward, through the skirting, and his voice came back, slightly muffled. "Here. Look. The boardwalk's raised up nearly two foot off the ground. We can crawl out under that, and I bet make it as far as the alley." He pulled backward again, out through the hole in the skirting, back under the building. "Get in there, Pigeye."

"Oh, God, you're crazy." Pigeye sounded despairing. "Why did I ever leave New Jersey?" He was moving, scraping and dragging himself along the ground; he grunted with effort, and his voice sounded from behind the skirting. "Which way?"

"Go left," King said, beside Lily. "Wait for me."

She said, "You can leave me. I'll take care of myself."

His voice fell to a murmur. "Maybe, but I'm not about to let you try. You stay here. Although, if we aren't back by daylight, I guess you got to take your chances." He fumbled around in the dark, and then the hand on her wrist was turning her hand up and a weight of coins slid into her palm. He said, "Stay away from Brand, girl, whatever you do." The hands left her and he was pushing out the hole in the skirting and gone, and she was alone.

◆ Chapter ◆

IV

Brand nudged the body on the floor with his toe. He recognized this one from the robbery: the man in the duster. Brand had never seen him before, but one of the men with him had.

"Jewell Viner. You say there was a girl with him? That ud be Lily, his daughter."

"Likely they're still right close by," said somebody else. "Get a big enough posse, we can scour the whole town."

Brand slacked his shotgun into the crook of his short arm, sorting out what he should do. So far he had been incredibly lucky in this. He had retrieved the silver almost immediately, when, riding up from the stage depot onto C Street, he had seen Rafe Cantrell and another man trying to shove a strongbox under the canvas cover of a wagon. In his hurry to catch up with King he had left the strongbox in an exposed position, chained up to a porch rail, out in the middle of the busiest street in Virginia City. Now he had to get it over to Wells Fargo. Meanwhile, he should use some of these eager hands. He swept a look around the men before him.

"You, you, and you. Start checking the liveries. Ask after anybody who came in late this afternoon, three somebodies and a girl riding double. I need some people to watch the road, too."

Half a dozen voices rose, volunteering. They knew the SP would pay them. He pointed to men and gave orders, and they went briskly off. The bartender from the hotel saloon gripped the dead man by his boots and dragged him out. Brand rubbed his palm over his stump. He was tired, but the burning anger in him drove him like an engine. He had the silver to attend to, and then he would tear Virginia City apart building by building. Now that King had separated himself from the heavy cumbersome silver, it would be much harder to catch him. Brand walked out through the saloon to get the strongbox.

Lily lay there in the dark, her hand full of gold money and her heart racing. She thought about spiders and rats. She was hungry. Before she did anything else she had to find out about her father. Carefully she closed her hand over the money, thrust her fist into the sugarsack, and dumped the money there. She rolled up the open end of the sack, tucked it beneath the books, and set the sack carefully down to one side of the hole in the skirting. Then she groped her way beneath the boardwalk.

Crisscrossed beams held the boardwalk up and level, but the ground here tilted so steeply, she fit easily under the middle. The two men had gone to the left, so she turned to the right. After a few yards the space shrank, and she hesitated a moment—then somebody stepped directly above her head.

The crashing footstep shocked her; she huddled down against the earth, quivering, while several people pounded by on the boardwalk just above her and she waited for the plank to snap and a boot to smash through and crush her skull. The steps rushed off, fading. She made herself see that the boardwalk would not break, she was safe under here—from the feet above her, anyway. The dim thunder of the city reached her ears. That reassured her somehow, as if she could hide herself in the noise. She inched forward on her belly. Someone else ran by just above her; she heard him coming, a growing clatter above her, and then the driving of his feet against the wood inches from her head, then the steps fading away. She wiggled along, her head down, her hands stretched out before her. Cobwebs raked across her face. She imagined she felt something scurrying across her arm. Something sharp scored her wrist. Then up ahead she saw an opening under the edge of the boardwalk, and she made for it on her belly like a worm, holding her breath to keep from inhaling spiders.

She reached the opening, where a gutter ran under the boardwalk, a shallow trough choked with silt and trash. Cautiously she inched up to the gap under the wooden walk and peered out.

At eye level the powdery dust of the street stretched away before her. Horses and people moved along it, stirring the top layer up into the air in a constant haze. Somebody was calling out nearby. Across the street ran the porches and doorways and light-yellowed windows of buildings: the Emporium, Caswell's Poker Salon.

Panic seized her. She was tiny and alone and helpless; there was nothing she could do. The terror passed without much effect. She was still lying on the ground under the boardwalk listening to footsteps tramp heavily toward her and she still had to figure out what to do next.

"He's got to be here someplace. They can't have just vanished into thin air." The voice swept above her and went on away down the boardwalk, underscored by the steady muffled boom of feet.

She lay still under the boardwalk, waiting for her chance. For a long while people went by almost constantly, to and fro. A band of horsemen galloped up, screamed and cursed a lot, and galloped away. A heavy coach rumbled by, the top heaped with sacks and satchels. For a moment the wooden telegraph of the boardwalk fell still, and she stuck her head boldly out, saw nobody on the other side of the street, either, then squirmed into the open and stood up.

All along each side of the street stood lamps on poles, each one shedding a globe of yellow light that did not quite fill the space around it; she came up in a dark spot. Quickly she dusted off her coat and the legs of her trousers. From somewhere behind her came a woman's uncertain voice singing. The lull in the traffic had been momentary and already there were wagons coming down the street in both directions and a crowd spilling out of the music house in the next block. Lily thrust her hands into her pockets and walked along the boardwalk toward the hotel.

The building was big but flimsy. Light showed through cracks in the walls, and the porch columns were tilting left. She put on a little hip-strut swagger in her walk, part of her boy disguise, then went jauntily in through the double doors, through the lobby, and into the downstairs saloon.

Half a dozen men slumped against the wooden bar that ran along the right-hand wall. The mirror behind the shelves of glasses and bottles was broken in several places. Out in the middle of the room a wagon-wheel lamp hung from the ceiling. Half the table lamps weren't lit and the place was fairly dark. The game tables were empty except for a man passed out on the faro table next to the door. The bartender was counting money into the till and had his back to her. She went quickly around to the back, toward the door to the storeroom.

In the rear of the barroom she came upon her father.

She stopped in her tracks. Her belly heaved. He was lying on a table, on his back. A lamp hung directly over him. The whole front of his body was blown to bloody ruin. His plaid shirt was indistinguishable from his flesh. His eyes were wide open, staring at the ceiling. She fought the urge to go to him, to turn his head and bring his gaze on her. She realized she had both fists to her face, like a child. She drew back into the shadows of the wall. She was shaking from head to foot and irresistible tears welled into her eyes.

Her father. Her body hurt; she ran one hand down her front, amazed to find it whole and dry, when his body was torn apart and soaked with blood.

Somebody banged in the front door. "Where's Brand?"

She jumped. She leaned hard against the wall, hoping she was out of sight. The bartender turned, money in his hands, and said, "He's asleep upstairs. I guess he has to sleep sometime. Any sign of King?"

"Naw." The other man went up to the bar. "You know King. He's like an Indian, he can disappear in broad daylight off a bare tabletop."

"Brand ull get him in the end," the bartender said. He put a glass and a bottle in front of the other man. "Brand never gives up. Whoever took off that hand left him with a permanent case of mad."

"Nah." The other man slapped his palm on the bar. "Pick the fox over the hound, every time."

The bartender brought him a bottle and a glass, sliding them along the bar. "Know who's got him really stung? Jewell's girl. Wouldn't want to be in her boots."

"Stuck-up little brat, that one," said the other man.

Lily turned her gaze again toward her father. He was so still, his open eyes glassy in the half-light. Her eyes leaked. Don't think about it anymore, she thought. Don't think about him anymore. Her body ached; she wanted to lie down somewhere and sleep and sleep. She watched the bartender and the man at the bar talking, and the bartender kept his back turned, and it occurred to her he had seen she was there and was warning her. She went quietly through the room to the door and went out.

On the street, she moved into the shadows, away from the hazy gilding of the streetlamps. Even in the middle of the night, C Street was crowded and busy. People went in and out of the saloons and restaurants that lined it and horses and carts moved steadily along the roadway. Lily crossed over to the other side and walked down until she was opposite the place where she had come up from under the boardwalk.

She could see the space where the gutter came out, a black hollow under the wooden planking. She knew she could not get under there without being seen. People tramped by her in a steady parade; a man with a shovel over his shoulder nearly knocked her down. Almost in front of her a big wagon collided with a smaller one and the two drivers got out and stood there in the street yelling. Other carts and coaches swerved to get by them and clogged the street and everybody started screaming at everybody else. She looked next at the buildings on the far side of the street and saw which one it was she had crawled under, following King, to reach the boardwalk. Crossing the street, she went down the alley.

The wall of the building came up flush against the hillside. There was no way to get around the corner. She went back out to the street again and went down the other alley, and there also found the wall butted smack up against the hill.

Through a door in the wall she could hear people talking; she could smell roasted meat. Her stomach hurt. She went back out of the alley and off down the street, looking for something to eat.

If she had that money she could go into any of these places and buy food. She had done that often enough with her father. You went in the door and they took you to a table and brought you roast venison, fluffy little rolls, and butter and jam if you were lucky. Her empty belly knotted itself around her backbone. She stood before a fancy house where she and her father had often eaten. She knew what the inside looked like, how the tables were jammed together, where the door to the kitchen was, even the names of some of the waiters. She belonged in there, sitting at a table, eating dinner. When the door opened to let in customers, a gust of warm air billowed out and she smelled onions, bacon, roasting meat, and warm bread.

Her mind flinched from these pictures, the memory of sitting at the table with her father. Of walking around beside her father, safe.

At Union Street she went downhill to D Street and turned north again. It wasn't fair. There was plenty to eat, but simply because she had no money she had to go hungry. A wild anger rose within her against the stupidity of the world. Nobody cared about her. She had to get the money King had given her. She trudged back up the boardwalk, her head hanging.

She started slowly down D Street. A ratty-looking dog bolted away as she approached. A horse ambled slowly past her, the rider slumped down in his saddle, his head rolling, asleep. Drunk, she thought. She guessed his horse would take him home. She wished she had someone to take her home.

Then, passing the big gaudy doors of the theater, she jumped at the sudden roar of voices inside. The show was ending. She went off to one side and watched the big doors swing open and the people stream out, talking and laughing and excited. As they came into the street, many of them winced at the cool air and bundled into their coats, but in the middle of the crowd others walked along with their coats over their arms. Down the street, a carriage pulled out of an alley where it had been waiting. Horses started moving off down the street.

Hiding in the dark of the wall, Lily stood watching them flood by her, all these people going somewhere, laughing and happy together. She felt cold and weary to the bone, too sad even to cry.

Her books. Abruptly she longed to be reading, to have the words running through her head, the world inside swallowing up this bigger, meaner one. She stood on the boardwalk in the dark, watching the people drifting away up and down the street, going into restaurants, getting into coaches and onto horses. Going home. Her stomach growled. What an idiot she was, to leave the money with her books. She trudged up to the next corner, her head down, avoiding the people bustling past her. People knew her here; someone might recognize her. She remembered what the bartender had said, that Brand was after her, too. After her especially.

She reached Union Street and turned uphill. The boardwalk climbed the slope in steps. Just below C Street where the climb was steepest there was a handrail. She reached C Street and stood on the corner looking around.

Up the street from the north a mule galloped, swerving around the lumps of wagons and people, a man on its back waving his hat and shouting.

"Fire! Fire in the livery stable!"

As he went by, the crowds on either boardwalk swirled into sudden excitement. Voices rose. Somebody ran past Lily toward a row of tethered horses. The man on the mule galloped on toward Union and whipped his mount up the steep short climb to B Street. His voice trailed him.

"Fire! Fire in the livery stable!"

A bell began to clang, somewhere down the hill. Lily ran along the boardwalk; men stampeded by her, heading north toward the livery stable. A crowd of horsemen thundered past her in the street, calling back and forth. Nobody would pay any attention to her now, and she dashed across the street, dodging a bolting horse, then stooped above the gutter and dove in underneath the boardwalk.

In the dark, with the rumble and roar muffled above her, she dragged herself along on her elbows. The dark was absolute. She wondered how far she had to crawl to get back to the hole in the building skirt. Suddenly she realized she had no idea how to find her way back to her books. She clenched her teeth. Everything had gone wrong; the whole world hated her. She inched forward on her elbows, trying to remember how far she had

crawled coming out. Reaching out her hand, she touched
the wooden wall beside her, feeling for the gap.

A hand clutched her wrist.

She went rigid. Her skin prickled like chicken skin
and her belly turned to a rock. King Callahan said,
"Faith, now. I knew you'd come back for the books."

She sobbed, relieved; her head drooped. He tugged on
her, and she followed where he led her, back through
the break in the skirting. Her free hand groped over icy
ground and brushed the yielding cloth of the sack, and
she clutched the books.

King said, "We got some horses waiting just outside
town. We got to get out of here fast. Come on."

"I—" She recoiled against his grip on her. She didn't
want to go with them, especially not with him. "You can
leave me. I'll take care of myself." As she spoke, her
belly wrung out a long painful growl.

He said, "I got something to eat."

"Where?"

"Come with me," he said, "and I'll feed you. Come
on." He pulled on her. She did not want to go with him.
But she was hungry. She thought about food and gave
up resisting, following him back through the crawl space
under the building.

◆ Chapter ◆

V

King said, *"Give me the* sack."

"No," she said.

King herded her along the boardwalk. There was certainly no future in calling attention to them by fighting over her books. Even with the excitement of the livery stable fire, C Street was still full of people. Most of them were going north, where the fire was; by the distant roar and the red glare in the sky King guessed it had gotten out of hand. Their fault for storing so much hay in one place. The wind was blowing up; the fire would keep everybody busy for a while. He went along the boardwalk, pushing the girl along with one hand on her shoulder, staying away as much as he could from the wells of light under the streetlamps.

He had given her a chunk of bread and three apples and she was eating them as if she had never seen food before. She clutched the sack of books under her arm as she walked.

"You can walk faster if you let me carry the books."

"No," she said, and gripped the sack with both hands. He gave up. His attention anyway was mainly directed toward the likely places along the street where a man could get a good look at the passing crowd.

Brand would certainly have posted lookouts; with all

that railroad money behind him, plus the stage company's reward, he could buy an army. King had gotten back into town without being seen, but Brand's men would be looking for somebody trying to get out. He steered the girl on down C through the thinning crowd in the block past Union, past Taylor, where they were the only people, toward the point where the streetlights ended and the main streets of Virginia City melded into the road that plunged on down through the canyon south toward Gold Hill.

The moon was full, bright enough to throw shadows, and the rising wind swept away the dust and smoke of the city. The long streets of Virginia City merged on the south in a dusty flat, gouged with ruts, at the head of Gold Canyon. On the uphill side of the flat was a boarded-up mine entrance with a pile of tailings in front of it, and two old ore wagons in front of the tailings. The curving ruts crisscrossing the flat were streaked with mud that glinted in the moonlight.

A sudden furious gust of wind howled down off the mountain, for a moment drowning the city racket; his hand still on Lily's shoulder, he felt her brace herself against it. He steadied her. On the far side of the flat the stage road began, plunging down into the canyon. Once they reached that, they were free.

A barn stood along the eastern edge of the flat, where C Street came out. As King and Lily walked up to the end of the boardwalk, a man suddenly appeared on the roof, a moving black shape against the moon-filled sky.

King stretched his stride longer and leaned toward the girl.

"See that ore wagon over there?"

"Yes." She hitched the sack of books up in her arms.

"When I yell, run there."

She stiffened, looking around, and then from the roof a voice rang out.

"Hey! You two, down there! Hold up!"

King said, "Now," and pushed her. She took off at a

dead run. He pulled the pistol out of the holster on his hip and shot at the man on the roof.

His aim was nowhere close but the lookout ducked down anyway. King sprinted toward the ore wagon; Lily was already behind it, leaning against the side. From the roof came another shot, and something burned across King's belly and smacked into the ground beyond him. The hot lick of the bullet put wings on him; he reached the shelter of the wagon's back wheel in two long strides like flights. Slamming into the side of the wagon, he slacked his weight against it, his hands on his knees, panting. The front of his shirt was wet.

The man on the roof opened up again. Clearly he had lots of ammunition. Splinters flew off the top of the wagon's plank side. The girl was hunkered down with her back against the front wheel, her head turned to face King; but in the shadow of the wagon he could not see her expression. He reached into the holster under his arm and pulled out the .46.

"Here."

She took the gun; he had seen before that she knew about guns. Another shot zipped by just over his head and wailed off a rock in the dirt beyond. He said, "I'll cover you. Head for the far bank of the stage road. When you get there, shoot—"

"I won't kill—"

"Miss all you want. Just make him duck. Shoot at the roof, three or four times. You got to cover me getting across that open stretch." He moved toward the front of the wagon, straightened behind the high back of the wagon bed and the seat where he could get a good look at the roof, and lifted the other gun, the muzzle pointed at the sky. "Ready?"

"Yes," she said. She had the sugarsack over her shoulder and the pistol in her right hand aimed at the ground.

Up on the roof, the man peered over the edge, showing only the top of his head. "Hey, down there! King Callahan! Come out with your hands up!"

King sighted on the bump in the straight line of the roof's edge that was the lookout's head. "Run," he said, and pulled the trigger.

He missed again. The man shrank down out of sight, and the girl raced away. She was gawky, all long legs and streaming hair, but she ran fast and straight. King shot twice more at the roof, keeping the man respectful up there, as she dashed across the wide dusty road and disappeared into the dark of the road bank.

King had his doubts that she would open up with the gun, and he started to yell orders to her; but before he could get the words out, bullets blasted out of the dark. He ran crouched across the road. As he reached the bank he could see her there, the gun in both hands, aiming very high. When he slid in beside her she lowered the Remington.

"Go on," he said. He took the gun from her, pointed on down the road with the barrel, and then thrust it into the holster under his left arm. "Follow that road south. Stay against the bank. I'll catch up with you."

She went off at once. He turned back to watch the roof. He was afraid maybe the lookout had already sent a runner to Brand, wherever he was, in which case their getaway time would be cut to a few minutes; and this girl was dead tired, he could see that. Game as she was, she couldn't go much farther without rest.

She was pretty damned game. He liked her. He was having some thoughts about her. And in any case he had gotten her into this, and he had to get her out.

The barn door opened, letting out a man with a rifle. This man looked wide-eyed around the empty street and started at a high-stepping run back into town.

King straightened up, away from the wagon, and raised the pistol with both hands. The shot was long-range but clear and dead level. He let the gun muzzle follow the man running until the little figure grew sharp and bright in the radiance of the first streetlamp on C Street. Lifting the bead slightly to account for the distance, he squeezed the trigger, corrected, cocked, and fired again. The running man bowed out in the middle, his arms flying up, staggered two steps, and crashed to the boardwalk. King went at a lope on down the south-bound road, into the steep decline of Gold Canyon.

They had brought Jewell's horse along for Lily. When King came jogging down through the bushes she was tying the sack of books to the cantle of the saddle. King stopped where he could see both ways along the road and shucked the spent shells out of his guns and poked in new cartridges. Pigeye watched him slantwise.

"You fired a lot of rounds."

"There was a lookout on the roof of the stage barn," King said. He slid the iron into the holster on his hip and thumbed the keeper down.

"You take care of him?" Pigeye said.

"Yes."

He saw the girl turn her head toward him; she had heard that. He went to his horse, checked the girths, patted the saddlebag full of money, and went around to Jewell's tall red chestnut mare.

"Can you ride?" He checked the knots she had made on the sugarsack; they were smooth and tight.

The girl said, "How did you take care of him?"

"Get on the horse," he said.

"You killed him, didn't you?" she said.

"Yes, I did."

"I hate you," she said.

"I don't give a damn," King said. "Get on the horse, now."

In the moonlight her face was set and grim. He expected her to argue, but she was too tired; she turned to the mare, gathered up her reins, and lifted one foot awkwardly toward the stirrup. King put his hands on her waist and boosted her into the saddle, and she turned to glare at him.

"I'm only going with you until I find someplace else."

"We'll see about that," he said. He went around to his horse and took the reins from Pigeye. "Let's go."

Lily woke up shivering in the first gray-blue dawn. Wrapped in her coat and her saddle blanket, she had slept between the two men, and in the night cold they had all crowded close together; she was huddled up against King in front of her, and Pigeye was lying against her back. She got up hastily, not caring if she woke them up. They did not wake up. She threw the blanket off and straightened the coat around her.

They had found a sheltered place to sleep, under the bank of a wash, but as soon as she went out more into the open, the wind slashed her. She filled her lungs with the cold pure air. The sun was coming up, the whole eastern sky swept white, the light streaming across the heights. Birds were singing. She could see them hopping in the spindly clumps of brush that grew along the wash. She should know the names of all these birds. She should know where to go now, and what to do.

She shivered all over. A gigantic possibility seemed all around her, just beyond her reach.

They had hobbled their horses and let them drift, but her father's mare was just across the stream. Her horse, now. She went across the shallow purling water and the mare lifted her head but did not try to escape her, and Lily patted her neck. The mare went back to munching grass. Lily wondered if the mare missed her master. If she even knew that her master was gone. Jewell seemed infinitely distant, as if he had never been. She thought of saddling up and riding off. Turning, she looked back toward her saddle, lying on the sandy ground near the sleeping men.

One of the men stirred, reared up, looked at her. She froze. After a moment he lay down again. She realized she was holding her breath. She stood still until he had not moved again for a long time.

She changed her mind about the saddle. She went off up the wash, along the edge of the thin little stream, found a sheltered place where the bank had caved in, and made water and washed her face and hands in the stream. She picked a twig off one of the clumps of brush and chewed it to make it fuzzy. The taste was delicious and her belly growled. She scrubbed her teeth with the twig. She wondered if the men had more food. She was afraid to drink out of the stream; she had drunk stream water that hurt. Slowly she went back to the camp, bored, now half hoping that the men had wakened.

The men still lay in their bedrolls in the lee of the bank. They did not stir as she walked toward them. She knew one of them had a canteen and she fished around the saddles until she found it. The water inside was faintly flavored with whiskey. She drank a lot of it, until her stomach began to feel it, and got a book from her sack of books and went away down the stream again, to her new place.

The sun was already warming the yellow sandy bank. The stillness of the desert was like a balm after Virginia City's endless racket. She felt good here, safe. She sat down and opened the book and sank into a distant, easier world.

After a little while a crunch of footsteps brought her back again. She looked up, and King came around the bend toward her.

All her muscles stiffened. She shut the book. King sat down next to her. He was not big or brawny, only a shade taller than she was. The red stubble of his beard hid his face like a mask.

He turned to her, his gaze on the book, and said, "You really like doing that or is it just a way to keep from talking to people?"

"What do you want to talk about?" Lily said. She remembered what he had done the night before. What they had all done the night before. "How you killed that man back there?"

He said, "No, not really."

"Doesn't it bother you to kill people?"

"Less and less," he said, and lifted his gaze to her. He had pale eyes, green or gray or hazel, direct and unblinking. "When they're trying to kill me I got no compunction at all. Could be that shooter on the roof was the one who did for your father."

She jerked around, away from him, and stared across the wash. Her hand clenched around the book. She said, "I hated my father. He was mean and he never let me do anything or go anywhere." She choked. She bit her lips to keep them from trembling.

If King said anything she would hit him. She would not cry. She would not cry in front of him. She had been stupid to talk about her father to him. Slowly the place around her flowed back in along her senses, the twittering of the birds in the stalky brush, the mutter of the stream, the good kind warmth of the sun. She felt suddenly tired, dull and used up. The man beside her said nothing. She wished he would go away and leave her to her book.

After a long while he said, "My father was hanged. He was caught poaching and the lord hanged him on the spot."

Lily turned her eyes toward him. "The lord."

"This was back in the old place. Ireland. I came from there. They had lords there. Englishmen. They'd've hanged me, too, if they'd caught me. But I ran faster than my father."

Lily looked away from him, out across the little stream. "How old were you?"

"I was ten. Some younger than you." His voice altered, steering the conversation somewhere else. "I take it you don't like me very much."

That startled her; she turned her gaze toward him. He

was scratching at the stubble of his beard, watching her. She said, "No. I don't."

He smiled, the long mean smile he had shown to Brand. He said, "That's your lookout, I suppose. Only I'm takin' you with me."

"What?" she said, alarmed.

His fingers nuzzled in his beard. His serpent's eyes were meditative. "You haven't got a Chinese chance on your own, darlin'."

"I'm not—" She stopped, running out of words, staring away again, across the stream, into the empty air, as if by looking hard enough she would make something appear there. He waited, patient, at the corner of her vision. She focused on him, and her temper swelled.

"No. I can take care of myself."

His smile widened a little. "I don't think so. Anyhow, it ain't up to you, you're goin' with me. I'm sayin' so, and that's all there is."

"Why?" she said hotly. "I won't—" She lowered her eyes, her face on fire.

"You don't have to do anything you don't want to do," he said. "I ain't goin' to hurt you. Pigeye won't. And nobody else will, either, if you're with me. Where I'm goin', there's women, girls like you, it'll be good for you."

"I can take care of myself," she said.

He didn't even bother to answer that; he got to his feet. "Let's go, we got to get moving."

"Is there anything to eat?" She rose, the book in her hand.

"No," he said. "That's one reason why we have to get moving."

He went ahead of her down the wash. She thought of turning and running the other way, and cast a look over her shoulder, out across the gray-green sagebrush, the sand, and the creek. She was very hungry. He would find them something to eat. He knew what to do; he had gotten them out of the trap where her father had died;

he had come back for her the night before and gotten them out of Virginia City. When she came around the bend, the horses were tethered in a line against the bank and Pigeye was already saddling up.

She thought, When I've had something to eat, I'll get away.

She stooped and put the book into the sugarsack by her saddle. King slid in between her mare and his sorrel and moved his horse away from her. She took a handful of grass and rubbed the rangy mare down with it, trying to straighten out the curlicues of her sweat-dried coat. On the far side of the row of horses, Pigeye said, "Any more food?"

"No, we got to cobble something up," King said. He lifted his saddle onto his horse's back.

"Where we gonna ditch this kid?"

"Nowhere. She's coming with us."

Pigeye squawked. "What're you, crazy?"

Lily clenched her teeth. Pigeye was dirty and loud and she hated him. She stooped and gathered the saddle in both arms and set it carefully on the mare's back. Her father had taught her how to take care of horses. She patted the mare again, happy with her. Her father had never named the mare and she decided to call her Jane.

"I don't like it," Pigeye was saying. "Jewell was loony, and she's pretty strange herself, the snotty little bitch."

"Yeah, well," King said, "from now on she's my snotty little bitch."

Pigeye's voice dropped; she realized he was trying to keep her from overhearing him, and she turned in time to see him lean inquiringly toward King, form his thumb and forefinger into a ring, and poke the other forefinger in and out of the circle.

She wondered what that meant. Whatever it was, King knew. He wheeled around, his arm flying up, and back-handed Pigeye so hard the other man sailed off his feet and hit the ground on his back. King leaped on him, grabbed him by the shirtfront, and flung him down again, and Pigeye screamed.

"No—King—I didn't mean it—" He thrust his arm out, trying to hold King off, scrabbling backward like a crab across the sand. King pulled the gun out of the holster on his hip, pointed it at Pigeye, and cocked the hammer.

Then abruptly he turned his head toward Lily. His face smoothed. He let the gun off cock and slid it back into the holster, then turned to his horse as if nothing had happened. "Get up, Pigeye," he said over his shoulder.

Pigeye scrambled to his feet. He lunged toward Lily, gabbling. His eyes were sleek with fear. He said, "Sorry, girl—sorry—I don't mean nothin'—"

"Stop, Pigeye," she said. She went to her horse and mounted. Her hands were shaking. She wasn't sure which frightened her more, King's attack or the speed with which he had shut it off. Even his rage was cold. She wondered what he would do to her if she angered him.

Her father had beaten her when she was bad. But only her father could do that, and now Jewell was dead, and she would never let anybody else beat her, ever.

She lifted her gaze; King was watching her, smiling, his face unreadable. No matter how much he smiled she could never trust him. She said, "Where did you say we were going?"

"South. Down near the ocean."

"The ocean." That was impossibly far. "How long will that take?"

"A week, maybe two." He shrugged. "Longer, if we don't get goin' sometime soon, now." He reined his sorrel around and started down the road. Lily followed him, having no other choice, and hastily Pigeye swung into his saddle and came after.

◆ Chapter ◆
VI

"Where is this?" Lily said. She nudged Jane with her heels and brought the chestnut mare up stirrup to stirrup with King. "Where are we?"

"El Pueblo de la Reina de los Angeles," King said.

Lily stood in her stirrups to look ahead of them. She had lost track of how many days had passed since they had left Virginia City, but in all that time she had not seen half as many signs of people as she had on this one single day, and now they were coming into a town.

It was dark, well after the time when they were used to stopping for the night. They had been riding since early morning, when they came out of the mountains onto this broad grassland. All during the day she had seen houses in the distance, groups of houses, smoke in the sky, and they had passed by settlements, which King had avoided. Now the road was curling over the shoulder of a hill, and there before her, spread out across the lower ground, lights glowed by the dozen, by the hundred.

She was tired, but she strained her eyes to see, to pick out the dark masses of the buildings in among the strings of lights. The air smelled like smoke and paint. Somewhere in the distance, in among the barking of dogs, a machine ground a long screech of metal noise. A roar went up in the distance, maybe a crowd, or maybe not. As the road descended, she lost her view of the whole place; she sank down into this city. The road reached the bottom of the hill. Off on her right now clustered a bunch of shacks; she smelled something strong and sharp that turned her stomach.

Pigeye rode up on her right. "Where we goin'?"

"Sonoratown," King said. The road led them down through a stand of small orderly trees: an orchard, she thought. A wagon rolled by them, going the other way. Two men sat backward on the wagon tail. Ahead, a flat-roofed building stood beside the road, and beyond it, another; a lamp shone in the window. A dog began to bark. Other people moved along the road, on foot, on horseback. After the bleak unpeopled desert all this swarming activity seemed confused and too fast. Yet Lily leaned forward, eager.

The road became a lane, winding down through clumps of houses. Delicious aromas floated past her nose. A woman flung open a door and called out in a strange language. Great heavy-headed trees leaned down over the road, spreading a peppery fragrance. King reined his horse into the deep shadow of one of these trees and said, "All right. We're here."

"What did you say this place was called?" Lily slid down from Jane's back.

King said, "Just be quiet and keep your eyes open and stay close. Pigeye, watch the horses. Come on, Lily."

He started off across the dark street. Lily followed on his heels. The street was deep in dust, rutted beneath the soles of her boots. She had to hurry to keep up with King, who went toward the long low building opposite.

The narrow door spilled light and people into the street. King waited a moment until the way was clear and then went on into the building, Lily just behind him.

The smell of hot rich food struck her. She blinked in the sudden light of the smoky lamps suspended from the ceiling; the rumble of a dozen conversations buzzed in her ears. She put one hand out blindly, caught King's arm, and held on. The place was full of people, most of them sitting at tables and eating; she had been eating raw meat and wild onions and bad coffee for two weeks and the sight and smell of this food brought tears to her eyes.

King did not stop here. He went straight to the back of the room, where along a waist-high counter several men were standing. He leaned across the counter and called, "Serafa!"

Lily clutched his arm. The men on either side of them were staring at her. Brown men, broad round faces, dark eyes. She felt ugly and strange in front of them. She wished she had stayed outside with Pigeye. The door in the wall behind the counter opened and a woman came out.

She was tall, dark-skinned, not young, with high cheekbones and a wide, full mouth; her hair was knotted up in a bun and she was dressed all in black. She came through the door and saw King, and she stopped. Her eyes widened and her mouth fell open, and then immediately she settled her face, as if she were putting on a mask, expressionless. Her hands disappeared into her shawl.

King smiled at her. "Serafa." He leaned his forearms on the counter and, to Lily's amazement, rattled off an incomprehensible speech.

Serafa spoke, in the same gibberish; Lily guessed they were speaking Spanish. King talked easily in it; by the way his hands moved and the look on his face, she knew he was asking for something.

The dark woman answered sharply, with a shake of her head. But she stayed where she was, watching him, her body turned toward him. Her voice said no, but her looks contradicted her. King said something more to her, wheedling, bargaining. He took his hand out of his pocket and dropped gold money onto the counter.

The woman did not look at the money. Lily saw that

the money didn't matter to her. She was staring at King so intently that she did not even seem to notice Lily, until King nudged her slightly forward, nodded to her, and said something.

Now the woman's gaze fell hard on Lily. She had the eyes of a witch, wide and tilted and black. Lily met her stare; they looked at one another a long while, neither speaking. King asked a question, his voice turning up at the end. The woman swung toward him, and her voice changed, softer, resigned. She shrugged. She stepped aside from the door and waved one hand toward it.

King thanked her with a lot of words, meanwhile pushing Lily on ahead of him around the counter and to the door; they went on into a back room full of barrels and crates and shelves of goods, and out another door into a dirt yard.

The aroma of the food was so strong here Lily's belly gave a painful longing growl. Several other buildings bordered the yard, one of them the kitchen. As she realized this, a big young woman with round arms and round full breasts burst out of the door across from them, each hand balancing a tray piled with dishes.

She saw King and stopped in her tracks, the trays swaying dangerously. "What are you doing here?" Her head swiveled toward the front building. "Does my mother know you're here?"

"Sure," King said. "Come on, *querida,* don't drop the profits. She's letting me stay in the old house."

"Oh, no," the woman said. "Wait until Josefa finds out. What is everybody going to say? This is terrible." She hurried off toward the back door.

One hand on Lily's arm, King piloted her on by, across the yard. "Don't worry about her, it's Serafa who counts around here."

"Where did you say this was?"

King did not answer her. He hustled her over to the farthest of the buildings ringing the yard, which was a ragged-looking adobe block with small square windows all along the front. The door was at the far end and they went in.

"I'm hungry," Lily said in the dark. "Are we going to eat? Who are these people?"

A match scraped alive. King held the flame to the wick of a lamp hanging from the wall on a bit of scrolled iron. "I used to know her husband. Serafa's. He and I did business together."

"They really don't want us here. She said no at first." Lily turned slowly, taking in the room, long and narrow under the low-hanging rafters. A jumble of furniture filled it, stacked bed frames, chairs, mattresses. A wooden cupboard against one short wall had a basin in it and a water pitcher.

"She's keeping up appearances," King said. "As long as I pay her she'll let us stay. She just wants to make sure I appreciate it."

Lily did not think much of this explanation. She thought that King and Serafa had known each other for a long time and that something else was going on here. She said, "This is nice. Beds, even." She swung toward him. "What about Jane?"

"Well, hell, darlin', there's plenty of room. You can move her right in with us."

"Really?" She looked around, dubious.

He laughed. "No. You been outside too long. There's a pen in the back where we can keep the horses. I'll have to buy some feed."

"Can I take a bath?"

"I thought you wanted to eat."

"All right," she said. She felt suddenly light and quick and not even tired anymore. A bed, a bath, good food, and all these people; she went toward the door as if some power drew her toward the lights and the voices. "Let's go eat."

⁂

King came into the cantina through the back door. Serafa was sitting on a tall stool behind the counter, watching the house while her girls ran around feeding people and collecting money. King leaned up against the wall beside her. She ignored him. In no hurry, he said nothing to her, looked out into the room.

Lily and Pigeye sat at one end of the back table; Lily was packing away the food like a track-layer. He would have to watch her, now that they were around so many people. In a busy place like Los Angeles she might be tempted to take off on him.

He had no intention of letting her get away from him. She was brave and smart, but by herself she would be prey for all the wolves; she needed him. The way he felt about her startled him. He wanted nothing from her except to take care of her, and that more than anything in the world.

He had felt this way before, a long time ago. He could not remember why.

Serafa said, "Who is this girl?"

"She's Jewell Viner's daughter. He and I did a job on a stagecoach up by Virginia City. Jewell got himself killed."

"Poor child." Her long eyes slid toward him. "Do you like her very much?"

"Not that way," he said, irritated. "She's just a kid, an orphan now. I got a soft spot in my heart for orphans."

She made a sound in her throat that was almost a growl. Her eyes turned toward the room again. "This word of a heart, now. This is news."

"Well," he said, "that's not true. I like you."

"You do? You have not been here in years."

He considered the interesting edge in her voice. "After Tiburcio died, I didn't think you'd want me around."

"Bah. And yet you are here now."

Glad of it, too, he almost said. He had always thought she was a fine piece of a woman. He and her husband had done robberies together in the gold country, hanging around the cantina sometimes between jobs, and early on Tiburcio had let him know what would happen if King took his interest past honest admiration. King had liked Tiburcio, more than any other man before or since. Some of that respect lingered on, after Tiburcio's one-way rope trick. Now he studied her through the side of his eye, and thought the period of mourning had come to an end.

She was older, but she would always be beautiful, her eyes magnificent, the bones of her face a like a sculpture. Her body was still ripe under the black widow's weeds; she still made all these people here stand up and salute.

He said, "Tiburcio wouldn't want you to wither away, Serafa."

She wheeled toward him. She had a quick, fierce temper, which he also liked. "What do you know about how I wither?"

"I know what life here is like," he said. He smiled at her, so she would take this next in the right way. "Tiburcio would have wanted me to look after you."

She gave a yelp of a laugh. Her black eyes flashed. She swung toward him, snapping her fingers in his face, and said, "Tiburcio would have slit your throat just for thinking of it." She went away down the counter, her head high and a little strut in her walk.

He leaned back against the wall, pleased. He had always thought maybe she liked him a little, too, and now he was sure of it. He looked around for Lily and Pigeye.

They were still sitting at the end of the last of the long tables that crisscrossed the room. Pigeye had broken out his deck of cards; Lily was slumped wearily on the bench. Her neck was bent, and there was something so tender and innocent in the look of her that King was going toward her even before he realized it. He'd have to get her out to the old house. Find her some blankets. She had said something about a bath, but that would wait.

Pigeye was dealing the cards; he looked up as King came to the table and said, "Wanna play?"

"T'll be out in a minute," King said. "Got to take care of my little girl." He scooped Lily up in his arms. She didn't wake up; she snuggled in his arms like a baby. He took her out to the old adobe to put her to bed.

Lily opened her eyes. A hazy pale light filled the house. The cot beneath her was so comfortable, the blankets around her so warm, that for a while she could not leave them; she lay still, watching the windows brighten with sunlight.

The room resounded softly with Pigeye's snoring. The room was different. The men must have moved things around; most of the furniture had been cleared down to the far end, and the beds were set along the walls. Pigeye lay in the bed across the room from her, a whiskey bottle on the floor beside him.

She twisted slightly, looking for King; she moved just her head, careful not to draw his attention. But he was deep asleep on the cot just ahead of hers, his face toward the wall.

She stole out of the covers, reaching down her bare feet to the floor, easing her weight upright. She still had most of her clothes on. Her boots and coat were on the packed earth floor. She picked them up and looked around for her books.

She had left the sack by her saddle, against the wall at the foot of her cot. Alarmed, she took a step toward the spot where it should have been. The sack was nowhere. She stooped and peered under her cot: nothing there. She swung her gaze wider, searching the room with her eyes, and finally saw the sack of books stuffed in under the head of King's bed.

She squatted there, frozen, for a long moment. If she tried to get the books out of there he would surely waken. He must have done that on purpose, to keep her from leaving.

She straightened. For a moment she thought of returning to bed. But her back rose against it, that he should hold her prisoner with her own books. He had forgotten the money he had given her under the building in Virginia City. She still had that. She could buy more books. She gathered herself up and went, step by step, across the room toward the door.

Neither of the men stirred. Quietly she slipped out to the yard.

From the kitchen building, across the yard, came the banging of pots and the smells of cooking, and smoke billowed up from the pipe in the roof. They were making breakfast in there. Her stomach growled. She was hungry again. Food took up so much time; no matter how much you ate, very soon you had to do it again. She hesitated, thinking she might eat breakfast here before she left.

The door to the kitchen flew open, and one of the two big round girls strode out, balancing a tray on each hand. Lily shrank back into the lee of the house wall, and the big girl did not see her, but marched away toward the front building. The great trays she bore gave off trails of steamy aromas. The smell was delightful, but the girls did not like her, she had seen that the night before. Lily slunk around the corner of the house into the back.

This was a broad dusty ground, bordered at the far end by a ditch full of water and fenced with stakes and poles. Inside the fence, four or five horses dozed. Lily stopped and put her boots on. It was too warm to wear the coat and she hung it over the fence rail.

"Jane." She kept her voice low. "Here, Jane."

The mare's ears flipped back and forth, but she stayed where she was, in among the other horses. Lily called her again, with no result, and finally climbed through the fence and went to her. The mare snuffled at her, mildly protesting, but when Lily took her by the forelock and pulled, the mare followed her obediently over to the rail. Lily hugged her.

"I love you, Jane. You're a good girl."

The mare's lips flapped at her hair. Lily went out to the lean-to against the back of the house and got her saddle and bridle. A few minutes later she was leading Jane around the opposite end of the house, into the narrow way that led to the street.

She drew a deep breath, exhilarated. She was free.

She climbed onto the mare and rode out into a busy stream of people. A man in a broken straw hat went by her, a hoe and a rake over his shoulder; ahead of her another man was walking along under a long wooden yoke, hauling water in buckets. She swung out to get around him and caught a glimpse of a dark face wrinkled like a walnut. Someone on the far side of the the street was shouting words she could not understand. King had called this place Sonoratown. These people must be Mexicans. He had called it something else, too, a long spill of Spanish syllables. They must have ridden all the way to Mexico.

She nudged the mare into a short trot. Her heart leaped. Being alone felt like flying. Although she had never been where she was going she felt that she was going home. She turned the mare up the street, which stretched away between small square dusty white houses with flat black roofs now steaming in the sunlight. Here and there a dark green tree grew. White stones marked the edge of the street. In front of one house there were white cow skulls instead of stones. Nobody among the passing crowd paid any heed to her.

Suddenly she realized she had left her coat behind. There flashed into her mind the picture of it hanging on the rail of the fence, back behind Serafa's place. She thought of the money and laid her hand on the pocket of her pants. The pocket was flat. In her mind's eye she saw herself days before putting the money into the pocket of her coat.

After a moment, the man with the yoke passed her, and she realized she had pulled the mare to a stop. She turned, looking back down the street, which stretched away through the long shadows of the heavy-headed trees. One of those adobes was Serafa's place, but she could not remember which; she had only gone in through the front door once, and that in the dark.

Good riddance to the money, then. She would take nothing away with her but what her father had left her, the mare, the saddle. She lifted her gaze forward again, resolute.

Ahead of her the street broadened, opened onto a wide expanse like a village square, crisscrossed with pathways and clotted with small trees. There was a church at the north end of it, the front wall steeply peaked; she knew it was a church because of the crosses on the doors. Jewell had told her a lot about churches, all of it flatly contradicted by everything else she had heard. Most of the other buildings lining the square were adobes, squat and small, but along the southern edge sprawled a huge stone structure with three layers of archways, on the top a big gaudy sign reading PICO HOUSE.

English. Or partway English, anyway, so this wasn't Mexico. She swelled her lungs with air, relieved. This wouldn't be so hard, after all.

Past this corner the street swarmed with people, on foot and on wagons and horses. She reined her mare around into this traffic. The street went off straight into the distance. The steady passage of horses and wagons kept the air thick with dust, yellow in the slanting early morning sunlight. The first few houses she passed were small and plain, but a block away from the square there sprouted up suddenly a great red brick building whose rows of tall thin windows were capped in white cornices like eyebrows. A man in a bowler hat was just opening the doors; as she rode past he bustled out with a stack of chairs and then some buckets: a store.

She let the mare carry her along. She had to find

something to eat soon and she looked for a market where she might be able to steal some food. She watched a team with no driver pull a wagon at a dead gallop down the street, several men racing after it, shouting. She watched a blacksmith open up his yard, folding back the fence gates, pumping up his fire. These people were speaking English. She was still in America. She rode past a stand of little trees, the branches all fuzzed with new green and the ground beneath spangled with flowers. In a few months, she could have eaten there.

She remembered Virginia City, jammed up against the flank of Sun Mountain so tight it was always halfway falling down. This place, whatever it was called, was the opposite of that; it had too much room, each building separate from all the others, sprawling without form or lan, like fragments of a lot of different cities all jumbled together. The long straight street began to bore her. She swung the mare off into a side street, narrower, without boardwalks, that led east through trees and fields and scattered houses.

The first few houses were square and ordinary, but the next was huge, towering up like a wooden castle, its eaves and wooden facings carved into fantastic lattices and ornamental scrolls. Two stone lions sat at the foot of the walk up to the front door. Hedges of green made tight little circles on either side.

She sat there staring at it, delighted, until a wagon rattling down the street reminded her where she was. She nudged Jane along at a trot, promising herself she would ride back by that house again often.

But she had no need. Every block or so there was another huge house, dressed in fabulous ornaments of wood and rising up like a temple out of the humble fields. She stopped in front of each one. They did seem to her like temples: she knew they were real homes, where people lived forever, forever happy. She imagined herself going up the walk of each house, climbing the steps to the porch, opening the door, and going inside.

She stopped longest before a house with a porch around one forward corner, whose front door had a glass window in it, and the glass window a white lace curtain, figured with the image of a peacock. She was daydreaming herself up to that door when around the side of the house a dog hurtled, wildly barking, and lunged up against the fence.

Jane spooked; Lily clutched at the reins. The front door of the house opened and a woman came out onto the porch. This woman was much older than Lily. Her iron-gray hair was done up in a bandanna and the hem of her dress was tattered. She carried a long broom in her hands. Lily gaped at her, startled.

"You!" The tattered woman shook the broom at Lily. "Get away from here, go on! Shoo!"

Lily swung the mare around, heading off. She wondered why such a bedraggled woman lived in such a beautiful house; she had taken for granted that the people inside the houses would all be beautiful, too, and rich. The woman shouted at her all the way down the street. She wondered what she had done wrong. Abruptly her spirits plunged. She had to get out of here.

"Hey!" A boy came running up behind her. "Hey, you! What are you doing here?"

She kicked at him. "Get away from me."

"Wooooo!" He dodged. Several other little boys were rushing up the street toward her. The first boy screamed, "Gypsy! Indian! Why can't you filthy people leave us alone?" Stooping, he groped in the dirt for a stone.

Seeing what he was doing, Lily reined the old mare around and charged him. He whirled and ran, and all the other boys turned and ran also, screaming. She chased them on down the street almost to the house with the porch, wheeled her mare and galloped away. She did not stop or slow down until she reached a broad thoroughfare, full of wagons and horses.

She turned into this traffic, going north. Beyond the jumble of buildings ahead of her rose low crowns of hills, the dun sand studded with dark green brush; some old building stood on top of the highest hill. In the distance, the mountains jagged up mottled blue in the hazy air. The mare picked her way across a set of railroad tracks and moved on, out across a wide dusty space that in a moment Lily recognized as the other side of the village square that she had seen before.

She turned to cross it. She was ravenously hungry. She longed for her books, the abundant hot food of Serafa's cantina, the comfort of the house. She would escape some other time. As she ambled the mare across the square, she passed by the front of the Pico House, and there on the steps, looking the other way, stood a man with only one hand.

She jerked her gaze away from him. Her spine prickled. The mare picked up her pace, and Lily reined her down again, not wanting to draw attention. She kept her eyes forward. Jane knew where they were going and turned before Lily told her to, into the street that led to Serafa's place. On the corner, Lily turned and glanced behind her.

He had come down the steps a little; and now she could see his face. It was certainly Brand. She faced forward again and hurried off into Sonoratown.

◆ Chapter ◆

VII

Josefa beat her fists on the table. "Mama, you must throw them out!"

Luz came in and sat next to her. "Yes, Mama. People were finally forgetting, and now this."

Serafa turned to face them, the big iron spoons in her hands. "People will never forget, and for one reason, I won't let them. Are you ashamed of your father? This is your father's friend."

"What about the Rosas?" Josefa cried. "Mama, I am being married in four months. Now suddenly here we are, taking in Anglo bandits—how will that look to the Rosas?"

"Yes, Mama," Luz said.

Serafa said, "I am not sending them away. You may depend on that, so stop pleading with me." She hung the spoons over the edge of the rafter.

She knew what Josefa meant. It had been five years since Tiburcio died, and she had put her life in order, quieter, calmer. Five years without much money: but then Tiburcio had never had any money, although he had always been just about to get very rich. Five years without a man: which meant without a master, nobody to yell, to hit, to argue. A good life, anyway, and now here was his friend come again, acting as if everything were the same.

Waking up all these old feelings in her, all these old itches. She had been bored until King walked in.

Josefa said, "Mama, please. I'm getting married!"

"I will not hear any more," Serafa said. "I have my honor. Your father's honor. This is his friend."

Josefa flung her arms up, her face dark with anger, and stormed out of the kitchen. Luz sat watching her mother, her mouth curling unhappily.

Serafa said, "What of this child? Do you want her turned out into the street?"

"She's gone," Luz blurted out.

"What?"

"This morning. She was gone. And her horse." Luz gave a little shake of her head. "Mama. We were almost respectable." She stood up, taking off her apron, and went out the door into the yard.

Serafa went after her to the threshold. From here two steps led down to the dirt yard. Luz was just turning the corner of the kitchen, going toward her room. The back door of the cantina stood open; Josefa would have gone in there to clean up. Serafa started that way, but instead turned and walked across to the door of the old adobe and knocked.

Unlatched, the door swung open under the impact of her knuckles. King stood there, in nothing but a pair of trousers, half his face covered with white soap.

She turned her back on him. "You are indecent. Put some clothes on."

"I'm sorry," he said. "I'm almost done. Pigeye!" He rattled off some English, which she had never troubled to learn; out of the deep of the room came a strange voice, saying something falsely cheerful.

She said, "What do I hear, that the girl has gone?"

"She'll come back," he said.

He had moved away, down along the wall to the sunlit window; she could see him through the corner of her eye, stooping to see himself in the mirror there. He was the only man Serafa knew who shaved his entire face. She folded her arms around her.

"What if she can't come back? Los Angeles is an evil place. She's only a child."

"I'll go looking for her if she isn't back pretty soon."

"Is she trying to run away from you?" Serafa turned and looked at him.

He pointed his chin up and scraped whiskers from his neck. "Probably. But she'll come back, woman, give her some time." He straightened, reaching for a cloth, and wiped off his face and neck. Picking up his shirt, he thrust his arms into the sleeves and came toward her, doing up the buttons. She went ahead of him out to the yard.

Outside, in the sunlight, he said, "I heard Josey yelling." He shoved the tails of the shirt down into his pants.

She shrugged. "Josey is bad-tempered. She has her father's humor."

He looked earnestly into her face. "We'll leave. I don't want to cause you trouble."

"No," she said. "Stay. I decide, not Josefa."

He smiled. With his cheeks skinned of beard, he looked younger, finer. He said, "I'm in your debt, Serafa. I'll make it good to you. Just tell me how."

She said, "Make yourself useful."

He laughed. "Faith, I always do that." As if by accident he brushed against her. "I'm a very useful man, Serafa." He smiled at her again, and turned and went back into the adobe.

She made herself walk on across the yard toward the cantina. Her arm tingled where he had touched her. He was a fool if he thought she didn't see through his smiles and his lies.

The cantina was a little forest of upended benches and chairs, Josefa on the far side sweeping down the rafter. The lamps were all lined up on the counter waiting to be filled. Serafa went down and took the chimneys off, all the while thinking about King.

She should have nothing to do with him. She should never let him live here, that was certain; since he had come in the night before, she had thought of nothing else. She was a respectable, righteous widow, with a very valuable cantina and two well-mannered and pious daughters, and she should not lower herself to entertaining the addresses of a bloody-minded, honey-tongued, redheaded Anglo bandit.

She poured a measure of oil into each lamp, and silently Josefa came and took it and hung it back up again on the rafter. Josefa was still angry and not speaking to her. But it made no difference; they knew their work so well they did it without words. In a few moments they would begin the midday meal, for which a good number of the people of Sonoratown depended on her. They had done so every day for years; for years, every day, the same.

Now here came King Callahan, with his wicked smile. With his talk all woven around with hints and meanings, teasing and tantalizing, if things could be different.

She wondered if she was hearing more in his words than he was saying. She went out to the back door again, looking out over the yard.

The door of the adobe was open. He was in there dragging furniture around, making room for himself. He was staying, then. Maybe he had only sweet-talked her so that she would let him stay.

That ruffled her. She was a woman of consequence, not to be played with: let him find that out. Henceforth she would ignore him until he proved himself true. She drew her eyes from the old adobe and, armored in her virtue, she went over to the kitchen to begin making the dinner.

☙

Lily came back early in the afternoon; the place seemed deserted. She sneaked into the kitchen for a fistful of tortillas and made a dash for the adobe house where they were living.

"You ungrateful brat." King came around the corner, caught her by the arm, and propelled her into the adobe. "I drag you all the way down here and take care of you like a cat with one kit and the first chance you get you run off."

She kept her feet, letting him muscle her into the room; she knew she had the upper hand on him. She said, "Brand's here."

In the middle of the room, he let her go. His eyes narrowed. His cheeks were smooth and pale: he had shaved. He said, "Really."

"How did he find us?" she asked. "We have to run away again, don't we? I don't want to leave. I like it here."

King sat down on the cot by the door, which was his bed. "Calm down. You saw him? Where?"

She told him. King said, "He hasn't found us. It's a coincidence. He wouldn't just be walking out of the Pico House in broad daylight if he was coming here after me. If he was after me, the first I'd hear of him would be when the gun went off in my face."

"What are you going to do?" She went over closer to him. His calm was reassuring. His cheeks were smooth as a baby's.

"I'm thinking about it." He reached out and gripped her by the shirtfront. "What you're going to do is get in line and help Serafa and the girls out, or I'll whack you black and blue."

She struck his hand away. "If you dare touch me, I'll kill you."

"I thought you didn't do things like that. What did you take off for? Where did you think you were going?"

"Just to look around. I came back, didn't I?"

"Sure," he said. "Your coat's over by your bed."

She was still tense, waiting for him to strike at her, but he did not. He wasn't all that angry. Bolder, she said, "Why can't I go looking around, if I come back?"

"Los Angeles is a rough place," he said. "Lots of stupid people with guns." But he was smiling at her. "Let me go with you. I'll show you where everything is. Right now I'm going to see about getting you a bath. Is that all right with you?"

"Yes," she said, surprised. "Sure."

He got up off the bed and went toward the door. She wondered why he was being so nice to her. She would never like him, no matter how nice he was. She went to find a book, to fill the time until the bath.

Serafa dipped her hand into the tub and tested the water. "It's getting cold. Tell her to hurry."

Josefa wheeled and spoke to the girl, who came uncertainly forward into the kitchen. She was very dirty, her hair clumpy and her nails black-rimmed. At Josefa's words she began to peel off her clothes, turning slightly away from the eyes of the three women watching her. The clothes were a man's clothes, in rags. As the girl took off each piece Luz took it between thumb and forefinger and dumped it in a growing heap on the hearth.

The girl came out of her clothes like a young corn sprout out of dead husks. She was made long and thin, her skin brown but not red like an Indian's or dark like an African's. Without clothes on she seemed older, a young woman, with her small dark-tipped breasts and long hips. She climbed into the tub and sank down, and Luz and Josefa poured buckets full of water over her.

"Give her the soap," Serafa said. "Ask her where her mother is, the poor child. Throw those clothes in the fire."

The girl soaped herself; when Josefa spoke to her she answered. Josefa said, "She says her mother is dead."

"The poor child," Serafa murmured, and crossed herself.

Josefa sniffed. Rudely she clapped one hand to the girl's head and shoved her under the water; startled, the girl slapped out with both hands and fought her way up into the air again, her eyes enormous and shiny with fear, and gasped for breath. Josefa went at her at once with the towel, scrubbing viciously at her hair and her face. The girl gave a single muffled yelp and then gripped the side of the tub and endured it.

Luz said, "Josey, don't be so rough, you'll hurt her."

"Bah," Josefa said. "Stand her up." She grabbed the girl's arm and pulled, and the child rose up out of the tub, long and thin and brown, and Josefa attacked her again with the towel.

Serafa sat with her hands folded in her lap, watching; Josefa's fury amused her. Luz murmured another protest. The girl herself made no sound, her eyes and mouth screwed tight. Her skin glowed ruddy. She kept hold of the side of the tub as if to a lifeline.

Josefa stepped back and spoke in English. The girl opened her eyes, wide and black, looked at her, and got out of the tub. Josefa draped the towel over her and gave a curt order, and the girl sank down and dried her legs and feet.

Luz came over with an armful of clothes. She spoke also in English, soft and gentle, maybe softer and gentler because her sister was so harsh. The girl said something and looked around toward the hearth.

Josefa was throwing her old clothes into the fire. The girl cried out, stretching one arm out for her things, and Luz caught her wrist, murmuring, "No, no," and pushed the new underthings into the girl's hands. The child looked down, blinking, and put on the clothes she was given: Serafa's daughters' threadbare cast-offs, every seam turned, but clean and well made.

Serafa said, "Ask her if that doesn't feel better than the old clothes. Those were men's clothes."

Josefa snapped out words in English. The girl shrugged, her eyes lowered. But she turned her gaze on Serafa and spoke to her directly.

"What?" Serafa asked.

"She wants to know if we have any books," Luz said.

"Books," Serafa said, surprised. "The Scripture? She doesn't look religious." She gave the girl a long curious stare.

Josefa snorted. "No—she means storybooks."

"Mary Mother," Serafa said. "What a scandal. Does she think we're nobility here, that we can lie around all day telling stories? Give her the comb for her hair."

Josefa took the comb from the counter, and the girl recoiled; wise now, she dreaded Josefa's touch. Luz said, "I'll do it," and held out her hand for the comb. With one hand on the girl's shoulder she got her to sit down on the stool and began to comb her long black hair.

"She looks very pretty," Serafa said.

Josefa said, "She's an outlaw's brat. You can wash her and dress her up like a decent woman, but she'll always be an outlaw's brat." She bent over the tub, scooped up a bucket of the scummy water, and hauled it away out of the kitchen, going to water the corn patch behind the adobe. The girl sat still on the stool; Luz was battling her way through the tangles and knots in the long hair, trying to be gentle, and yet yanking and tugging; the girl made no sound, but her face twitched with pain. Serafa got up and went to see to the chickens roasting in the oven.

While the women gave Lily her bath, King withdrew to the cantina, quiet and empty in the midafternoon. The chairs and benches were turned wrong side up on the tables and he lowered one chair and pulled it into the corner by the back door, where he could sit with his back against the wall. He took the .46 out of his shoulder holster, laid it on his lap, and read the newspaper.

He had not read a newspaper since he left Virginia City, nearly a month before, which was unusual: King loved newspapers. He had taught himself to read out of the newspaper, in the first year he was on his own, and he read them everywhere he went. They were invaluable in his line of work, for one thing, as in the matter of Brand's appearance here in Los Angeles.

Brand belonged to the Southern Pacific, whose track ended now in Tulare County in the San Joaquin Valley, far to the north on the other side of the Tehachapi Mountains. As everybody knew, the great Railroad was looking for a southern Terminus to anchor its swing east across the lower edge of the country. Brand was in Los Angeles: therefore the Railroad was considering Los Angeles for its southern terminus. And here in the paper was proof of that, two articles about the Railroad on the front page.

Brand's job was guarding things—big money, important men. King hoped there was a big heap of money somewhere in Los Angeles, but he thought it more likely some SP nob was coming down, and Brand was here to get things ready for him.

He wondered if the Railroad was serious about Los Angeles. The city did not strike him as a good choice for the southern terminus. It was barricaded away behind its mountains, had no harbor and not enough water, didn't mine gold or silver. It had nothing but lots of empty space. Since the big dry spell just before the war, even the cattle ranchers had gone broke here, and during the war the city had been so Dixie that the Union government had put troops in the old fort on the hill to keep order.

He had read that the SP would choose San Bernardino, down on the desert, which was closer to the silver mines of the eastern Sierra, and a lot easier than Los Angeles to build in to. He knew also that the city of San Diego, south on the coast, had been negotiating with the

Texas Pacific, to anchor another railroad between the Pacific and the East to rival the SP.

King had a double-sized interest in all this. First of all he had a war on with all railroads. When he first came to America he had worked on a crew laying track for the Pennsylvania. They had ordered him around, starved him, beaten him up, cheated him of his pay, worked him almost to death, and then turned him off in the middle of nowhere; everything he had seen since convinced him that this was every railroad's going practice, not just toward skinny ignorant helpless Irish boys but toward all working men. He always looked for ways to take shots at the Railroad.

Plus, the Railroad meant money. He liked money.

The back door creaked. He lifted his head, brought out of an article about the Chamber of Commerce meeting. Serafa came across the room to the front door and opened it; people began to flood into the cantina. King folded the newspaper and paid attention to what was going on around him.

Serafa's customers were Sonoratown people who came in every night for dinner, always sat in the same places, talked to the same people, said the same things. They paid with a monthly sack of cornmeal, chickens, eggs, some baskets of tomatoes and squash and oranges out of the fields and orchards they worked along the banks of the river. As they filtered into the cantina a few of them glanced at King out of the corners of their eyes, but most of them ignored him. Because he had a white skin they thought he was an Anglo. He doubted they would have appreciated the irony of that.

Pigeye came in the door, sidled down between the long tables toward King, and sat down on the bench beside him. "Any sign of the little girl?"

"Yes. She came back." King dropped the folded newspaper onto the floor beside him. Serafa's daughters came in through the rear door, bearing the great trays crowded with coffee mugs, and began to set them down two at a time in front of the customers.

"Oh, she did. You cuss her out?"

"Some. Brand's in town."

"Brand!"

"Don't get worked, it doesn't mean much. Just watch out. Don't let on to anything. I got my doubts he even knows you. But better to be on the safe side."

"How you know?"

"Lily saw him."

"Damn. Son of a bitch don't leave us alone."

King said nothing. Luz had come in through the back door carrying a big tray heaped with tortillas; at her appearance the people waiting around the tables let out a low breathy cheer. The smell of the roasted corn tortillas reached King's nose and his mouth watered and his stomach groaned.

Pigeye said, "I went up to the real city last night. Lotsa good places up there."

"If you like booze halls," King said.

"There's a couple fellows I met want to talk to you."

"Why would I want to talk to these couple fellows?"

"They got an idee for getting rich."

"Oh, God."

"I just told 'em I'd ask."

"I got money now," King said. "Tell 'em I'll think about it when I'm broke. Who the hell are they?" He picked up the newspaper. "What do they know about me? If you told 'em who I am, I'll kill you."

Pigeye was taking out his deck of cards. "Hell, no, you think I'm crazy? I just tole 'em I had a partner. They're white men, they live someplace near here called El Monte. You wanna play? They gonna feed me?"

"Sit here long enough and they'll feed you." King stood up. "Stay out of trouble. I got to get a line on Brand." Behind Luz, Josey was coming around from table to table, laying down dishes of food. She swept by Pigeye without breaking stride and left him staring down at the dish of beans and steaming *colorado* that had suddenly appeared before him. King went off through the bustling cantina toward the back door. He belonged here: he would eat his dinner in the quiet of the kitchen.

In the kitchen, he found Serafa sitting like a queen on the stool, her long spoon in her hand. At the far end of the table sat Lily, shoveling food into her mouth.

King eased onto the edge of the bench, his gaze fastened on the girl. She was remarkably clean. Her hair shone. She lifted her head and gave him a single swift, angry look, and went back to eating. His heart jumped: he saw that she was beautiful. He had forgotten; he had grown used to the layers of dirt and he had forgotten. Something in him yearned toward her, some deep tender heart, longing and caring, secret and infinitely sweet.

He said, "What's the matter?"

"Why do they hate me?" she said, looking up again, and he saw her eyes brimmed with tears.

Serafa said, "What is she saying?"

He turned toward her, angry. "What happened? What did you do to her, damn it?"

The older woman lifted her head, looking down her nose at him, barricaded behind her years and power. She said, "Josefa scrubbed her a little hard. What is she saying?"

"She thinks you hate her." He turned back to Lily, getting to his feet; he was hungry, but that could wait. "Come on," he said. "Let's go."

"Where are you going?" Serafa asked sharply.

King shook his head at her; he went over to the girl, took her by the arm, and drew her along out of the kitchen.

The night was coming down, slowly, as it did in the summer, deep and cool and blue. The laurel trees in the back of the yard stained the air with their strong spicy scent. He let go of Lily and she walked along beside him toward the little old adobe. He said, "Josefa's getting married. The older daughter. She's scared us being here will queer things for her."

"Will it?" Lily asked.

"No," he said. "They're all *pobladores*, Serafa, her kids, whoever it is Josefa's marrying. That means more'n anything to them, keeping it all together."

"*Pobladores.*"

"The first families that came here from Mexico. The people who started Los Angeles." He hung back to let her go through the door into the adobe. "But like as not they're giving Serafa and her kids some gaff about us and Josefa is taking it hard."

She flung herself down on the cot where she slept. "I hate it here." Suddenly she began to cry. "I hate it. I hate it."

He got busy lighting the lamp. Her sobbing tore at him, as if it were his fault. He had said he would take care of her. Easy to say it. She was lying on the bed, her face pressed against the cover, silent. Her shoulders quivered. He was afraid if he touched her that she would scream at him, push him away. He looked around the long, narrow room; he had moved everything they wouldn't use back into the far end, and he went there, taking the lamp, and looked over the supplies.

When he came back, she was sitting up, her eyes swollen and red, her nose stuck in a book. He put the lamp on the windowsill above her head so she could see better. She paid no attention. Her cheeks were slobbered with tears. He went back to the other end of the room and dragged the spare bed and the chest back against one wall, out of the way. Not finding what he wanted in the stack of lumber against the wall, he went out to the shed behind the house, next to the corral, and got an old fence post.

This he hauled back inside, into the center of the long room, and there wedged the fence post upright between floor and ceiling. He had to jam another piece of wood under the upright post to keep it in place. The big cupboard just inside the door was full of blankets and linens, and he fastened the biggest blanket he could find across the space between the wall and the post. It hung down all the way to the floor, leaving a good space on one side for a doorway. He tucked the blanket under the piece of wood on the floor to hold it there.

Now she was watching him. "What are you doing?" she said.

"Making you a room," he said. "You should have a room of your own."

She said nothing. He went into the new room; the blanket shut out most of the light.

He restacked the pile of old lumber so that it lay closer to the end wall, out of the way, as he did so choosing two good flat slabs, which he laid against the side wall. He went out to the yard. The cantina gave forth showers of light and bursts of laughter and talk. He was still hungry, but he was doing something more important now. He went around behind the adobe to the shed and found some adobe bricks.

When he came in she looked up, her face bright with interest. He took the bricks in to her new room and set two spaced apart on the floor and laid a slab of lumber across them, set two more bricks at either end, and laid the second piece of wood across them. As he did this, the light swelled and grew around him; she had brought the lamp in behind him.

"What's that?" she said.

"Shelves. For your books," he said. He turned and looked at her. "Whyn't you go bring 'em in?"

She put the lamp down on the floor and went back out to the front room. King went after her; she brushed past him, the sack of books in her arm. In the lamplight he saw her face shining. She had forgotten to be unhappy. She went to her knees beside the new shelf and began to take books one by one out of the sack and set them carefully in place.

"Come here and help me with this bed," he said.

She got up, turning, purposeful, beautiful when she moved, like a young animal, and came in and got the foot end of her cot, and with him lifting the head they lugged the bed into her room. They put it head up against the wall next to her bookshelf. He brought in the lamp and set it on the end of the bookshelf.

"Be careful," he said. "Ain't nothing nailed down here."

She plopped down on the bed; her eyes shone like the lamp. She looked up at him and a smile lifted her mouth and her voice sang. "Thank you, King."

"Yeah," he said. He felt warm from his head to his toes. "I'm hungry. I'm going to eat." He went out of the adobe, feeling enormous, and high as the fresh new stars in the sky.

◆ Chapter ◆

VIII

Out on the quiet blue water the steamship floated like a giant wooden wedding cake, its wheel stilled. Bearing the first of its cargo and passengers, three lighters skittered over the water toward the wharf, which extended the natural curve of the shoreline out across the bay toward the little hump of an offshore island. Brand sauntered along the edge of the wharf toward the painted bollards and the little gang of waiting workmen. The light wind ruffled his hair and stroked his face like an airy wing.

Inland, back in the city, the summer heat had laid everybody low, but here the ocean breeze cooled the blazing daylight to a balmy basking glow. The blue sky lay behind a faint veil of clouds. South across the bay, the white beach spread away toward the south, with the soft waves purling along the edge. An osprey hovered over the marsh, just beyond the wharf. Even the dull whine of the machines in the railroad yard was lost in the roll of the waves and the purring of the breeze.

This was like paradise; Brand thought it would be easy to lie down in the sun here and sleep forever. The delicious mildness of the air lulled him. Even the prospect of dealing for days—weeks, even—with Joseph Hyde, soon to disembark from the steamer, was mo-

mentarily less burdensome. Nothing seemed impossible.
Nothing seemed very important.

He knew this for seduction, and resisted it. This
paradise was nothing but a wide, unused, slumbering
space, which the Railroad would burst into and bring to
life. Only, it was beautiful to stand here in the sweetness
of the day, the lighters a way off yet, Joseph Hyde not
yet a sliver under his skin, and enjoy the sunshine.

He sauntered along the wharf a little way. Wilmington
was in itself interesting, it belonged mostly to the man
who had built the little railroad, Phineas Banning, who
had come from Delaware. To landward, over beyond the
grassy dunes, the top of Phineas Banning's house was
just visible, a great city mansion, standing alone in the
middle of a sand barren. Banning's many enterprises
filled the narrow stretch of firm flat ground that lay just
north of the railroad station and the wharf; there were
foundries, warehouses, and factories for making railroad
cars, boats, machine parts, machines.

The coastline here stuck a rocky headland out into the
Pacific, sheltering just to the south a little patch of shallow water, not a good harbor, but close. The wharf ran
lengthwise of the top edge of this cove; where the shore
curved, the wooden platforms of the wharf gave way to
the railroad tracks stretching away inland. South of the
wharf, behind a narrow sandspit, the shore was marshy,
flooded at high tide; the railroad ran out across this on
a series of trestles like wooden knees. Beyond, the yellow hills took over.

Brand could see the old wagon trail denting the high
grass at the edge of the marsh; the wagon trail skirted
the soggy swampland, while the railroad's wooden legs
ran it straight across, as if the marsh weren't there. This
pleased him warmly, like a good drink.

Brand loved the Railroad, not the iron and the loco-
motives and the ties, certainly not the men in boiled
shirts and silk hats who thought they were the Southern
Pacific, but the spirit, the sheer will that blasted tunnels

through mountains and spun track across empty space, the power that nothing could stop. The Railroad was pure force, true force, that never failed. The Railroad had given him a job, a way to live that did not require two hands, a way to compel other men to look up to him even if he was a cripple. Because of the Railroad, as the lighters bobbed over the waves to the edge of the wharf, and the workmen ran to swing around the gangplank and connect it, Brand could stand there with an even mind, a man who belonged where he was.

Then Hyde came up the gangplank onto the wharf, like a cloud across the sun.

Hyde was a negotiator, a big soft man who worked sitting down. He wore his plentiful chestnut hair curled like a woman's. He had small close-set eyes and a mouth bent into a permanent sneer. Brand had met him a couple of times before and hated him.

At the foot of the gangplank, Hyde stopped, looking around importantly; hurrying after him came two other men in the same kind of clothes: dark gray coats, silk ties, white collars and gloves. Nabobs. Brand started forward. Hyde came to the middle of the wharf, took a wide look around him, and swung back toward the men following him.

"This is your harbor? Mr. Newmark. Governor." Hyde laughed, swung around again. "Where?"

The other two men hustled up to him. Brand recognized one for John Downey, who had been governor of California, which was less a distinction in this state than in some others. Now that they were all stopped, a stream of porters rushed past them, hauling off the boxes and trunks that were the men's luggage. Hyde was still laughing. He caught a glimpse of Brand, and the laugh froze on his lips.

Brand went up to meet them. He said, "Welcome to Los Angeles, Mr. Hyde." He put one finger to the brim of his hat. "The train's just over here."

"Brand," Hyde said. He clasped his hands together in

front of him. "I didn't—I expected someone else." He looked at the train waiting in the station at the end of the wharf and his breath exploded out of him in a contemptuous grunt. "Hunh."

Brand turned, stretching out his right arm to catch the nearest porter, and dropped a half eagle into the man's hand. "Make sure all Mr. Hyde's baggage gets into the last freight car, and keep it together."

"Yessir."

Hyde said, "What is this?" His voice whined with annoyance. He was striding along toward the train. "A narrow gauge?"

"I assure you, sir," said the Los Angeles nabob who was not Downey. "Our railroad is one of the finest in the land. We're very proud of her. Aren't we, Governor?"

Downey said nothing. Clearly Hyde's company had already told on him considerably. He strode after Hyde toward the train, while Brand collared a second porter and gave him another five dollars to shuffle the few remaining, unimportant passengers into the forward car.

When he caught up with Hyde, at the step up to the last passenger car, the railroad man turned on him.

"I am accustomed to traveling in a private car, as you very well know."

"They don't have one," Brand said. He waved his hand at the steps. "You want to stand out here on the wharf until somebody gets around to building one, why—"

Hyde tramped up the steps past him into the car. The governor and the other man followed him. Brand went after them. The car had been built here, on the model of a Pullman Golden Palace, with the Pullman's wide windows and elegantly finished interior. Brand had made sure that the bar at the far end was stocked, and he had hired a black attendant to serve the drinks. But the car was small and the seats were hard and narrow. Even the harsh fresh tang of soap didn't hide the general stink of chaw tobacco juice. Hyde went grumbling toward a seat in the car's waist; the governor took the bench opposite him and turned his stare resolutely out the window. The other man sat next to Hyde.

"As I said, we're very proud of the Los Angeles and San Pedro. Before she was built it took half a day to get freight in from the coast, and now it's there in the depot in an hour. Faster, sometimes."

Brand went toward the end of the car. Expressionless, adjusting the white napkin on his arm, the attendant went up the car toward the three nobs; Brand reached across the shiny maple bar, where the liquor stood on a gim-balled shelf, and took down the square bottle of bourbon. With his stump he pinned the bottle and with his fingers jerked the cork.

Behind him, Hyde said, "Mr. Newmark, are you lec-turing me on the wonders of the railroad?" He gave a throaty chuckle.

The attendant brought all the men drinks and that shut them up. The train captain looked in the door, and Brand caught his eye and nodded and the man left. The whistle blew. Brand took a long slug of bourbon. The train gave a jerk, fell still again, and then lurched into forward mo-tion, steadily faster.

"Actually," Newmark said, in a sudden burst of jo-viality, "we could use a private car. I'm surprised Gen-eral Banning hasn't ordered one himself."

"Expensive," said Hyde, who was staring out the win-dow. "God, what a dismal landscape." They were crossing the trestle over the marsh, and cattails whipped by past the windows. The little narrow gauge was mov-ing along at a fair pace but the car tended to sway.

"All the cars are made right there in Wilmington," Newmark said. "I'm sure the expense would not be be-yond our railroad."

"I understood the railroad belonged to Banning," said Hyde. He sniffed. "Excuse me. *General* Banning."

"The city has a commanding interest," Newmark said airily.

Hyde gave another irritating laugh. "Better an interest than an obligation, I'm sure."

This comment affronted Newmark into silence for the rest of the trip. The train barreled across a road, a dent in the endless yellow grass, running off to nowhere. The tracks led north across the broad savanna that lay between the San Gabriel Mountains and the Pacific. Here and there dark islands of oaks and cottonwoods broke the monotony of the broad yellow plain. The train let go a long sorrowful whistle, and a moment later they were rushing through a tiny town, two or three bare board buildings, a railroad platform with a sign reading COMPTONVILLE.

Brand settled himself more easily in his seat. Wherever a railroad went, it seeded towns along its route. Hyde could bad-mouth this little road all he wanted, but it was certainly the heart of the deal he was here to make. The Southern Pacific fattened itself by gobbling up short lines and stitching them together into one road. The Los Angeles and San Pedro Railroad gave the SP track here even before they laid a single rail of their own.

In the distance the mountains were low blue ridges. They flew through another crossroads stop, this one only a shack with a sign reading FLORENCE dangling off the eave of the roof. Almost at once they were coming to the city. They passed a field, where brown people stooped among the rows of corn, then another field, then an orchard, and then they were chugging down, sliding into the city past empty lots and the long rickety-looking building of the brewery, a livery stable where the tethered horses reared and shied to the ends of their ropes away from the train, and into the station.

Here again, Hyde had some remarks. Brand went around paying off people to haul the Railroad man's luggage over to Pico House; he had already arranged for a carriage, which was waiting in the usual jam of people and vehicles on the other side of the platform. Hyde was grumbling, his fat lips pursed. His little eyes glittered behind the plump rolls of his cheeks. Newmark and Downey muttered their farewells and hurried off, looking relieved. Hyde dumped himself into the carriage and Brand got into the seat across from him, pulling the door shut.

Hyde glowered across the space between them. His plump fingers paddled at the front of his vest and produced a cigar. He said, "I hope you've done better with the accommodations than you did with the train." He took a clipper from a vest pocket, nipped off the end of the cigar, stuck it into his mouth, and waited, staring at Brand.

"I don't smoke," Brand said. "I don't have any lights."

Hyde made a nasty sound in his throat. From a vest pocket he produced a little pack of lucifers and tossed it over. Brand caught the box in his hand, slid it open with his fingers, negotiated one of the matches out, and struck it on the edge of the seat. He held the flame toward Hyde, who leaned forward slightly, laying the tip of the cigar into the flame. He puffed. The rich smoke rose into the air. Brand shook the match out and Hyde took the cigar from his mouth, looked at it appreciatively, then leaned back again. He frowned.

"Why aren't we going anywhere?"

"Traffic," Brand said. "It'll ease up in a minute."

Hyde growled under his breath. His eyes glinted. He leaned back, chewing the cigar. "Well. You've been using your time here profitably, I hope?"

"I'm still looking around," Brand said. The carriage lurched suddenly and rolled forward; they swung away down Alameda Street. Hyde was still staring at him.

"Opened an office yet?"

Brand twitched. He had not thought that was part of his job. "I don't have any money."

"Well, you'd better get to it. We've got a lot of work

to do here." Hyde shifted on the seat. Abruptly his face slumped, sad folds drooping along his jowls. "Lot of work and no money. Nobody's got any money." He stared out the window at the new buildings they passed. Everything in Los Angeles was always new. "Is this all there is to this place? God, what's Stanford think he's doing?"

The carriage wheeled around into the plaza and pulled up before the Pico House. Brand got out; while porters fought to take down Hyde's baggage he sauntered around stretching his legs. Hyde was just blowing air, he thought, complaining about the SP being broke. But Brand was already out of pocket some two hundred dollars, and they owed him three months' pay. Somebody somewhere had to have some money. When Hyde came down from the carriage Brand tramped away into the hotel with him, saying nothing.

The hotel manager was waiting for them, made a big ceremony out of greeting the Railroad's man, and ushered them up to the top floor and the best suite in the place, two big rooms furnished in European woods and Chinese drapery and a Persian carpet. Hyde took it all in with a sniff. He plopped himself down into a big wing chair as if he had not just spent hours sitting. Brand paced around the room, uneasy, while the porters brought in the bags.

The porters lingered, their eyes shining, their hands discreetly cupped before them. Brand tossed them each a half eagle as if he had a thousand more. When they left, he said, "I'm running short of cash, Mr. Hyde."

"So is everybody else," Hyde said. "Get me a drink."

Brand bit back his temper. He went to the tall lacquered cabinet between the windows and opened the double doors.

Behind him, Hyde groaned. "Look at this place. What a dump. I hope there's a maid to keep the dust down. God, this is the end of the world. I don't know what Stanford's thinking. Bringing the line in here is like pouring water down a bottomless hole. Los Angeles will never amount to anything. We should be going into San Bernardino. This is just going to be a way station en route to San Francisco. I get all the dirty, low-down jobs."

Brand brought him the glass of bourbon. Hyde glared at him even as he reached for the whiskey.

He said, "I told them to send somebody else, Brand. I don't know as how you can handle this assignment. I thought they'd fire you after that fiasco up in Nevada."

Brand jerked his head up and a rush of anger heated his neck and face. "I got that silver back the same day."

"Yeah, but a highway robber made a fool out of you." Hyde laid the cigar down on a tray on the table next to his chair. "You foul up here, Brand, and I'll see you never work for the Railroad again. You understand me?"

Brand wanted to sock him; the end of his stump throbbed. He stared into Hyde's face a moment. "You can't fire me. If you fire me, you got to pay me my back wages."

Hyde harrumphed. "We can't pay anybody. There's no money. The Road's broke, Brand. The SP is three days from being bankrupt, and the three days are today, yesterday, and the day before that."

Brand turned and went back to the liquor cabinet. "Relax. There's always more money. They'll just sell some more bonds. What're we doing here, if the Road's not building into Los Angeles?" He poured himself three fingers of the amber sourmash.

"This is the worst it's ever been," Hyde said. "Crocker and his brother want to sell out, I understand Hopkins wants to sell out, but they can't find anybody to buy them out. Huntington in New York is peddling bonds just to raise working capital and nobody will buy them. Why should they? Everybody knows railroads are terrible investments. Half our track ends nowhere, half our cars travel empty, the gold is mined out and the silver's going. The Mexicans will have the whole place back in twenty years."

"We've been here before," Brand said, lifting his glass. "Huntington will get us through."

"I don't know about that. The Road's twenty-five million dollars in debt."

"Get it from the counties," Brand said roughly. "Like before."

"The legislature's passed this damn bill saying we can't take money from the county governments until we've built fifteen miles of track actually inside the county in question. And then we get only as much money as we've spent. We've got to build track to make money, we've got to make money to build track. It's crazy."

Brand paced around the room again, sipping the bourbon. "Nothing can stop the Road. We'll make it."

"We have to get control of the legislature. That's Stanford's business. You and I have other fish to fry. We need to screw everything we can out of Los Angeles, and fast. I'm going to negotiate a subsidy. Your job is to make sure nobody gets in the way. There'll likely be a vote on the subsidy and I expect you to help manage that, too."

Brand turned toward him, glad to have something he could handle. He hated Hyde, but they both worked for the Railroad; it was like hating his brother. "That won't be hard."

"Make sure it gets done right," Hyde said. He picked up the cigar again and sucked on it, but it had gone out. He contemplated the cold tip. "I'm having dinner tonight with the mayor and the Chamber of Commerce. I'll get some money out of them. We need a temporary office, at least until after the election, and then for a while if we win."

"When we win," Brand said.

Hyde smirked. "You'll need some people to help you handle the opposition."

"Right," Brand said. The tightness in his throat eased a little; he felt the inexorable power of the Railroad begin to flow through him again. With the Railroad behind him he could do anything.

"Get the maid in here to put my clothes away," Hyde said. He waggled the cigar at Brand, who went to the liquor cabinet again, found a match, struck it, and crossed the room to light the smoke. Hyde leaned back, releasing a stream of blue smoke into the air.

"God, what I do for Collis Huntington and Leland Stanford."

◆ Chapter ◆

IX

In the morning, after breakfast, Serafa took Lily into the kitchen and put her to work, first bringing in the wood for the hearth and then hauling water. The other girls disappeared at midmorning, but Serafa stayed in the kitchen, perched on the stool by the door, and watched Lily impassively.

This woman was baffling. She never smiled, but she never frowned either. Her wide black eyes were either serene or secretive. She always seemed to be staring at her, but maybe she was staring into space and Lily simply got in the way. She never said anything. And yet Lily felt her presence as if she shouted.

Late in the morning, the two girls rushed back in, and with Serafa they made the midday dinner and took it out to the cantina. They worked with a furious silent efficiency that left Lily out entirely. She slipped away out the door and across the yard to the old house where she was staying. Pigeye had not come back the night before, his saddle and bedroll were missing, and she was beginning to hope he was gone for good. King had also disappeared. She had finished *Villette* and she fished a new book out of the sugarsack and sat down on her bed to read.

A few moments later the door burst open, and the tall

girl, whose name was Josefa, came into the room. She scowled down at Lily. "What are you doing? Mama says you must come."

"I did work," Lily said.

"You did a little work," Josefa said, her hands on her hips. "Come back now, we need help, there are many more people here because of the fandango." When Lily did not move, she said sharply, "We are all at work. You have to help us."

Lily slid off the bed and followed her out the door. "What's a fandango?" she asked, but Josefa strode on ahead of her, back pike-upright, and swept into the kitchen. One arm thrust out toward the table.

"There! Wash these dishes and dry them, quick!"

Lily went into the dark kitchen. Instantly the heat from the great hearth brought a sheen of sweat to her skin. Beside the washtub on the table stood towers of dirty dishes; the full tub steamed.

Josefa turned and stared at her. "Well?"

Going around the table, Lily picked up the top dish and slid it into the water; she winced at the heat. Quickly she brought her hands up out of the tub, scrubbed the dish, swished it back and forth through the water and set it down to her left, then took another dish. Josefa stalked past her, went importantly once around the table, and left.

Lily washed dish after dish. Serafa came in, stirring, tasting, pulling things off the fire and putting them on. Josefa dashed in once more. She always made a lot of noise, Lily noticed. She took over the table, dropping her tray onto it, shoving the dirty dishes off into the heap in front of Lily. She shouted, "Wash these dishes, girl! We need them right away! Right away, you lazy *cholla*." Serafa ladled steaming meat and red sauce onto a row of clean plates, and Josefa arranged the plates onto trays and bore them swiftly off. Lily glared after her, realized Serafa was watching, and reached hastily for another dish. The heap in front of her was as big as ever; she would never get done with it.

Luz came in. She was quieter than Josefa and smiled all the time, and when she set her tray down she moved off the dirty dishes into orderly stacks.

She said, "Let me help you," and came around the table to Lily's side and plunged her hands into the wash-tub. "*Aiyyah*," she said. "It's too cold." She went to the fire for the kettle and poured boiling water and steam into the tub.

"It's too hot." Lily yanked her hands out of the water.

"You have Anglo hands." Serafa's daughter gave a laugh; she put down the kettle. Her own wide brown hands moved expertly through the dishes, washing faster than Lily ever could. Lily watched her, trying to imitate the way she handled the plates. Luz said, "Dry them—the cloth is there, hanging on the hook."

Lily reached for the thick white cloth. Luz said, "Haven't you ever had to work before? Who did the work where you used to live?"

Lily had it on her tongue to tell her that she had scrubbed and washed up after her father ever since she was five. Instead, she said, "No, we had servants."

Luz glanced sharply at her. "Really. Where did you live?"

Lily was drying dishes and stacking them; she kept her eyes on her hands. "We had a huge house, with twenty rooms, and a lace peacock on the front door. There was a front stairs maid and a back stairs maid, and a cook, and two butlers and a footman." She lifted her gaze to meet Luz's, this picture blooming into full color in her mind. "I had two rooms to myself, a bed-room and a place to sit and read overlooking the garden. But we had to leave because it was entailed away." She had no idea what "entailed away" meant, but she thought Luz wouldn't, either.

Luz gaped at her, astonished. She said, "Where was this?"

"New York City," Lily said. "But when my uncle—he was the one everything was entailed away for—when he came into the estate he chased me and my father out here. His gang nearly killed us several times."

Luz blinked at her. Lily smiled, delighted with this story; she shook the wet cloth out and reached for another dish. Luz began to say something, and Serafa came in.

Lily at once bent to her work, thinking that with Serafa's presence there the game was probably over. Luz and Serafa spoke back and forth in Spanish. At any moment, Lily thought, Luz would round on her, angry, and accuse her of lying.

Instead, she turned to Lily and said, "My mama wants to know if you are coming to the fandango."

Lily put the last dish on the stack. "What's the fandango?"

The mother spoke again, nodding to her daughter and pointing to Lily. Luz turned to Lily again. Her face was carefully bland. "My mother wants me to give you one of my dresses to wear, if you are going to the fandango."

"I don't know what a fandango is," Lily said, coming down hard on the last word; they seemed to her to be deliberately confusing her, taunting and teasing her.

Luz said, "It's just a party. It is the day of admission, when California became part of the United States." Now her voice was definitely edged with malice. "Didn't you have parties in New York City?"

Lily looked away. "Why should I go to a party? I don't have any friends here." Suddenly she longed with her whole heart for that house in New York City, where they had parties every day. She reached for another of the infinite plates heaped before her.

Luz shrugged. "As you wish." She and Serafa set out clean plates and ladled the steaming food onto them. Luz hurried off with the heavily laden trays.

Serafa said something to Lily in Spanish. Lily shook her head, morose. "I don't understand you." She turned away, not wanting to understand. Nobody understood her anyway. Nobody knew her.

Serafa came around the table to her, took the dirty dish out of her hand, and drew her around to the far end of the table. She set a dish down before Lily, spooned the rich meat and sauce into it, and waved her hand at it. Suddenly Lily's mouth was full of sweet water. She had not eaten since breakfast. "Thank you," she said, and sat down and ate.

Serafa spoke a string of syllables and went over to her stool. Lily devoured the food and felt better. She decided she liked Serafa. She wished she could speak Spanish.

But usually Serafa wasn't there. All afternoon, Lily washed dishes while Josefa shouted at her that she was lazy and stupid, and even Luz, who helped her often, laughed when she dropped a plate and broke it. "Silly girl—you ought to have done that before you washed it." Hot with rage and shame, Lily stooped to pick up the pieces, threw them into a basket, and stormed out of the kitchen.

She expected them to call her back and determined that she would not go; but they left her alone. She went into the old adobe, cool and quiet after the kitchen's steamy heat, and got out her book. Through the door she could hear Luz and Josefa laughing, and she knew they were laughing at her. These people were mean and hateful and she had to get away from them. She sat on her bed, propped her book on her knees, and sank gratefully into its otherness.

In the late summer dusk, the street was a stream of fuzzy yellow light. Strings of lanterns hung along the eaves of the houses and clustered in the branches of the laurel trees. Every door and window spilled out light and noise. People sauntered along the street, stopping to talk, laughing, knocking on doors, and calling out to their friends. The day had gone by and the evening air was warm and soft and ripe with the smells of food and of flowers.

King rode in from the south, where he had gone to look around. The sun had just set and the air was the color of clear water. He could hear fiddles playing. Arm in arm, the village girls were walking up and down the street, talking to one another, while the boys stood around, pretending not to look at them.

He remembered when this had been all of Los Angeles, this *Calle* and the plaza just beyond, only a few years ago. When the streets ran south only to vineyards and fields, and everybody knew everybody else. Then he and Tiburcio had been lords of the place, spending money and doing as they pleased, stepping aside for nobody.

The rest of it, the factories and saloons, the stores and boardinghouses and mansions, had grown up in the last few years. This new Los Angeles had eaten up Tiburcio; King was bound it would not get him, too. Sonoratown, he thought, was safe enough; he drifted along the side of the street, enjoying the colors and sounds of the fandango.

Nearby a fiddle burst into a long zigzag of music. An old memory stabbed him, the shrill of another, different fiddle. Someone dancing in the street. He did not want to remember it. He rode around behind Serafa's place, to the corral there and the shed.

He had ridden his sorrel horse, used it hard all day, and he brought the animal a bait of hay and rubbed it down well and picked up its feet. They were low on hay and he would have to find some more. He put the horse in the corral with more feed and went around to the adobe.

There was a long white dress hanging in the doorframe. He slid by it into the dark room beyond; Lily's lamp shone through the blanket wall. He went around to the doorway between his side of the adobe and hers.

"What's this dress here?"

She was sitting on her bed, her head in her book. She mumbled something at him, not looking up. He leaned against the wall, looking her over; she looked unhappy.

"Why don't you go to the fandango?"

"I don't want to go to the fandango!" she snarled at him. Her eyes were pink.

He said, "Well, there's a dress here, looks like just your size. I bet you'd look pretty good in it."

"I'm not going to the fandango," she said. "I hate these people. I hate everybody. I hate you. Just go away and leave me alone." She slammed over the next page in her book.

He slid back out of the doorway, giving up. He had something he planned to do this evening, anyway, for which he definitely did not need her. He went back out to the clear blue air and the music.

Lily could not force her eyes to read; the book was like a block of nothing in her hands. Her face was hot. She hated them all. Far off, a lot of voices all went up at once in a long cheer. People were laughing. She hated them. She hated the whole world. She hated life.

She put the book down. Her heart was beating in an odd galloping way. Her ears strained after the distant music. Suddenly she wished she had listened to King, put on the dress, and gone to the fandango.

She got up and went to the opening in the blanket.

The dress hung there, white in the gloom. It was simple as a nightgown, long, with a wide neck, long flowing sleeves. She took it down from the doorframe and held it against herself.

Somewhere beyond these buildings a yell went up, and then applause and laughter. Suddenly she could not move fast enough; she rushed into her room, pulled off her clothes, and put on the dress. It was very loose. The hem brushed her bare feet when she moved. She whirled around once, and the long dress swung around her, its hem ruffling.

She went out the door into the yard, her feet bare in the dust. She could hear music beyond the cantina, in the street; she wondered how to get there. Then the back door of the cantina opened and Serafa came out.

She saw Lily at once. Lily drew back, wary; but Serafa had been kind to her. She thought Serafa might like her. Lily gave her an uncertain smile. The older woman looked her over from her bare dusty feet to her hair. Lifting her eyes, she said something in Spanish. Her voice was husky, and there was a note of laughter in it.

Hopeful, Lily came forward a few steps. "I'm going to the fandango," she said.

"Ah." Serafa held up one finger and went away across the yard to the building past the kitchen, where she and her daughters lived.

Lily stood where she was, not knowing what to do. After a moment she started off again, going around the building, but then Serafa came back. She had a brush in her hand and a piece of red cloth. She beckoned Lily over to the rear door of the cantina, where the light from the lantern shone, and with one hand on her shoulder made her sit down on the step. Quickly she gathered up Lily's hair and brushed it, a few abrupt hard strokes. Lily put her hands up, and Serafa said something softly, pushed her arms down, and laid down the brush beside her. Lily subsided, her hands in her lap. The strong tugging on her hair felt good; she could feel Serafa coiling up her hair, twisting it around, and then the soft weight on her head and the small pokes of the pins going in.

Serafa came around in front of her, held out her hands, and brought her up onto her feet again. Her tilted black witch's eyes snapped with good humor. Lily put her hands to her head. The smooth rounds of her hair felt like silk under her fingertips. Pleased, she said, "Thank you."

"De nada," Serafa said. She took the strip of bright

cloth from her apron. She wrapped the cloth twice
around Lily's waist and tied the ends just in front of her
right hip. Standing back, she swept her gaze over the
girl, smiled again. Bending, she picked a flower from a
clump of wildflowers beside the stoop and tucked the
stem into Lily's hair.

"*Vaya.*" She urged her off with both hands. "*Vaya,
florita.*"

Lily laughed. She tingled all over, warm and vibrant.
Serafa's touch had made her pretty. Whirling, she ran
around the end of the building and out to the street.

The street blazed with lights. The number of people
startled her. She stopped abruptly by the corner of the
building. In front of her and to her left, along the wall
of Serafa's cantina, three men were playing guitars,
while two long lines of people surged along the street,
bowing and kicking and spinning around. Lily hung
back by the corner of the building, shy again.

Between the line of dancers one couple pranced beautifully from pose to pose. They were all in pairs, she
saw; they turned and bowed to one another, each pair a
man and a woman. She saw Josefa, spinning on the arm
of a tall young man with a thin black mustache. Josefa
wore a look of calm unconcern, as if she were above all
this, watching. For once her mouth was closed. Lily
looked for Luz, but did not see her.

Other people swarmed along the sides of the street,
standing around talking to each other and going in and
out of the buildings; they had to shout to be heard above
the music, and the people listening bent toward the
shouting mouth, a hand cupped to catch the words. Their
clothes glittered. Lily ran her hand down the plain front
of her dress. The other women had colored figures all
over the tops of their dresses. She was too plain. She
would never dance. She watched couple after couple follow the first in their intricate twisting and turning down
the long line of bodies. Then the music flourished to an
end and the dance stopped.

In groups, the dancers went wandering off; two children ran out into the suddenly empty street and began to reenact the dance in energetic graceless jerks. A ripple of laughter spread through the people watching. Two of the guitar players slung their instruments on their shoulders and walked away and the third stood, his head down, picking out a little bit of music, over and over. A fiddler stepped over to him and played the same little sentence of notes. Lily looked off down the street, wondering where Josefa had gone.

A strange voice startled her, coming from just behind her, and she spun around. A young man stood there smiling at her. He spoke again in Spanish; she said, "I don't understand you."

"Ah," he said. "But you understand English. I am saying only that you are the most beautiful creature on earth, and I beg your permission to worship at your feet."

Lily's mouth fell open. He was holding his hand out to her. She reached out and took it, and he drew her into the street, where people were gathering into lines again.

She looked up at him, panicked. "I can't dance."

"I will show you," he said. He smiled at her. Here in the light of the lanterns she saw him more clearly. He was a little older than she was. He had smooth dark skin and dark eyes, and a mouth so shapely she had the sudden urge to kiss it. At that thought her whole body seemed to surge upward with excitement. She put her hands out to him.

"Show me."

"My name is Raul," he said. "Raul Rosas."

"My name is Lily."

Behind her the fiddle scraped out a sudden long cascade of notes. She laughed. Raul held her hands up. "Ready?"

"Yes!"

King leaned against the wall of the cantina, watching Lily; he had never seen her laugh so much. The boy who was her partner had taught her half a dozen steps in two minutes and now she was bouncing and kicking along with the rest of them, her eyes blazing. Every man there was looking at her, and her partner was holding tight to her hand.

She's beautiful, he thought. And: I'll kill anybody who touches her.

The fiddler strolled up and down along the wall, streaming out the long sonorous tune, and the dancers swayed back and forth in the grip of the music. King shifted his feet, disturbed. Something in the music rubbed on his memory, a few notes that sounded like another, alien song. But the fiddle was wrong. The rhythm wrong. He edged away from the dance. The music pursued him. He wanted it to be faster. It made him uneasy. Suddenly he wanted not to hear it at all.

In a gush of notes the forgotten song came back to him, the quick jig of the old tune, and the deep memory welled to the surface. A great piercing ache. Fiddler, play faster. In another dusty street, half a world away, a little girl danced for coppers. This here-now fiddler's song ran off down its Californio path, but the Irish song clung to him on the shrill of the strings. He reeled away, unable to stand and hear it. The song in his mind. The pad of bare feet on the stony dust and the coach full of people watching. He flung himself into the cantina.

The room was dark, save for the lantern hanging over the bar. Beneath it, Serafa stood alone, wrapped in her shawl so that the perfect oval of her face seemed to float in the air. Her wide black eyes fixed on him, unsurprised, remote. He went up to her, his blood rushing.

"*Señora*!" He would make a game of it, cage it in some joke. "Dance with me."

"Dancing is for girls," she said, but her eyes gleamed. She put out her hand to him.

He gripped her hand, swung her around. His feet

stumbled a few steps. He had forgotten how to do this.

Serafa laughed. "Silly man. That is not how to dance."

"Oh, yes, it is." Now suddenly his feet remembered. Da-da-dit-da-da-dit—he spun her around by the hand, dancing faster and faster to the song in his mind.

"King, you go too fast!"

"Never!"

He kicked out the steps, nimble as a goat even in his boots, gripping her two hands in his, and she laughed, throaty and wild, trying to keep up with him, her face tilted back, fierce with effort. Fiddler, play. He shut his eyes and wished himself away, away; the wish would carry him home, wasn't that how it went? He opened his eyes, and saw Serafa.

Sweet and good Serafa. He pulled her against him and kissed her.

For a moment she kissed him back, her body, heated from the dance, pressed against his; then abruptly she twisted away from him. Her eyes were brilliant. She said, "How dare you do that."

He said, "I only did half of it, *señora.*" He grabbed her again and held her, although she pushed against his arms. "Let me."

"Ah," she said. "You are heedless of me."

"Oh, no," he said, "that's exactly what I am not," and held her fast and kissed her again. She was fighting, but she wasn't fighting very hard. Her lips parted. He ran his tongue into her mouth and felt her shudder all through her body.

Her hands pushed on his chest and he let her go. She drew back away from him a few steps, turning away, and then looked back at him again. Her tongue ran over her lips. He reached for her hand.

"If I come to your window tonight, will you let me in?"

"I am an honest woman, I do not let common bandits in through my bedroom window." But she smiled at him;

she tipped her head forward and looked quickly up at him. He got hold of her hand and held it.

"But let me come talk to you, at least," he said. "I'll sing. Or something." He put the ends of her fingers to his lips.

"I suppose you sing like a nightingale."

"More like a corncrake. But for you, *querida,* anything."

The door burst open; several people bustled into the room. King turned away from her, dropping her hand, and Serafa went swiftly in behind the counter to bring up the punch and the brandy and the glasses. King let the crowd push him back toward the door. After a moment he watched her lift her head and look for him. Their eyes met through the noisy, shoving crowd, but then he reached the door and went out.

Somewhere across town they were shooting off Chinese fireworks; most of Los Angeles had gone there to watch. Still, the Crystal Palace was jammed with men, and Brand had to work his way through to the bar and with his elbows wedge open enough room to stand there.

He leaned up against the scarred wooden counter. The mirror behind it reflected the packed bodies, the brilliant lights of the room behind him. He had trouble picking himself out of the mob, and his face startled him when he did find it: he had imagined he looked better, not so ordinary. He lowered his eyes. The barkeep brought him a glass and a bottle.

"The usual, sir?"

"Sure."

The bartender poured sourmash into his glass. Brand had been coming in here for a week now; they knew who he was and respected him. Still he kept his left arm below the level of the bartop. He drank the first shot off fast, to take his edge off, and set the glass down with a thump and a nod. The bartender was there at once to fill it again.

"There's somebody here who wants to talk to you, sir."

"Yeah?" Brand had been expecting this. "Where?"

"I told them to wait. I can send them over—"

"No. I need a private room. You got a card room?"

"Just a moment." The bartender went purposefully off. Brand nursed his second drink; he had to keep his head clear. He kept one eye on the mirror, watching his back by looking forward, a nice work.

A few moments later the bartender was ushering him around to the back staircase; he went up the steps by himself and in the corridor at the top opened the first door and stepped inside.

The four men sitting at the table there all swung toward him at once; a fifth slouched in a chair in the corner. Brand said, "My name's Brand—I work for the Southern Pacific. I'm looking for some hands. Are you fellas what I'm looking for?"

The big, bluff man directly across the table said, "We're your boys, Mr. Brand. Ain't we, boys?"

Their voices rose, a chorus of agreement. The big man stood and stretched out his hand toward Brand. "My name's Elmo Bryce."

"Pleasure." He didn't shake the offered hand. Reaching for the nearest empty chair, he pulled it to the table and sat, and big Elmo sat down on his left. He scanned the other men—young, rough, dressed in working clothes, carrying handguns. None of them looked very bright, which suited Brand fine.

"Where you boys from?"

"El Monte, most of us," Elmo said. He fisted his big hands together on the tabletop. His knuckles were flattened and lumpy with scar tissue. His thick black hair still carried the indentation of his hat, and his tan ended abruptly in the middle of his forehead. "George there's just got into town from the silver country." He nodded toward the man slouching in the chair in the corner.

Brand gave him a probing look. "You into this?"

"Unh—sure." George lifted his head. He had scanty yellow hair and eyes like pinpricks. His mouth worked nervously, as if he were getting ready to spit, but he didn't.

"Get over here, then," Brand said.

George dragged his chair to the table. Elmo chuckled. "George has some big shot partner was going to give us work, but turned out the partner wasn't such a big shot after all. More like small gauge."

George flushed. Taking their lead from Elmo, the other men crowed and jabbed at him with their elbows. Brand listened to them, getting a feel for them: stupid country boys, sick of cows and plows, looking for some quick money, they would do anything that paid well. Brand had money now, too. Hyde had fixed him up with a war chest that afternoon—not all that much, actually, but to these hayseeds a double eagle looked like a fortune.

He said, "What about you?" and looked at the next man, who mumbled a name, and so it went around the table. He didn't bother to remember any names but Elmo's. He would deal through Elmo, let the big man boss his friends. He faced Elmo now, eye to eye.

He said, "All right. I need some work done. Mostly it ought to be pretty easy. Most people down here seem to be on our side already. There seems to be a couple people may want to fight it, but we're going to deal with that."

Elmo's mouth pursed with the effort of thought. His eyes flicked toward his friends. "You mean, beat people up."

Brand laughed. "Well, no, I hope not, anyway. I hope it won't come to that. For starters, though, somebody's been putting up posters around town talking up some big rally against the SP. I want all those posters torn down, and any others like it too."

Elmo pushed out his thick lips. "Sounds like work," he said.

"And if you happen on people putting up posters," Brand said, "then you want to discourage them. If you get me."

At that Elmo grinned, relaxing, and nudged George with his elbow. George jumped; clearly he was a nervous sort. Elmo said, "I got you. We'll make 'em sorry they ever said anything against the Railroad. Won't we, boys?"

"Don't mention the Railroad," Brand said sharply. "Don't say anything at all to anybody, in fact. Just get those posters down. I don't want three people showing up at that rally. I don't want any talk, any at all."

"Oh." Elmo looked perplexed. "Well, you're the boss."

"That's right," Brand said. He took the sack of gold money out of his coat and tossed it onto the table. He had kept his stump under the table the whole time, but now, deliberately, he brought it out into sight. He saw them all stare, wide-eyed; he let them look all they wanted. He opened the sack up with his fingers and poured out a little pile of the gold money and with his stump flicked a coin at each of them.

"This is for starters," he said. "Every time you do a job for me, when it's done, you'll get more."

"All right," Elmo said. He fondled the pretty yellow coin in his fingers, his eyes greedy on the sack lying on the table, still plump with gold. "We're your boys, Mr. Brand."

"Good," Brand said. He jerked the strings tight on the sack and slid it back into his coat. "Now, listen up."

There were three fiddlers now, and two guitar players. Night had fallen, a black whispering depth beyond the smokey yellow of the lanterns. Lily was tired of dancing. She sat down on a bench under a laurel tree, and Raul brought her a glass of lemonade and a plate of cakes.

Josefa and Luz were sitting across the street on the bench in front of their mother's cantina. Josefa's young man sat next to her, and sometimes she turned and spoke to him, but often she stared at Lily, and Luz watched her all the time. Lily decided that the next time she had the chance she would tell Luz that she was a princess of the blood and only waiting for her grandfather the king to recover his throne from the red revolutionists.

Raul hovered behind her. He had not left her side since he drew her forward out of the shadows. She had found out, with some pleasure, that he was the younger brother of Josefa's soon-to-be husband, now lolling there on the bench across the way, letting Josefa hand him sweetmeats and bat her eyes at him.

Raul knelt down beside Lily and tried to take hold of her hand; this bothered her, and she kept out of his grasp. She said, "What else is going to happen?"

He said, "For me, beautiful one, the most wonderful thing has already happened, which is that I have met you."

Lily laughed. "I think you have a very boring life." His attention annoyed her; it was like a fence he threw around her. She slid off the bench and went a few steps down the dusty street.

Raul followed her; he said, "Let me walk with you, beautiful one."

"Oh, come on," she said. "I'm not beautiful."

"Oh, but you are! You are the most beautiful girl in all of El Pueblo." He tried to take hold of her hand again. She pulled out of his grip.

"Well, I'm not," she said. She knew what beautiful girls looked like; they had long yellow ringlets, and deep blue eyes, and red lips like Cupid's bows. She looked around for King, who might get angry if he saw her walking along with this strange boy. King was not in sight.

"Will you dance with me, then?" Raul reached for her hand and she moved away from him.

"No. I don't want to dance anymore. I wish there was something else to do. What else can we do?"

Behind them, the fiddles and guitars struck up another tune and a cheer went up. Lily turned around to watch. Was that all there was, then? Dance and watch other people dance?

"Tomorrow we'll have horse races," Raul said. "I'll ride. Will you cheer for me?"

"Maybe," she said. "Is your horse fast?"

"Oh, the fastest horse in the country!"

She looked away. Raul seemed a collector of superlatives. "What else is there?"

"Oh, well, barbecues, of course, and more music." He sounded strained, as if he were trying to conjure something else up. "The Anglos have fireworks, but we never have such things here, of course."

"Fireworks," she said, turning toward him. "When?"

"I don't know." He shrugged. His jacket was trimmed down the front with flashing silver disks and silver thread, and when he moved the lamplight ticked off him in all directions like sparks.

"Well," she said, "how can we find out?"

"*Señorita,*" he said, sounding alarmed. She laughed. She went on into the dark, her back to him. She knew he would come after her, but even if he didn't, she would find the fireworks somehow.

◆ Chapter ◆

X

Serafa leaned against the window frame, the night wind cool on her face, and said, "If you come in, everybody will know."

She could still hear the music and laughter from the street, where the fandango continued, but here it was quiet: here, they were alone, and she could bask in the heat of his interest.

He had his head and shoulders in through the window, his forearms on the sill. "Oh, Serafa," he said, his smile spreading wide across his face. "Everybody already knows." When he smiled at her, she saw the devil glittering in his eyes. She loved his eyes, which seemed to share some joke with her alone. He had his hat in one hand; leaning in across the windowsill, he tossed it into the room onto her bed. "Just let me in. Who cares who else knows, so long as we're happy?"

Serafa laughed. The thought lingered that, once he had what he wanted, he would not want it so much anymore and this pretty game would be over. He reached out and took a tress of her long hair in his fingers and tugged, and she bent down and let him kiss her lips.

His mouth against her mouth, he whispered, "Let me in, Serafa."

Somewhere else, outside, Luz's voice called, rising in a question.

Serafa stayed bent over in the window. She spoke with her mouth against his, so that their lips brushed together. "And if I let you in tonight through the window, will you expect to come in through the door whenever you want?"

"Whatever you wish." His fingers teased her hair. "All I want is to make you happy, Serafa." The lightness of his touch seemed to draw her skin quivering after his fingers. Her heart was pounding. She knew she would give in, sometime. Steadily she was growing more eager. But she would stretch it out, as long as she could, sip every juice from anticipation.

"What I wish—"

Then, louder, Luz called, "King?"

With a jerk he straightened, looking over his shoulder into the dark, Luz was behind him in the yard somewhere, very close. When he faced Serafa again his smile was gone. He said, "What's that?"

Serafa leaned out the window and called, "Luz! Lucita!"

Luz rushed around the corner of the building, coming from the direction of the kitchen. "Mama, I must find— oh." She came up beside King, now standing to one side of the window, out of the light. The light fell full on the face of Serafa's daughter, revealing every line brimming with suspicion.

She said, "What are you doing here?"

"Serafa mended my shirt," he said, in a perfectly grave voice. "I came to thank her."

Luz's brows flew together. "Your shirt isn't torn."

"Faith, no, I told you, girl, she mended it. What's the matter?"

"I can't find Lily."

"Oh, Christ," he said.

Serafa moved back, away from the window. "This little girl of yours is a lot of trouble."

Luz turned to her. "Raul Rosas is gone, too. When he got his horse out of the remuda he asked old Verdugo where he could find some fireworks."

"Fireworks!" Serafa said.

Still frowning, King gave a little shake of his head. To Luz, he said, "What kind of horse does young Rosas ride?"

"Oh," she said. "A big Overo piebald. The most beautiful horse."

"That should make it easier," he said. He was going. Serafa drew back into the room; a pang of jealousy knifed through her. She wondered why this girl was so important to him. Suddenly he seemed worth more, a prize that was slipping away.

"I'll go find them," he said. At the edge of the light, he looked back over his shoulder at Serafa, and his mouth quirked with amusement. "Keep my hat," he said, and went off into the dark.

Serafa said under her breath, "Damn that girl."

Luz swung toward her, her face vivid. "Mama! What are you doing? What did he mean by that?"

"Bah," Serafa said, and reached out to draw the shutters closed.

Raul said, "I will get you a better horse than this nag. I will find you the most beautiful horse in all of California!" His horse was magnificent, black on its shoulders and back and legs and white on its sides, its long mane braided with rosettes of ribbon, the ends of the ribbon trailing down to flutter whenever the horse shook its head.

Lily patted Jane's neck. "I like my own horse," she said. They were riding along the edge of the plaza. Throngs of people swarmed by them on either side, mostly boisterous drunken men shouting and singing and falling on their faces. Before the Pico House two big coaches were drawn up; she veered in that direction, curious, thinking perhaps there were great ladies after all in Los Angeles, who might ride in such coaches. Remembering Brand, she turned quickly away, cutting across the broad irregular square with its stubby trees, its blocky water tank in the middle.

The lights from the big houses and the hotel spilled across the open ground. She swung her mare past a man lying sprawled on the ground, either dead or drunk. Raul caught up to her.

"Look at this. They are animals."

She glanced up at him, surprised at the vehemence in his voice. A dense wall of bodies jammed the way before them and he nudged her off to the left; over the heads of the massed men she saw a wagon with two kegs standing on the open bed. The crowd in a waving forest of arms held up cups to the two boys on the truck, who took cup after cup, dumped them first, whatever was in them, into a box, and then dipped each cup into a keg and handed it back. She realized what went first into the cup was money.

Raul grumbled something else. His horse was skittish, snorting, its ears laid back; she admired how effortlessly he controlled it, almost without paying attention. While he scanned the crowd she glanced shyly into his face. He was certainly handsome, dark, like the hero of her favorite novel, and probably rich, since he had silver on his clothes. When she thought that, she liked him better, and she also felt a little guilty, and looked away.

Out there in the center of the square, a man stood on a box, shouting, "The Railroad will bleed us dry and send it all to San Francisco! That's where it's all going to go—all that money—a hundred dollars for every man, woman, and child in Los Angeles!"

"What's he talking about?" she asked.

Raul shook his head. "Anglo matters. Of no interest." He faced her, his expression taut with indignation. "We were here first. By God's will this all still belongs to us, the *pobladores*, who made it. These Anglos, they all came here in the last few years. They won't take root here, God does not want them here, before too long they'll leave again, and then everything will be as it was." His face softened. "Except you must not go, my Lily."

She laughed, half angry, although she wasn't sure at what. Not *his* Lily. The mention of God made her uneasy: did he know something she didn't know? Jewell had said God was a lie. She turned toward the man ranting on the box again. "Why is he talking about the Railroad?" She remembered that Brand worked for the Railroad. She turned to sweep her gaze over the crowd; suddenly she felt exposed and visible, sitting up on her horse above all these eyes. She nudged the mare quickly toward the dark on the far side of the square.

When they were halfway across the square, suddenly on Lily's left there was a flat boom, and a billow of smoke went up and a streak of light whistled into the sky, and the crowd all shouted softly, as if sucking their voices inward, and looked up. For a moment the whole plaza was hushed. Then above them lights bloomed, red and blue and white, and hung a moment, and then spilled down in streams through the darkness.

The crowd greeted this with a bellow, and many people clapped. Everybody around her still looked up into the sky, but Lily looked where the boom had come from, the smoke cloud, and saw a man bent over a little round pot on the ground.

Somebody cried, "Over there!" and she wheeled around. Across the plaza, on the front of one of the adobe buildings, lights glimmered and grew stronger, a ring of lights, and then the ring began to spin, casting off showers of sparks. Faster and faster it whirled, a great white rose of lights, while the crowd shrieked and applauded and pushed toward it, as if to warm themselves in the glow.

There was no heat from these fires, and no lasting

light either; she watched another rocket burst overhead, disappointed. Raul reached out to her.

"Isn't this wonderful? See, I have brought you what you wanted!"

"Yes," she said, and smiled, so he wouldn't see she didn't want this after all.

She wondered what was the matter with her, that nothing satisfied her. Obediently she watched and cheered the gaudy show, until her neck began to ache and the urge to be somewhere else overwhelmed her. She reined her mare around. She would go look for beautiful houses. Raul jogged his horse up beside her.

"We should go back. They'll miss us."

"Who cares?" she said.

"My father will be very angry with me," Raul said. "I have my family name to consider."

She shrugged; who knew his family name anywhere but this tiny corner of nowhere? She said, "Have you seen the big houses here?"

"Which houses?" He tried to herd her to the left, riding his horse up slightly ahead of Jane and then reining across her path, but Lily kept the mare straight ahead, leaned her into Raul's horse, and so forced him to ride to the right.

She said, "There are some wonderful houses."

"New ones," he said disdainfully. "Anglo houses. They don't matter."

They left the plaza behind. She had come this way before, she remembered, in the daylight; the broad thoroughfare stretched away ahead of her between rows of yellow lamps on tall posts, vanishing into the dark distance like an invitation. A block ahead of them a lone man walked wearily away. She tried to remember which of these streets led to the wonderful house she had seen before. Raul crowded up beside her again.

"We should go home. It isn't safe here."

She shrugged him off. At the edge of her hearing someone was shouting and she thrust that aside also, her gaze searching the darkened street for the way to the beautiful houses. Someone was shouting somewhere. She turned her head, frowning.

Raul said, "I think it's that way," and reached for her reins.

"No," she said, and kicked the mare on. "Listen. Hurry!" She trotted the mare toward the far side of the street.

"Help," someone was shouting in the next street. "Help!"

She gave a yell. With a clap of both heels she sent the mare at her nervous pace toward the corner, not looking to see if Raul followed; she took for granted that he would. The mare leaned around the corner and shied hard from the swarm of men there, the wild flutter of papers.

Sliding off balance, Lily clutched at the saddle; for a moment all she could see was a circle of white faces gawking at her. She thought somebody was running away. Then a hand grabbed her by the arm.

"Let go of me!" She struck with the quirt on the end of her reins. "Leave me alone. No!" They were all around her. Abruptly she was afraid; they were trapping her, grabbing for her. She kicked at them, and hands caught at her feet; somebody clutched her skirt and pulled.

"It's a girl! Get her down!"

"I'll show her how to kick!"

"Wait," cried a voice she knew. "Wait—let her go, damn it." This man pushed forward, dragging away the big man who clutched her arm. "Let her go, Elmo."

She twisted in her saddle, looking for Raul; he was back there, somewhere. Elmo still had hold of her leg. She shouted, "What are you trying to do? What are you, robbers?" If she yelled someone might hear her. Her skin was cold. She tried to act angry, for the power in it. She yanked on her reins and with her free foot kicked her mare forward.

"Let her go, hell!" cried Elmo, still clinging to her leg. He reached up and got her by the sash around her waist and dragged her down out of the saddle.

"You don't know who she is," cried the voice she knew. She fell into the midst of these thrashing bodies, went to her hands and knees, all the breath knocked out of her. Pigeye, that was, screaming. Something banged her side. What was he doing here? She tried to call his name, but she couldn't get her breath. Somebody caught her arm, hauled her up onto her feet, and pushed her.

"Run!" Pigeye said in her ear.

She turned, looking for her horse, for Raul, and stumbled a few steps forward. She went to one knee. Looking back, she saw big Elmo strike Pigeye across the head. "Out of the way, George!" Pigeye staggered, and the other men rushed past him after her. She lunged to her feet, ran toward the streetlight at the corner, hearing Elmo only a step behind her. Panting, she looked back over her shoulder and saw him reach for her, his eyes hot.

She ran headlong into an immovable body like a tree in the middle of the street. An arm went around her, gripping her tight. The voice that rang out above her head she knew instantly.

"You stop right there, boyo!"

She slumped against him, wobbly with relief, her head against his chest. Behind her, Elmo's big bawling voice said, "Hey. We saw her first. Who the hell are you?"

King's arm shifted, still holding her tight; she heard the ratcheting click of a gun cocking, and he said, "You didn't see her at all. Get running."

"Who the hell—"

The gun went off, so loud, so close she jumped. She turned inside the circle of his arm, looking around, and saw the men pounding off down the street in the dark. King lifted his six-gun again and shot into the sky. He looked down at her.

"You got anything to say to me?"

"Thank you," she said uncertainly.

"No!" He pushed her away; she realized how angry he was, and a trickle of fear went down her spine, different than being afraid of Elmo. He said, "I told you not to come out here alone. I told you—"

"I wasn't alone," she said. She looked around her for Raul.

There he was, she saw, grateful; he had caught her horse and was leading it back up the street toward them. "I came with Raul," she said, and pointed.

King thrust the gun into the holster under his arm. He took her by the wrists and put his face inches from hers. "I told you not to come into the city without me. He's a worthless fool, that one, I'd be doing him a favor to shoot him. You should be glad I'm not wearing out my belt on your backside, darlin'. Get on that horse."

Her face burned. She looked at Raul, who was leading her mare up toward them, and by the rigid set of his shoulders she guessed he had heard a lot of what King had said. King pulled the mare's reins out of his hands.

He spoke curtly in Spanish; Raul answered him in English. "I was going to help her."

"When?" King said. "Get back to Sonoratown." He reached for Lily with both hands.

"You take your dirty paws off me," she said. "You aren't my father."

He got her by the waist and lifted her into her saddle. "Shut up, Lily. I may smack you yet." He led the mare off; Raul was riding away, his head sunk down between his shoulders.

She thought, He deserves it. He is worthless. But he looked so downcast her heart ached for him; she wished she could make him feel better. We're both worthless, Raul. King's horse was standing under the streetlamp, watching them approach, its ears pricked up and its reins trailing. She started to tell King about Pigeye and changed her mind. She could keep some things secret. Her dress was filthy now, filthy and torn and ruined.

Abruptly her eyes filled with tears. Everything she did came out wrong. She had gotten Raul in trouble and ruined Luz's dress. King swung into his saddle and looped her reins over the mare's head and over her saddlebow. She remembered suddenly how safe she had felt in his arms; she wanted to say something, to thank him, but he had yelled at her. He had no right to yell at her, no matter what she had done. She didn't like him anyway. But she remembered Elmo chasing her, and she followed King meekly along the street, glad to be going back home.

◆ Chapter ◆

XI

When Luz saw her dress her face slumped. "Oh," she said, and put her hand out toward the ruined fabric. "Oh. It was so pretty."

"I'll get you another," Lily said desperately.

Luz gave a deep sigh and shook her head. "It looked pretty on you. It made me look like a pillow."

Josefa said, "Ask King to buy you some cloth. The fashion is simple enough. We'll make another." She took the dress and tossed it into a corner of the kitchen. "That will do for rags."

"King's angry at me," Lily said. "I don't think he'll give me anything." She stood by the table, watching the other two girls make tortillas; before them on the table-top was a great bowl full of dough, and several little wooden rollers. She said, "Should I be doing something?"

Luz sighed. When she looked at Lily her eyes were sharp with annoyance. She said, "Here. Come help." She reached into the bowl and scooped up a handful of corn-meal dough, flattened it on the table, took a roller, and with three or four quick short strokes turned the dough into a little yellow sun. She laid it on top of the stack between her and Josefa. "Like that."

Lily reached for a moist yellow fistful of the dough.

"I'll get you another dress," she said again. "I have some money." She thought about the gold money in her coat. If it was still there, if King hadn't taken it. She squished the roll of dough on the table and it fell into chunks. When she applied one of the rollers to it, the way the other girls did, the chunks crumbled away into pieces.

Josefa gave a noisy snort of amusement. Lily tried again, with no better luck.

"I can't do this," she cried; her hands were coated with crusty dough.

Luz shoved the bowl at her. "Mix more dough. Over there, the big basket."

Josefa said, "Stir the sarsa again, while you're at it. And bring me a cup of lemonade. Raul is in much greater trouble than you, so consider yourself lucky. He's having to rake hay and clean corrals."

Lily hadn't thought about Raul since the night before. "I'm sorry. It was all my idea." She ignored Josefa's commands about the sarsa and the lemonade and took the bowl to the powdery sack and scooped up the flour. She liked the idea of mixing the dough. Pouring in a measure of water, she churned the dough around for a while with the spoon, put that down, and used her hands to work it all into a dense mass.

"Well," Josefa said, "he is coming here this afternoon with Andrés just to see you, so I suppose he forgives you."

"What?" Lily said, alarmed. "He's coming to see me?" She saw her siesta, the only free moments she had all day, disappearing into boring chitchat, mostly in incomprehensible Spanish. "Isn't he in trouble? Shouldn't he stay at home?"

Luz looked up, wide-eyed. Josefa said, "What, my lady has something better to do?"

"Yes, in fact," Lily said. "I was going to read."

Josefa sniffed. "I'm sure you can find some other time to read." She picked up the stack of tortillas and went to the hearth.

"I like to read," Lily said.

Luz was still staring at her. "Don't you like Raul?"

Lily shrugged. "He's nice enough." The work and the fandango had kept her from her book, but she had been thinking about it all the while, waiting for her chance to go back to it. She thought Raul could fit himself into some other corner of her day. She put the bowl of dough on the table in front of Luz and went around the kitchen picking up dirty dishes.

Luz said, "What do you read, Lily?"

"Stories." She heaped dishes into the water basin and poured hot water over them.

"Love stories?" Josefa was browning the tortillas on the hot bricks in front of the oven. The delicious aroma of the toasted corn flooded the kitchen.

"Sometimes." The hero of the Dickens novel she was reading had fallen in love with the silliest girl Lily had ever heard of. She decided suddenly that she liked Josefa and Luz much better. She watched them with a new interest.

Josefa was flipping the toasted tortillas from the bricks into the dish, and then putting raw ones onto the empty spaces on the bricks; her hands moved so fast Lily could not see what she did, and the tortillas flowed as if by themselves from stack to brick to the round crock. In a voice that quavered violently, Josefa said, "That's sinful. Reading stories like that."

Luz glanced toward the door, obviously looking out for her mother, and swung toward Lily again, her eyes bright. "Will you read them to us?"

"I—" Lily cast a quick look at Josefa.

"Not me," Josefa said roundly. "I've got better things to do." Her hands moved, keeping the river of tortillas flowing. Lily was suddenly desperately hungry; she wanted to grab one of the tortillas, dip it into the bubbling sarsa, and stuff it into her mouth.

"Please," Luz murmured, and put her hand on Lily's arm. "Will you?"

"If you want," Lily said. At least then she would be reading. "Today?"

"Yes!" Luz glanced at Josefa. "During siesta. Mama will be in her room."

Josefa grunted. Her eyes narrowed, and her mouth twisted into a nasty smile. "King will keep her busy."

"King," Lily said. "How?" The other two girls broke into stifled giggles and covered their mouths with their hands.

Lily sniffed at them. They didn't like her, and she shouldn't care what they thought. But they wanted her to read to them. In spite of herself she began to be excited. She could not read them the novel she was reading now; they would be lost. Anyway, what she wanted most of all, had wanted, she thought, for a long time, was to read someone else her favorite story. Her hands were still caked with dried dough, and she rubbed her gritty palms together, considering how to do this.

The beginning was a little slow; she might lose their interest if she started from the very beginning. She had to get quickly to the best early part, where the book really began anyway, the moment when the guest in the old bedroom heard the rapping of the ghost on the window.

She would explain the beginning to the others, tell them only what they needed to know. Already, in her mind, she was going over what she would read and how she would read it, the tone, the gestures. A shiver of delight passed through her. She realized that this was going to be fun. She turned quickly and dipped her hands into the basin of water to clean them.

From the kitchen doorway Serafa looked out across the dusty yard to where Lily was sitting on the step of the bunkhouse, the book on her knees, reading to Luz and Josefa on either side of her. Serafa's daughters sat immobile, tilted slightly toward Lily, their eyes fixed on her face, captive.

"This is not good," she said. Now here came Andrés Rosas and his younger brother, Raul, walking across the yard toward the girls. Serafa folded her arms over her breast. This would be all around town by the time the church doors opened in the morning. She asked, "What are these books of hers about?"

King sat at the table behind her, swabbing his plate clean with a piece of a tortilla. "I've never asked her." Popping the tortilla into his mouth, he got up and took his dish to the basin and washed it.

Leaving no traces. Serafa watched him narrowly. It still rankled that he had left off their dalliance to chase down this beautiful young wastrel girl with her strange ideas and her sinful books. He came up beside her, his gaze directed out the door to the little group of people on the bunkhouse step.

"She needs new clothes. Shoes." He leaned on the doorway. "She should go to school."

"School," Serafa said. "She's female. What does she need with schooling?"

"She likes books. She'd like school. Is she going to wait tables all her life?"

"No," Serafa said. "She'll marry and have babies."

She turned toward him, laying her hands side by side on his chest, and guided him back into the dark of the kitchen. His arms went around her. She tilted her head back and he kissed her, soft and sweet, one hand on her hair. Then his hand moved to the front of her dress, undoing buttons.

She whispered, "Tonight. Come to my window after dark."

"Ummm." He pressed his lips to her temple. He had undone several buttons and his hand slid in through the opening. She gasped at the shock of his touch, not on her skin, but on the thin cotton just above her skin. His hand on her chin tipped her face up again. His kiss was eager, his mouth moving against hers, insistent. Her body flushed, warm and full.

"King." She stiffened, alarmed. His hand cupped her breast and she felt the nipple tighten. "The girls."

"They're busy," he said. His free hand went to his belt buckle.

"No." But she held tight to him, the idea thrilling.

"Yes," he said. "Yes. You know you want me. And I want you, more than anything." Then suddenly he whispered, "I love you, Serafa. I love you."

The words shocked her, as if, expecting a candle, she had seen the sun. Her whole body yearned toward him. She lay back in his arms. He half carried her to the table. His mouth was hard on hers; he would not let her go now, she thought. She wanted him to go on, she was past stopping him. She shut her eyes, greedy, leaving it all to him. He whispered, "*Querida.* Serafa. I love you." He lifted her onto the table, drawing up her skirts around her waist, parting her knees, and took her there, in her clothes, on her own table, in the middle of the day.

The street coursed with people, mostly men, surging along in packs from one saloon to the next, where all the drinks had been flowing free for hours. Brand was staying upright and clear-headed, but with some effort. He walked along through the lamplit night, hidden in the crowd, trying not to get sucked into the aimless feverish excitement of the mob. He had been in a lot of boom-towns, and they were always wild. Los Angeles didn't even have all that much of a boom going on.

In the upstairs room at the Crystal Palace Bar he made stacks of double eagles in front of Elmo. The big man's eyes followed every movement of his hand. Brand said, "How did it go? There wasn't any mention in the newspaper."

"Unh—" Elmo shot a glance at Brand's face. "You said not to hurt anybody too much."

"No, no, I like it that it didn't make the paper," Brand said. "You did that part of it right."

Elmo blinked. "Everything went right," he said.

"Good," Brand said. "Your friends all did their parts?"

"Yeah, sure," Elmo said. He scratched his beard, shoving out his jaw to facilitate that, so that his whole lower face shifted sideways. He said, "There was George."

"Tell me about George," Brand said quickly. George had stuck in his mind. He had the feeling he had met George before. "You said he came in from the silverlode country. When?"

Elmo shrugged. "I don't know. He's an all right one, George is." Whatever he had against George, he had changed his mind about telling Brand. "Any other jobs?"

"Stay in town," Brand said. He tied up the money pouch. Elmo's eyes dropped to the pouch again, to the gold, Brand thought. Brand stood up, stowing the pouch in his pocket; Elmo's eyes followed, not the hand with the money, but the left, the hand not there. Quickly he looked away.

Brand said, "Something on your mind?"

"Naw," said Elmo, and lifted his eyes to Brand's. Their eyes met, only for an instant, and then Elmo looked away, but Brand saw the challenge in his eyes, half curiosity and half contempt.

"You sure about that?" Brand said.

In the doorway, leaving, Elmo turned and gave him a thin smile. "Sure, boss," he said, and slid out like a departing snake.

Brand's gut tightened. He wanted to bash Elmo's skull in. Instead he was giving him money. He choked down the urge to kick the furniture and swear. He needed Elmo, anyway, for now; but a time would come for getting even with him.

He needed Elmo because, as Hyde himself had predicted, the huge subsidy that he had negotiated with the Los Angeles City Council was going to a ballot in a few weeks. The local pols insisted they could pull this election off, but having a few thugs around on voting day never hurt. Brand caught himself scrubbing the butt end of his left arm. He hoped the local men knew what they were doing. The Railroad needed this subsidy, which, besides giving the Southern Pacific control of Banning's little narrow-gauge line to San Pedro, supplied them with land for an office and a station, and a huge amount of cash.

Brand clicked his tongue against his teeth. He went out of the room and walked down the corridor toward the stairs. Hyde as usual had made an astonishing number of enemies in the course of his visit, and his farewell to Los Angeles was going to make him many more. As part of the preliminary agreement, Hyde had managed to get the Los Angeles & San Pedro Railroad to promise him, for his twenty-mile trip from the city to the harbor, "a private car, suitably outfitted for an important traveler." This one was going to be a regular rolling parlor, a whole car richly outfitted to carry a single man twenty miles.

People were already rankling over the City Council's offer to the Southern Pacific; the luxurious car was fat in that fire, loud and flashy, catching everybody's attention. Brand had been working steadily to cool down the opposition to the Railroad, but Hyde by himself could revive a good deal of it. The fat negotiator was insisting, also, that Brand accompany him on the trip to San Pedro. The only good thing about the whole matter was that Hyde was leaving. Brand reached the stairs. Below him the room boiled with lights and smoke, excited laughter and the bellows of gamblers, all charged with the aimless enthusiasm that seemed to possess this whole city, with its constant breathless feeling that surely something wonderful was about to happen, a gold rush fever without the gold. He went down the stairs into the heat and turbulence.

ꝏ

"Where are you going?" She tightened her arms around him, holding him down into the warmth of her bed. At once he stopped going away. He lay down against her, pressed against her from foot to face, and kissed her.

"You don't love me," she said. "Or you wouldn't want to go."

He nuzzled her hair. When she had taken down her hair he had wound it around himself, buried his face in it. His appetite for her reassured her. He licked her skin, sucked on her fingers, handled every part of her. He stroked his whole body against her, curling around her. His attention was like a magic balm that made her young again.

"I have to go," he said, propping himself up on his elbow next to her. "Do you want Josefa and Luz walking in on us?"

"They won't," she said.

"They will." He ran his fingers down the side of her throat and over her breast to her nipple. His eyes followed with an absorbing interest. She felt beautiful in his eyes, even this old, worn, used, mothering flesh, beautiful. She arched her back toward him and he lay down again and held her and stroked her, his legs twining around hers.

His hand slid between her thighs. "Once more," he said.

Once more. Afterward he lay there drifting toward sleep, and she thought she had him, but suddenly he started awake.

He said, "I have to go, darlin'."

"King," she said. "How soon before you go for good?"

He sat up. Curled beside him in the bed, waiting for him to answer, she put her hand on the arch of muscle above his hip.

He didn't answer. After a while she said, "For the

girl's sake, for your own, for mine too, you should stay."

He turned toward her and their eyes met. He said, "I'm staying as long as I can." He kissed her on the mouth, and then he straightened and turned away and was gone into the dark.

She lay down again, taut as a fiddle string. As soon as he was gone she wanted him back. She felt giddy, although she was lying down. She had not felt so well in years, so vigorous, so excited. He would come back. She would make it impossible for him to give her up. He needed her. The girl, too, needed her. She shut her eyes, incapable of sleep; her mind leaped through the days to come, planning how to get what she wanted.

Lily heard the bunkhouse door opening; she looked up from her book. The lamp on the shelf by her bed shed its light into her little space on this side of the blanket, but on the other side it was dark. She heard him groping around, just beyond the cloth wall, and then he said, "You still awake?"

"I was reading," she said.

"You should be asleep," he said. She heard his bed creak. "What's in those books?"

"Stories," she said. "Do you want me to read to you?"

He laughed, a rumble of slightly fatigued amusement. There was a thump, then another thump. His boots hitting the floor. That reminded her that he had rights in another bed now, and she said, "What are you doing in here?"

"This is where I sleep," he said. His bed was just the other side of the blanket wall. She could tell where his head was, that he was stretched out on his back. "This is where I live."

She said, "What are you doing with Serafa?"

"That's none of your business."

"I think it is my business, since you seem to have elected yourself my parent."

There was a brief silence. She shut the book and laid it on the shelf beside the bed. He said, "It's still none of your business. How do you know about me and Serafa?"

"Josefa and Luz say you are lovers."

"They don't know anything either."

"And tonight, the way she put her hand on you when you were standing next to her. As if you belonged to her."

"You're too damned smart," he said.

"Do you love her?"

"That's between her and me, and anyway if I told you, you wouldn't understand. Now, listen, now, you remember the other night, when those hardcases jumped you?"

"Yes," she said.

"Did you recognize any of them?"

"No," she said swiftly, thinking of Pigeye.

"Why did they crowd you?"

"Because—we came down the street, they were beating somebody up. I went to help."

He gave another easy, weary laugh. She turned onto her side, facing him through the blanket wall, her head propped on her hand. "What's your real name?" she said. She liked asking him questions.

"What?" He sounded startled. She liked that, too.

"Is King your real name?"

"It is now," he said.

"What was your real name?"

"Real name. What's that? Everybody calls me King. When I was a kid my mother used to tell me to be proud, to remember I was descended from the kings of Ireland. I told that to somebody once and he started calling me King and it stuck."

"What did your mother name you?"

"Why do you have to know this?" He sounded irritated.

"Why can't I know it? Why won't you tell me?"

"I don't know," he said. "All right, I'll tell you. Colum. How's that? Colum Callahan."

"Colum. I think I like King better. Are you a king's son?"

"Sure," he said. "Son of the King of the Beggars and Thieves, Son of the King of Ireland."

She tried to imagine this other place, this Ireland. She thought it was somewhere over the sea. "How did you get here?"

"Are you ever going to quit? Here where?"

"You came over here from Ireland, didn't you? How did you get here?"

"I swam," King said.

"By yourself?"

"Yes. By myself. You're getting in a lot of questions. Let me get one in, all right? Just try to remember, did you know any of those bully boys who jumped you?"

She realized he knew about Pigeye. But she had lied for too long to tell the truth now. She said, "No. I didn't. What do you think was going on? There was somebody else, wasn't there? Were they trying to kill somebody?"

"I'm not sure," he said. "I think they were pulling down posters and somebody caught them. There's nothing in the newspaper about it."

"Posters," she said. In her mind's eye she saw dramatic masks, scrolled with ribbon.

"Calling a rally against the Southern Pacific," he said.

"The Railroad," she said. "It was Brand, then."

"Brand wasn't there. But the SP's money was, I'd bet on it. They've got the election sewn up anyway, but they're lookin' to make sure." His voice flattened, harsher. "Damn them. That burns me. They think they can come in here and everybody will drop down on his face in front of them and worship."

"Are you going to do something?" she asked.

"What?"

"Are you going to rob them?"

"If I did, would I go telling a green little girl, now? Did you have fun, readin' your stories?"

"Yes," she said. "It was wonderful. Why won't you tell me?"

"Because it's no business of yours, darlin'. What was the book you were readin'?"

"Wuthering Heights," she said. "I could read it to you."

"Maybe," he said. "Maybe, someday. Meantime, go to sleep. Good night."

"I still want—"

"Good night," he said with emphasis.

She stared at the blanket wall, not sleepy; her curiosity rubbed. If he was planning another job, she wanted to know. She could help him. She had done perfectly in the stagecoach robbery. Green little girl! He had no right to call her that. She knew if she kept at him about it now he would only get angry, and when he got angry he scared her. She would find some way to make him see she was no green girl. She pinched out her lamp and lay down, her head pillowed on her arm.

◆ Chapter ◆

XII

Serafa leaned back, her eyes half closed; King was brushing her hair, long slow strokes of the brush from her crown to the tips of her hair that flooded every nerve, left her boneless in his lap, quivering. He bent over her and kissed her brow. She shuddered.

"Querida," he said. "I'll make snares to catch angels out of your hair."

She laughed; his hand lay against her cheek, and she turned her head to stroke herself against his fingers. "Ah, just listening to you is a sin."

His fingers grazed her cheek, her throat. "I have a few other sinful ideas for you."

She lifted her face toward him; they kissed upside down. She knew what he wanted. They lay back in her bed, twisting together in the rucked linen, and enjoyed each other. The summer was over, but the country lay in the grip of a late heat; everybody had gone indoors to escape the sun, and the siesta would go on for hours. She lay on her side and put her hand on his chest.

"Your skin is pale as milk."

He only smiled, his arms folded behind his head, his legs crossed at the ankles, his body stretched and easy. His eyes were shut; she knew he was drifting off to sleep. Escaping her. She felt a sharp tug of fret.

She said, "What will become of this girl Lily?"

His eyes opened. "What do you mean? I'm taking care of Lily."

"For how long?"

"For as long as she needs it." He rolled onto his side, facing her. "What's the matter? Don't you like her?"

"I like her very much," Serafa said. "The girls like her, too, more and more. She is a good-hearted girl. But she is wild, and rude, she needs to learn manners."

"Good," he said. He nodded at her, as if that were his idea. "You teach her that."

Such a clever man, so sweet-tongued, he had walked right in where she wanted him. She said, "If you wish." She put her hand on him again. Hers. "I will take her to Mass."

He made a sound in his throat and frowned. "Well, maybe," he said.

"She needs clothes. She cannot wear the girls' cast-offs forever."

"Not at the rate she goes through them, at least."

"You should have some new shirts." Not red, which would go to war with his hair. Black. She would stitch designs into the sleeves, to ward off bad spirits. Lawmen, and other women. She had done this for Tiburcio. The charms had worked excellently against women but not against lawmen. She would do better this time. King was falling asleep again, his head cradled on his arm. Hers. She laid her head down, her hand on his chest.

Pigeye scratched nervously at his jaw. Across the table, Elmo was grinning from the thicket of his beard at him, the battered cards gripped in both hands.

"Well? Call or fold, Georgie?"

Pigeye hated the name George and wished he'd chosen a better one. He was fairly sure his three jacks would eat up Elmo's likely two-pair hand; the matter was whether he actually wanted to win this. He had already taken twenty dollars from Elmo tonight and if he won much more the big man would sweat it out of him one way or another: the last time Pigeye had cleaned him out, Elmo had spent the next three days punching him in the shoulder whenever he came within reach.

Pigeye was sick of Elmo. He hated the city entirely, the noise and the stink and the constant uproar. He wished he could go back to Sonoratown. But if he did, King would certainly catch wind of him, and King had seen him in the gang attacking Lily Viner. Between Elmo and King, Pigeye preferred running afoul of Elmo.

Strengthened by this consideration, he said, "I'll call." He pushed two more dollars out into the middle of the table.

On his right, Roy sighed and shifted away from the table with a creak of his chair; Roy was Elmo's brother. Elmo said, "Beat this, Georgie." He spread out his hand, showing two aces and two tens.

Pigeye lifted his hand, ready to show it; his gaze caught on Elmo's glittering bloodshot eyes, and his nerve failed him. He tossed the hand in. "Beats me."

With a loud gusty snort of triumph, Elmo raked the pot in. Pigeye got up. "I'm quittin'."

"Can't quit yet," said Roy, wide-eyed with wonder. "Mr. Stumpy is supposed to come and give us some work."

"I'm tired," Pigeye said. "Fill me in later." Between Brand and King, he'd favor leaving town.

He took his hat off the back of his chair and went around through the rear of the saloon, circling through other tables of gamblers, the men clenched down over their fists of cards or dice, their eyes fastened on piles of money. A tall girl in a ruffled yellow dress brushed by him, carrying a bottle by the neck in one hand. She smelled strongly of sweat and perfume. He paused, looking out toward the big room, soaked in the light of the three big lanterns hanging from the ceiling. Layers of smoke hung in the upper air; as the crowd churned through the room, the smoke writhed and coiled lazily around the lantern chimneys. The piano player in the far corner began to jangle out some tune. Pigeye went on to the back door and out to the cool clean night.

He was out of money. Likely Brand would give them some up-front money for this new job, but if Pigeye wasn't there to collect his, Elmo would pocket it. He hunched his shoulders. Maybe it was time to quit, to head on north again. He knew people in Panamint City, they owed him, he could get a stake, maybe pick up some work.

He was standing on the steps at the back of the saloon; before him in the dark was a deep yard, half full of broken beer barrels and trash, with an old cottonwood growing up at the very back. He started down the steps, thinking of going for a walk in the dark, and behind him suddenly somebody moved and a voice he knew said, "Pigeye."

He jumped, cold to the soles of his feet. "King." He wheeled around toward the door into the saloon, which was still open.

King reached out casually and flicked it shut. "Brand in there yet?"

"Jeez," Pigeye said. "You scared me. Haven't seen you for a while." In a panic, he wondered what he dared say, if anything; he wondered how close he was to dying.

"Stand down, will you?" King came forward around him, headed for the alley. "I ain't mad at you, Pigeye. I saw you there in the street the other night, but I saw you were tryin' to stop these other blades. Come on, I got to talk to you."

Pigeye's body deflated; weak with relief, he nearly fell over following King into the alley. They walked into the dark between the saloon and the boardinghouse next door. Pigeye couldn't keep from babbling.

"Jeez. Am I glad to hear that, King. I was real nervous you'd think—you know, I'd never do anything to Lily, she's a great kid, I like her a lot, I knew her dad, you know, for years. Haven't I always said how much I like her?"

King said, "Yeah, yeah, yeah. Forget it. Right?"

"Right, King. Jeez. Glad to see you. I been scared, you know, thinking of leavin' town."

"Yeah, well, you do one more thing for me, and then leave." King stopped at the mouth of the alley, looking out across Primavera Street. The street lamp twenty feet away cast its light across him; he glanced at Pigeye, grinning.

"Anything," Pigeye said.

"Railroad's opened an office over on Hill Street. Scout it for me."

Pigeye groaned. "Anything but that, King. Look, he's on to me. He recognized me. I don't know how, but I saw it in his eyes, he knows me somehow. He's just waiting to jump me."

King faced toward the street. He was packing a gun on his right hip, and Pigeye knew he always carried one under his left arm. In spite of the summer heat he wore a coat, probably to hide the cannons. The trouble with King was the way he could take out one of those guns and shoot you with it and not even blink. Killing people meant nothing to him; he didn't even like it.

He was getting ready to pull another job, Pigeye thought. Which reminded Pigeye how broke he himself was.

He began to think he would fall back in with King; everything King did worked out for money.

King said, "You know, like as not Brand won't even be there. Just go up and look over the layout, where the desks are, the windows, the stairs, the safe, things like that." He turned and gave Pigeye a sunny smile. "Come down to Sonoratown tomorrow around dinnertime, fill me in. Best food in Los Angeles, anyway. For you, free."

Pigeye muttered something. Thinking of Brand made him queasy again. King was already going away, strolling right out there into the street like nobody in particular, certainly nobody the Southern Pacific and Wells Fargo and some other banks would pay gold money for, in good condition or not. Two plowpushers coming up the boardwalk swung slightly out of the way to let him pass. In the street, riders and a wagon ambled by. King went to the horse rack in front of the boardinghouse and mounted up; he was riding the rawboned dark red mare that Jewell had ridden, and then Lily. Pigeye wiped his forehead on his sleeve. He knew he should have left Los Angeles. Now King had a hook into him. Glumly he trudged away down the alley again, trying to find someplace where he could relax and forget his troubles.

King had watched Brand go into the Crystal Palace; knowing where Brand was made him feel a lot easier. He let Jewell's old red mare sidewheel down the street, pulling a little at the bit. She needed to be ridden more; she was out of shape, popping a sweat already. He reined her into First Street, heading down across a dried-up arm of the *zanja* toward the train yard.

The old water ditch was full of sage and here and there a sprouting cottonwood. On the side street, dark and quiet, he drew the mare down to a walk, glad to get out from under the spotty glare of the streetlamps.

He let the mare pick her way across the dry *zanja* and up the short incline. On the far side she broke into her ambling pace again, her neck extended. Ahead, pocked with light, surrounded by a fence, a big house stood beside the street. As he approached he saw a little group of people walking up the front path to the door, and the door opened to meet them and light flooded the porch. He heard the rising chatter of voices. Quickly the big house gathered all these people in.

He eased the mare down to a walk. He wondered what it was like to live like that, in a house where you could walk right in the front door, with people who knew your right name.

The lit windows were veiled in some kind of lacy white cloth; he could see shadows moving behind them, but he could not tell what was going on. Suddenly the urge seized him to draw his guns, to blast through those windows, to let in the dark.

The idea faded. He nudged the mare forward again, down the street, past two other big wooden houses where lawabiding people lived. If he lived like that, he could stay here, settle down with Serafa and Lily.

When he thought that, as he had now a couple of times, the idea leaped away from him, drew him on through pictures and dreams. Settle down, yes, but not here, not in town. Get a little ranch, up some draw in the hills where there was water, trees, good hunting in the back country. Raise some horses, run a few head of cattle. Grow corn and tomatoes, chiles, squash. Send Lily to school. Eat Serafa's tortillas and *colorado,* lie in her arms every night. For a moment, as it always did, it looked so good, that dream.

But he could not stay King Callahan and do that; he'd have to get some other name. And it couldn't be here, where too many people knew him. And it would take a lot of money. He only knew one way to make money. As soon as he stopped to think it over, the dream collapsed.

He didn't think he'd much like himself that way, anyway. Sitting on a porch somewhere in the sun, smoking a pipe, reading a newspaper.

He shifted in the saddle, uneasy. He already spent a lot of time sitting around reading newspapers.

The street cut across another light-spangled thoroughfare. He knew where he was now, and he turned right, went two blocks, and then crossed a vacant lot to the back edge of the railroad yard.

Banning's railroad, the Los Angeles & San Pedro, was a toy compared with the Southern Pacific. Its main yard stood on Alameda and Commercial next to a grocery store. The morning's train was drawn up at the station platform, the narrow-gauge locomotive, the tender, two freight cars, and a passenger car. At the end of the train, smelling of new paint, its trim shining faintly in the distant streetlamps, was the new luxury car, which would convey the Southern Pacific's agent out of Los Angeles in style.

King let the red mare drift along the street. The sight of the private car roughened him up. All these struggles in his mind fell back behind a surge of pure hatred. The Railroad would squeeze every penny it could from the blood and sweat of ordinary people; working men would build the railroad and then sit on the hard benches of second class, while the nobs and nabobs who never raised a callus enjoyed cushioned chairs in rolling parlors.

The mare took him off along the street toward the edge of town. But into his mind leaped a sudden thread of an idea, and he had to stiffen himself against the impulse to twist around and look back at the private car.

The mare stretched into her peculiar gait again, her ears pinned back; she had caught some of the tension in him. He let her ramble along the deserted unlit street while he thought this over. There were several things to consider. He saw no way to make any money doing this. It was a lot of risk for no money. Also, if he did it, he was throwing a serious hobble onto the notion of going straight and becoming an anonymous nobody who was only Serafa's husband and Lily's father.

He hated the Railroad. He hated nabobs, who had everything and thought that meant they were better than everybody else. He remembered standing on the hill looking out across an English landlord's grain, yellow and lush as far as a boy could see, and in the ditch behind him his mother and sister chewing grass.

That was cold, old and cold, that memory, and he shut

it quickly down before other old, cold things opened up on him.

Instead, he thought how Brand would take an attack on the private car. That decided him. A slow pleasure spread warmly through him. He would relish giving Brand a cut.

He let the mare stretch out down the road, rocked along in the big Mexican saddle, while he sorted out the details of the plan in his mind. There would be an uproar and he would have to get out of Los Angeles fast. He'd have to bring Lily. Brand would remember her; if he saw her he would go after her. As for Serafa, King just had to hope she wouldn't give up on him entirely, and that she would let him come back when the hunt died down.

He lingered on that a moment; he liked Serafa a lot.

But he could do this job on the private car. Somebody had to take the SP down a notch, she had to see that, and King knew exactly how. He had read about the luxury car in the newspaper. He remembered there was an icebox in it. The first place to go would be the icehouse in town.

The second place would be the Giant Powder Company.

He went on patiently thinking it through, over and over, tracking down the trouble spots and working out solutions. The mare had carried him out as far as the crossroads before the plan satisfied him completely. Swinging around, he traveled back, not along the road but through the paths and fields of the *pobladores,* laid out south and east of the city, where the *zanja* still flowed and the orange groves that the first settlers had planted grew. He felt very good. This was going to work. Serafa would take him back, in the end; he was even sure of that. In her heart she was an outlaw, too. He let the mare pace along toward Sonoratown, taking him back to her arms.

"Where's George?" Brand asked.

Elmo guffawed. "He needed a little air." Thinking of George gave him another little jolt of pleasure. He had backed George down like a crawfish. He leaned his forearms on the table, his gaze on Brand; this was another one who needed to find out who was the real boss here.

Brand said, "Well, I doubt you'll need him for this next job." He took out his wallet and began to count twenty-dollar gold pieces onto the table. "There's a rally tomorrow night, supposed to be in support of the Texas Pacific. I want you men to show up and make a lot of noise whenever anybody tries to speak."

"We need more money," Elmo said, and behind him the other men shuffled and grunted, eager.

"Hell," Brand said, his voice mild. "I'm already paying you more'n you're worth." He slid back in his chair, his face smooth. The stumpy arm lay on the table before him, behind the stack of gold money. The end looked rough and pink. "Twenty dollars now, twenty dollars after."

Elmo said, "We want forty dollars up front." He glanced over his shoulder at the others and faced Brand again, excited. He felt a surge of strength through his arms and shoulders. "Forty dollars after."

Brand smiled at him. "Hell, no. I can find fifty men to do this work for twenty apiece. You're lucky I'm using you, don't you realize that?" His eyes were bright. The railroad man leaned forward toward Elmo, still smiling. "You're stupid, Elmo. Don't think too much. Just do as I tell you."

Elmo glowered at him. He was a hand taller than Brand and much heavier and Brand ought to be sucking up to him, not sticking his nose in Elmo's face. He said, "I ain't as stupid as you think I am," and pushed his chair back and stood up.

Brand glided up onto his feet. "Oh, yes, you are. In

fact, I'm thinkin' you're even stupider." He came around the table in two strides and swung his fist at Elmo's midsection.

Elmo yelped, leaping back. This was not going well. In fights he liked to have the other man running away, or at least backing up. Brand came hot after him, and Elmo aimed his knuckles at the smaller man's nose.

Brand dodged, slippery, quick on his feet, and Elmo's arm flew harmlessly by; then Brand was toe to toe with him. Elmo grabbed him, meaning to hold him still and pound him, but Brand cocked his short arm back and drove the stump four inches forward into the pouchy belly just below Elmo's breastbone.

Elmo would have screamed if he had had any wind left; he had the horrible sensation he would never breathe again. His legs crumpled and he sat down. His eyes swam. He could see the slight figure of the man before him, coming toward him, and he thrust out one hand to stop him.

"N-n—" His lungs wouldn't work; in a panic, he fell over onto his side, trying to suck air into his chest. Hands gripped him from above and hauled him up, first to his knees, and then onto his feet. His brother muttered, "Come on, El, straighten up." They shoved him into his chair. He faced Brand again.

The railroad detective stood on the other side of the table, watching him with detachment. "You're too easy, Elmo. Take some advice, never jump somebody unless he has his back to you." He lifted his gaze and swept the other men with a cool look. "Twenty bucks each."

The other men murmured, "Yeah, yeah, fine, twenty bucks, all right, fine." Elmo was getting his breath. He wiped his hand over his face.

"You ain't so tough."

Brand broke into a smile. "Hell, no," he said. "But you are that stupid, Elmo. Just do as I say, keep your mouth shut, take the money. Got that?"

Somebody bumped Elmo on the shoulder. He rubbed

his face again. It hadn't been fair, Brand had tricked him, that hadn't gone right, and therefore it didn't really count. In front of his friends. His brother. He would have to pound some heads just to get back in right with them. He said under his breath, "Sure. I got that." Grimly he bit his lips together, feeling hot.

Brand's stump hurt; he cupped his hand over it. He watched Elmo and the other thugs bundle themselves away down the stairs. He wished Elmo had put up more of a fight. A residual temper still burned sulfurously in his veins. Alone, he tried to shake himself loose, to relax, but the fight had wound him up like a spring. He stuffed his money pouch into his pocket and went downstairs to get a drink.

◆ Chapter ◆

XIII

They went to church early in the morning, with the sun just coming up, the sky pale behind the black outlines of trees and buildings. They walked out of the cantina and into the street and joined a steady stream of people flooding along toward the plaza. The church bell began to toll, as if the worshipers made it ring, coming to Mass.

Lily stayed close by Serafa; the older woman kept a firm grip on her arm part of the way, but even when she let go, Lily stayed near her. She had heard a lot about God, and none of it good. All the people seemed to be staring at her. She wished she had a shawl, like Serafa's, to bury herself in.

The church was huge, its ancient adobe patched; inside, the air was cold and smelled strange. The door opened into the side of a long room; as the people flowed into the space they turned to the right and knelt down, forming rows across the room. Serafa nudged her on across the room, and with one hand and a murmured word urged her down to her knees.

In front of her, people were standing up again. First they made a busy twitching with one hand. Rising, they stood in ranks, like soldiers, facing a space like a theater, with a railing to set it off from those watching.

Serafa rose; Lily got up, her knees aching.

This was like a playhouse, she thought. The stage they faced now was a raised table against the back wall. There were no actors, only statues of people. Rows of candles stood against the back wall but their light reached only to the front edge of the table. There was a cup on the table, a big gold cup with a cloth over it, and an open book.

Then a man in a wonderful cape came out, followed by four boys in white dresses. The man turned to the assembled people and raised his arms and spoke, and all the people said something in answer, and in unison knelt down.

Witless, Lily did not move, and for an instant she was suspended above the whole crowd, the only one left standing. Serafa got her hand and pulled, and she sank down on her knees. Serafa smiled at her. Took Lily's two hands, and put them palm to palm before her, and with a hand on her hair tipped her head forward over her hands. Facing frontward again, Serafa assumed this same posture.

Lily stayed as she had been put, which was clearly the best protection. Through the corner of her eye she surveyed the people around her. Startled, she saw that they were not watching the stage, even now, when the man in the cape was saying things in some language she had never heard, not even Spanish. The people were looking all around, at everyone else, but most of them were watching her, and Serafa.

She glanced at Serafa, and saw her smooth expression, her bright and gleaming eye. Serafa knew. Serafa made a sign with her hand, up and down, back and forth, the same finger business they were all doing. Uncertainly Lily imitated her.

They rose again. The man in the gorgeous clothes went to a raised platform to one side, which had a little desk on it, and began to speak. Lily understood none of it. She was more interested anyhow in the way the people around her murmured and nudged each other and watched Serafa.

And how Serafa stood there, her head high, smiling, warming herself in it all.

They knelt again. Got up again. Everybody said incomprehensible words. Knelt, got up, knelt. She watched the man on the stage. Was that supposed to be God? Or an actor playing God? Above the stage on the wall was an image of a man hanging by his outstretched arms from a piece of wood, his body dangling and his head bowed. She wondered who he was. He seemed so tired, hanging there, as if he had given all he had at some heroic task. They should take him down, she thought, and let him rest. But he was just a statue.

People walked up to the railing, and the actor playing God went along from one to the next and fed them.

Serafa laid her hand on Lily's head and firmly pushed it down again. For Sarafa's sake the girl put her hands together and bowed her head. It made no sense to her, but for Serafa's sake, she could wait and see what happened.

All through the Mass, Serafa could feel the weight of the stares; she went on as she always did, praying for the souls of her parents and grandparents, and for her children. She prayed also for Lily, beside her, and for King, who needed it the most.

She prayed first to the Lord God the Father, to Jesus and Mary and Joseph, and to the Holy Spirit. Then she made her prayers to the saints of her mother's people, the Rainbringers, the Ocean, and the Old Woman of the Moon.

Let the people around her stare and talk. She had learned long ago that they had only the power that she allowed them, and she would allow them nothing, no care, no concern. They gave her power, with all their attention, a power she knew how to use.

After the *missa est*, as she went out the door, Lily beside her, the priest met her. He was an old man, his fleshy face drooping into a permanent frown, and meeting her he bent his brows double. His face looked like melted candlewax. He said, "Serafa! What is this report I have of you?"

She stopped. In a niche on the wall beside him was a bowl of sacred water and a yarrow sprig. She put her fingers into the water and crossed herself, picked up the yarrow and dipped it into the water and sprinkled Lily beside her. She faced the priest again.

"Father, God be with you." Taking Lily by the hand, she walked steadily on, out of the church.

In the plaza, people gathered to talk, but she did not stop. She spoke to them as she passed.

"Good morning, Clarita."

"Good morning, Serafa."

A chorus followed: "Good morning, Serafa." Nobody wanting to be left out of anything, here. Waving and smiling and nodding.

"Good morning, Don Pedro."

"Good morning, *madama*."

They might talk behind her back, but they would stay kindly to her eyes, which was all she asked. And she had done many favors all through the years, fed this one and that one through hard times, given quietly to some others, spoken up at the right time for several. They would remember, take the long view. She could endure this.

Behind her Josefa and Luz walked, surrounded by their friends; she heard Josefa's high ringing laugh. Serafa turned to Lily and took her by the hand.

"Did you like the service?"

Lily smiled. She knew no Spanish yet, but she would if Serafa kept on speaking it to her. Although they had very few words together, Serafa understood her very well. She saw how quick the child was to learn. How she blossomed in the warmth of a little kindness. Serafa

would train her out of her wildness, show her how to sit
properly and hold her head high and keep her feet together, as if she were her own daughter. She would be
her own daughter. She tucked Lily's hand over her arm
and, smiling, went on down the *calle* toward the cantina,
to serve breakfast to her people.

When Pigeye reached the cantina it was closed for siesta;
he knocked lightly on the door, and in a moment King
opened it. Pigeye's gut knotted up. He had been hoping
King would not be here after all.

"Good," King said. "I've been waiting for you. I hope
you had a good trip to the railroad office. Come back
over here, the light's better."

He took Pigeye on across the cantina to the corner,
which was dark and close to the back door and separated
from the rest of the room by the end of the bar. Reluc-
tantly Pigeye followed him. He scrabbled with his fingers at his beard. "King, I don't want to do that, I done
tole you that. Ask me anything else."

"Sit down," King said, and slid into the chair against
the wall, leaving Pigeye with his back to the room.

Pigeye's spine prickled. He sat down; behind him, the
door sighed open and he jumped. He looked back over
his shoulder and saw two brown men shuffling into the
cantina. They took their hats off as they came in. Pigeye
faced King again and began to talk, fast and soft.

"I'll do anything else. Ask me. Elmo and his boys
broke up a meeting against the Railroad. You see—"

One of the girls pushed suddenly in through the back
door to his left. She stood there, looking out across the
room. Pigeye blinked. It took him a moment to realize
that this was Jewell Viner's daughter, the girl Lily,
whom he had seen last on a dark street in Los Angeles.

He stiffened in panic; he turned and looked at King,
who was watching him hard. The girl surveyed the room,
turned, and recognized Pigeye.

"Oh. Hello," she said. Now she too looked wide-eyed at King.

"How y' doin', girl?" Pigeye cried, and got her hand and wrung it. "Good to see ya. Y' lookin' fine, girl." He glanced at King again and let go of her hand like lit dynamite. "Good to see ya," he said to Lily, sliding back into his chair. He looked at King, hoping he was convinced of Pigeye's good intentions.

"Go get Pigeye a beer," King said to her. "And bring me the bottle of whiskey and a glass."

She went away behind the bar. Pigeye leaned across the table, keeping his voice down; behind him, people kept on coming into the cantina all the time, and he kept wanting to turn to look over his shoulder. He had to get out of here. He leaned toward King, needing to convince him.

"You see, King, Brand's halfway on to me. I could tell when I met him. If he sees me again he'll recognize me, I know it. Recognize me from Virginia City."

"Shut up," King said, with a glance at the girl, who was bringing the drinks over to them.

Pigeye couldn't shut up; he blurted, "Ask me anything else."

Lily said, "What are you talking about?"

Pigeye looked up at her and turned his gaze away, mumbling, "I dunno." He reached for the beer, glanced over his shoulder again, and buried his upper lip in the foam. King took the shot glass and the bottle of Old-timers.

"Thanks," he said to Lily. "Now get out of here."

She went out the back door, which shut firmly behind her. Pigeye watched her go, wondering if she would hang around out there and listen. King splashed a little whiskey into the glass and drained it off. When he faced Pigeye again his gaze was unreadable; he had his head back and his eyes half closed.

"Pigeye, how you doin' for money?"

Pigeye shifted in his chair, suddenly hopeful. This

could be taking a better turn. "I'm dry, King."

"You do this, I'll stake you. You can take off for someplace cooler. Understand?"

"That's all I want to do, King. Like, a couple hunnert—"

King reached into his coat and Pigeye stiffened, alarmed, but the other man withdrew a wallet instead of a gun and shook out a dozen coins. King counted this money swiftly into two heaps of about twenty dollars each. He pushed one toward Pigeye.

"Scout the railroad office, come here and tell me, you get the rest."

"King." Pigeye had his hands out toward the lovely little heap of money and it was all he could do to stop. He said, "I can't do it, I'm telling y—"

"Make it good."

"I—"

"If you don't do it, I'll take it personally, Pigeye."

Pigeye licked his lips. King's narrow pale eyes never blinked. His smile hung on his lips as if he had forgotten it. Pigeye's back crawled. There were people shuffling around behind him; the cantina was filling up for dinner. He could not sit here anymore and he had to get away from King. He bolted up onto his feet. But the money, the money, he couldn't leave that. He gathered it quickly up.

King said, "Don't come back here without what I want, Pigeye."

"I'll do somepin'," Pigeye said, and fled.

The train's whistle blew, startling every horse in the street, and the bright red and yellow wheels on the locomotive began to turn. Smoke poured out of the diamond stack. King looked at his watch. As he had already observed the Los Angeles & San Pedro ran dependably on time. The locomotive chugged steadily up the tracks, drawing after it three freight cars, two ordinary passenger cars, and the private car in which the Southern Pacific's agent was leaving Los Angeles.

King's horse tossed its head, trying to get hold of the bit, and he turned it on up the street. A swarm of people was spilling out of the railroad yard, mostly idlers come to watch the train leave. It was still only midmorning. He followed an ore wagon full of empty rumbling barrels on its way to the brewery; behind it trailed a sour stink of stale beer.

When King got back to Sonoratown Serafa had the girls in a row at the table in the kitchen, all making tortillas. Lily was digging a handful of dough out of the bowl in the middle of the table; when he came in, she called out, "Watch me! I'm doing better." Her hands worked busily at the dough.

"I'm glad to hear it," he said, watching Serafa mostly. "But I got to take you away from it for a while."

Serafa lifted her eyes to him, her brows drawn down. Her voice grated. "What have you done?"

Living with Tiburcio had given her some experience at this. He switched into Spanish. "I have to get out of the village for a while. Nothing serious."

"Nothing serious," she said, strident. She was angry, he saw, which surprised him. She came a step toward him. "What did you do? Did you kill someone?"

"Hell, no, darlin', I just played a little joke on somebody, that's all. But I got to get out of here." He slid back to English, looking at Lily. "Go get some clothes and a couple of your books and let's go."

"Right now?" she said. "I'm hungry."

Serafa said, "A little joke, is it? Did you rob someone? Are you going to get all of us in trouble?"

Lily glanced at her, at him, and went swiftly out of the kitchen. King sidled toward the door. "Serafa, I'll be back," he said.

She rushed at him. "Don't be so sure I'll take you back!" She swung her arm around and aimed a slap at his face. He jerked his head out of her reach. Luz came up beside her mother and grabbed her arm.

"Mama!"

"Why should I love you?" Serafa shouted; she shook off her daughter's grip. Both the girls stood beside her now, their arms around her, murmuring to her. She ignored them. Her gaze never left King and her face was sharp and fierce with rage. "You're going to hang, just like Tiburcio. Get out!"

"Yes, *señora*." He touched his hat brim to her and went.

Lily was in the bunkhouse, stuffing books into her sack. Her face was white. She had heard the shouting. She said, "Should I bring all my books?"

"No need," he said. "We're coming back." He had gotten everything ready the night before, some food and some other gear and all his guns, and stashed them out in the horse shed under the hay. He went to his bed, rolled up the blankets, and turned the frame over against the wall. Going past the hanging blanket into the back of the shed where the scrap lumber was stacked, he dragged some of the boards and the big oak chest out into the middle of the room. Lily was watching him, her face set.

"Go on out to the horses," he said. "Take your blankets." He rolled out a cask of nails beside the chest. When she had gotten her bedroll and gone, he turned her bed against the wall.

She had left some of her books on the shelf. He thought of moving them, but there was no place else to put them. Probably he was being too nice about this anyway. He took the lamps and set them against the wall and went out to the horse shed.

Lily had her mare saddled already. "Where are we going?"

"Just out of town for a while. It's no major issue, I don't know why Serafa is making so much of a fuss about it." He dug his gear out from under the hay and loaded the horses.

"Where are we going?" she said again. She followed him out to the sunshine and they mounted up.

"Not very far," he said. "And we're coming back. Bank on that." He led her off down the lanes that wound through Sonoratown to the main road.

The train was spinning along toward Wilmington. Hyde unknotted his tie and sat back. "Stop complaining, Brand. You can catch the train back into Los Angeles tonight. Or rent a horse. I'm sure Banning keeps a string there, as the man seems to think he owns the entire public conveyance of Los Angeles County." He groaned and stretched, and his peevish voice ground on. "I'm leaving you in charge here. You can do me the respect of seeing me to the ship."

Brand slumped into the big soft chair opposite. He hated Hyde, and he hated riding on trains. This car especially annoyed him. The small dark rectangle was crowded with furniture and the window curtains were drawn, holding in the summer heat and the deep, fruity aromas of good coffee and whiskey and tobacco. He rubbed his bruised stump, which hurt. This place made him feel as if he couldn't get his breath.

The attendant came in and opened the windows on the right-hand side of the car, away from the sun. The soft sunlight spilled across the intricate dark patterns of the carpet, the fat, self-satisfied shapes of the chairs and the cabinet and the icebox. The train was rolling along past the tilled fields and little stands of orange trees, gliding swiftly toward monotonous dun hills and cloudless sky. The attendant broke ice from the icebox generously into a silver bucket and deftly twisted a green bottle into the middle of it.

With his thumb Hyde wedged tobacco from the leatherbound canister on his table into the bowl of a German pipe. He poked the pipestem at the near window. "This land will be a desert forever. The Big Men are making a mistake, this time."

Brand was thinking the land had a nice look to it, empty golden grassland, dotted with dark oaks, sweeping up toward the jags of the gaunt treeless mountains. He had heard there were tar pits out here, full of great bones. He aimed his gaze out the window, wondering what a tar pit would look like.

Hyde drew on his pipe. The attendant put a glass at his elbow and poured champagne into it. Hyde waved him impatiently off.

"Leave the bottle."

"Yes, suh."

"Leave us alone."

"Yes, suh." The attendant went softly, quietly out of the car.

Hyde stared at Brand. "How's the campaign going?"

"Oh, we'll win," Brand said. "They've got too much money into it now."

"You collected that second installment?"

"Oh, yes. That'll do."

"Keep it locked up. I don't trust this place. These people are money-mad."

Brand grunted, amused. He had heard Harris Newmark's version of the money issue. His nose tingled, and he sniffed.

"What's that?"

Hyde pulled on his pipe. "What?"

"Don't you smell anything?" Brand straightened in the fat chair, little warnings going off all over his skin, and looked around the car.

"Just good sweet-cured Virginia tobacco," Hyde said. "You should learn—"

"No. Look there," Brand said, and leaped out of the chair. A film of smoke was filtering out of the upper edge of the icebox.

Hyde said, "Oh, my God."

Brand bounded toward the end of the car and jerked

open the door. Behind him, Hyde shrieked, "Oh, no—
it's on fire! God, we're on fire!" Brand pulled his gun.
Outside the door, the attendant was sitting on the platform, his hands on his knees. He looked up at Brand,
his face wide-eyed and astonished, shot a look into the
car, and let out a yelp. He sprang nimbly across the
coupling, onto the platform of the next car, and burst
through that door, heading for the front of the train.

Brand looked rapidly all around; there was nobody in
sight, no armed gang, no horses galloping up. Not a
robbery. He turned back into the car.

Heavy dark brown stinking smoke billowed through
the car behind him. Hyde hacked a desperate cough. The
icebox was invisible in the heavy rolling pall. The train
lurched; the front end of the train, at least, was braking.
Brand holstered his gun. He rushed to the nearest window, shoving the curtain aside; when he couldn't get it
to stay out of his way he ripped it away. The window
latch was stuck shut with fresh paint and he jammed the
end of his stump against the frame, lifted it, twisted the
catch open, and thrust the window up, then went on to
the next and opened it, and the next.

Hyde sank to the floor, heaving and choking. Down
there, close to the ground, he would be safe enough; the
smoke was rising, boiling beneath the ceiling of the
car, flooding out the windows. The train's wheels were
shrieking against the rails. Everything leaned hard toward the front; Hyde's wine bottle tilted and fell and
rolled across the carpet, spouting champagne. From outside, maybe from the ordinary carriages in front of this
one, came faint screams and cries. The train skidded
along, trying to stop; the private car wanted to keep going, bucked and jerked against the slowing weight blocking it. Leaning against the pull, Brand went to the
platform, leaned out over the railing to the side, and
caught hold of the iron ladder going up to the top.

He scrambled up the ladder. Letting go with his hand,
he reached for the top strut, and the car lurched and

nearly threw him off; he swayed out over the rushing
ground, but hooked his short arm over a rung of the
ladder and stayed on. At the top, he staggered bent-
kneed across the domed roof of the car to the brake
wheel. His boot soles slipped on the smooth wooden
roof and he went to one knee. From here he could see
all around, across the yellow grassland on either side,
and over the train screeching along its curving track. Up
ahead, by the track, were three or four little buildings
and a loading platform crowded with people. There was
going to be quite an audience for this. Scrambling to the
brake wheel at the end of the car, he wrenched it around,
hung on it to keep himself in place, then turned it again,
steadying the car down to a stop.

He looked all around him again, cautious, but he no
longer expected to see a gang of robbers bearing down
on him. This was a prank, a dirty trick, an effort to make
Hyde, Brand, and the Southern Pacific Railroad look
really foolish. And it had worked. Already, in the car
ahead of them, he heard laughing. On the station platform ahead, people were leaning out to see. The back of
Brand's neck felt scorched. His hands tingled. The train
had at last come to rest, with a jerk and a shudder, and
he went to the ladder and climbed down into the car to
drag Hyde out to the open air.

◆ Chapter ◆

XIV

King moved too fast. He kept them at a quick trot almost from the moment they mounted their horses. Lily shifted her weight in the saddle; she was getting sore, and she was hungry. They had left behind the last buildings of Los Angeles. The road unrolled through stands of fruit trees and strips of planted ground. She wondered where they were going to stop. When. Where and when they were going to eat and sleep.

She thought they might not stop for a long while, that this might be the end of living at Serafa's place, and thinking that, suddenly it all became precious to her, Serafa herself, the company of the girls, the wonderful food, her bed and her lamp, even the work.

The sound of Serafa's voice stayed with her, the shrill righteous rage; she felt that like a blade cutting across her whole connection to Sonoratown. She was afraid to ask King anything.

She was alone with him now. The back of her neck tightened. Now he could do whatever he wanted with her. All he had done that was kind and good evaporated in her mind into a single anxious fume.

They rode along a trail that ran beside the railroad track. Even the gardens had fallen behind them now; the broken plain spread out around them in seas of yellow grass. Bored, she began to think about the book she was reading, to imagine herself into it, living the high life in London with Pip, the book's hero. The railroad tracks crossed a dry arroyo on a wooden trestle, and they rode down the arroyo's sandy bank and across to the other side.

Angling up the bank, her mare shied suddenly, plunging back down the slope, and Lily, daydreaming, nearly fell off. When she got back into her saddle, King, on top of the bank, pointed toward a spot halfway up, and she caught an instant's glimpse of a thin brown shape writhing swiftly into a crevice between two rocks.

"Watch out," he said. "There's lots of snakes."

"Was it a rattler?"

"Yes."

She gave an uncontrollable shudder. Now she began to look around her more. Anyway the wide rolling plain was not the dull place it had seemed to be at first. From a distance the land looked flat, but as they rode over it she saw the dry washes, the hollows, the sandy ridges like frozen waves in the grass. They passed a stand of tall scraggly bushes sprinkled with yellow flowers; she saw a line of tiny tracks running through the bare dirt below. A bird flitted away just above the brush. The mountains were fading shades of purple, featureless, as if someone had laid flat ragged strips of color against the edge of the sky. The wind smelled spicy and strong.

She glanced at King again, wondering where he was taking her. Why. Her muscles tensed; she jounced around on her saddle, and the mare Jane laid her ears back. The iron arrow of the railroad tracks led straight away toward the sky's margin. The unwavering streaks of the rails felt like an omen; she was going headfirst and breakneck into the invisible distance.

Near noon, they came to another road, cutting north and south across the railroad and the parallel path they were following, and a cluster of paintless buildings. At the crossroads there was a pump and a trough. Three horses and an oxcart were already gathered around the water. King slowed down, and she saw how he looked these people over before he led her forward toward the watering hole.

Lily was suddenly afire with thirst. Letting King take her horse she went up to the pump end of the trough. A big man in a floppy hat was already jacking the pump handle up and down, talking to a skinny boy standing beside him. She leaned over and with her cupped hands scooped up water and drank, and then splashed water over her face. In the water on her lips she tasted salt sweat.

"Morning train come by yet?" King asked, behind her.

The man with the floppy hat jerked upright. One cheek bulged prodigiously; his voice came slightly muffled past it. His eyes blazed with enthusiasm. "Damn train, sir, went by here trailing smoke and screeching, and stopped right over there." Her thirst slaked, Lily backed away, glancing sharply at King.

"It caught fire?" said the man by the oxcart. "I'm not surprised, the damned thing goes so goddamn fast—"

"Hell, no," said the man in the floppy hat. "It was that private car that got wrote up in the paper. The one they made special for the railroad man."

"It was on fire?"

"Not exactly." The bulge migrated across to the other cheek, and the man turned his head with a grave courtesy and released a long brown arc of juice six feet into a tuft of bunchgrass standing solitary beside the dusty road. "Was a smoke bomb. Somebody booby-trapped it."

Behind Lily a man guffawed. She looked around, seeing how the rest of the people were listening. Laughter spread among them. An old man said, "Well, I'll be damned." The skinny boy gave a low whistle.

The man with the oxcart said, "Glad somebody got to the son of a bitch."

King said, "A lot of people hate the Railroad."

"Whole lot of people got cause," said the man in the floppy hat.

Lily looked up at King, suspicion hardening into certainty. He stood beside his horse, which was drinking in long steady swallows. Opening up the flap on his saddlebag, he got out a handful of tortillas and divided it in half and gave half to her. When their eyes met, he winked at her.

Later, they rode off across the railroad tracks and turned almost at once from the main road onto a thin white string of a path running west through the grass. She said, "You did that, didn't you? Booby-trapped the luxury car."

He said, "They made me mad, is all."

She laughed, amazed. "How?"

"Just a little black powder," he said. "I stuck it in the icebox with a phosphor squib. Phosphor burns in water."

"How do you know how to do that?" She remembered how those people had admired this deed. Everybody hated and feared the Railroad, but only King actually did anything. "What if Brand finds out?"

"Oh, I think Brand likely will find out."

"Oh," she said. "Is that bad?"

He shrugged. "It's bound to happen sometime." Turning in his saddle, he gave her a keen look. "You let me worry about Brand."

She rode up next to him. "Serafa will take you back, though. Won't she? It's not like a robbery."

"I don't know, she surprised me, howling like that. I never made her any promises. She's actin' like we're married."

"When she finds out what you did she won't mind." Suddenly she felt better about being with him. She wanted to keep talking. "Where are we going?"

"Down by the ocean. I found a good hideout, water, grass for the horses, you can see anybody coming a mile away."

"How long will we be there?"

"Oh, we'll be back in Los Angeles by Election Day. Wouldn't miss that."

"Good."

"You like Los Angeles," he said.

"Yes," she said. "A lot."

"Well, then," he said, "Serafa will have to take us back."

They rode steadily along. The warmth of the sun lulled her. She took her feet out of the stirrups and let her legs dangle. The mare carried her along through stands of scraggly green brush, each branch tipped with tiny yellow flowers. They angled down the side of a dry wash onto a river of sand meandering off westward. The bank of the wash was pocked with holes, the burrows of animals, like round doorways in the pale sand. They followed the dry watercourse, picking their way around barricades of driftwood, broken trees, and clumps of brush. The wash widened out onto a broad shelf of a beach that stretched off in a curve sweeping for miles to the south. All along the low edge of the beach, the blue ocean rolled.

Lily trotted her mare straight out toward it, exhilarated. This was the edge, the limit, the end of the continent. The salt air stung her sunburned cheeks. She felt she had at last come somewhere important.

"Down there," he said, and pointed off to the south.

"How did you find this place?" The mare broke into her pace, keeping up with his sorrel gelding, and she bounced gently up stirrup to stirrup with him.

"Just lookin' around," he said.

They rode along the edge of the ocean. The broad blue water muttered and pulsed beside her, its mild little waves turning the white sand brown. Out over the even, orderly waves a flock of tiny dark birds swooped over the water; all at once, all together, they turned, and for an instant they disappeared.

She picked them out again instantly, a white cloud in the air. They whirled around, coming back, presenting her again with their dark undersides, so that they stood out against the blue sky. Their wings and backs were white, which was how they disappeared; when they reversed, they lost themselves in the blaze of the sun. Her gaze followed them, eager for the next transformation.

"See the pelicans?" King pointed.

Dutifully she watched some big ugly birds plow along through the air. She liked the disappearing birds better. She looked around inland, across the wide stretch of windblown green that lay behind the beach.

"That's marsh," he said. "Up there's where we're goin'."

Ahead, just behind a limb of the beach, lay a broad shallow lagoon, brilliant blue under the sky. Giant stalks of grass stood all around the inward edge. At the southern edge of the lagoon the land ridged up into a sandy dune. King rode along the beach around the lagoon, and she followed him down beneath the hollow flank of the dune and into a grassy meadow. He swung down from his horse.

"Water's over here." He walked through the grass toward the back edge of the lagoon. Lily followed him. In through the cattails a little stream wound down to the lagoon. King dropped flat on his belly, put his mouth to the water, and drank, like a horse, and then plunged his head completely under and leaped up, shaking his wet hair back, suddenly exuberant. He strode back across the meadow toward his horse and began to unsaddle it.

"We'll build the fire in the lee of the dune," he said. "We may have to look some to get good wood, but there's usually driftwood on the beach." His voice sang, the accent stronger. "There's game all over. This grass will last the horses a couple of days at least, and then we can move down the beach to another place almost as good."

She dismounted. Stripping the saddle off Jane, she used the saddle blanket to scrub the horse's sweated back and sides. When she took off the bridle the mare went at once toward the grass, her head down and her long tail swishing. Lily took her gear to the lee of the dune, where King wanted the camp to be. Sitting down, she took off her boots and socks and rolled up the cuffs of her pants.

King's sudden happiness worried her. She did not understand him and she wished she knew what he wanted with her. She went back around the side of the dune toward the beach, looking for the disappearing birds. The ground was warm against the soles of her feet. Along the bank of the lagoon there were heaps of sand, old worn mounds like little graves. She sank down on her heels beside the shallow, brackish water, looking for live things.

Something glinted in the sand just at the rim of the water. She poked her finger at it and pushed it deeper and it vanished into the sand. She dug down with her hand, lifted up a palmful of the sand, and washed it gently away in the lagoon water. Out of the last of the sand a tiny white tooth appeared. Not a tooth: iridescent, like a pearl. She picked it up. A hole pierced it. A bead. She let out a yell for King.

"What is this?"

"That's a bead," he said. He had a hatchet in his hand. His horse stood behind him. "You goin' to help me make camp?"

She didn't want to help him make camp; besides, the bead enchanted her. "Where did it come from?"

"Indians," he said. "Here. Look." He bent toward one of the mounds along the lagoon shore and, digging into it with the hatchet, turned up clumps of empty shells. "There's mussels and clams in the lagoon. The Indians came down here to dig them. Probably stayed here awhile, at certain times of the year. All these piles are their leavings."

"Indians," she said, and looked all around. "Where are they now?"

He shook his head. "Not here no more, darlin'. I'm

goin' for some wood." He swung up onto his horse and rode off.

She turned to the mound and dug into it, turning up dozens of shells. Tiring of that, she squatted by the lagoon shore, looking for more beads. She tried to imagine the people who had come here to dig clams. Although she had lived all her life in this country she had seen few Indians, a couple of drunken beggars here and there in the silver towns, a few long glimpses of digger families living in their hovels in the desert. Brown-skinned. Half naked. Most people despised them. She wondered what they had been like before white people got here. The bead was so beautiful. Could you make something beautiful without being good?

Squatting by the lagoon, she put her hands down, palms against the sand. They had stood here, in this place, their feet where her hands were.

After a while she got up and wandered back toward the meadow. King's saddle, saddlebags, and bedroll were heaped up next to hers. A few feet away he had scraped out a hollow in the sand for the fire. She walked along the foot of the dune. Halfway across the meadow, the mare Jane champed down the tall grass. Against the green her red coat looked bright and strong.

Lily stepped on something; she bent down and dug a piece of woven stuff out of the sand. It was not cloth, although the fabric was tight and even, a weaving of grass, fastened at intervals with knots. She felt a rush of possessiveness. Excited, she dropped to her knees on the dune and dug down through the mats of morning glory and strawberry plants, but all she found was sand.

When King came back she showed him the basket. "What kind of Indians were they?"

"Darlin', I don't know. I don't think anybody knows. They were here when the *padres* and the *pobladores* came, a hundred years ago. But they're all gone now."

"But where?"

"They're dead, darlin'."

She was still. Maybe there had not been many of them. She stroked the woven grass with her fingertips. Some woman had made this; men didn't do things like this. Some woman like her.

She must have felt herself safe here. She must have thought her world would go on forever.

Lily shivered. King was chopping wood for the fire; the light was bleeding out of the sky and night was creeping in. She went over closer to him, picked up some bits of the wood, and began to lay out the fire in a circle as she had always done.

Abruptly she thought of her father, Jewell, who had taught her to do this. With a shock of guilt she realized she had not thought of him in a long while. She had forgotten her own father. That seemed worse even than his dying, that she should have forgotten about him. She imagined him small, distant, as if she were looking at him through the wrong end of a telescope. She willed herself never to forget him again. Her chest ached.

She lit the fire. King cut the wood and stacked it, and she built the fire into a slow blaze that would last them a while. She said, "I'm hungry."

He dragged his saddlebag over and brought out tortillas, cheese, some *colorado* wrapped up in corn husks. She fell on it, her mouth watering.

Stuffed, she lay back, now abruptly so weary she could barely keep her eyes open. He had brought along a bedroll for her. He had planned this, all of it, she realized, long before he told any of them; she could see why Serafa was angry with him. But she was tired, so tired, she could not even get up to spread the blankets. She dragged them over her, cradled her head on her arm, and was immediately asleep.

◆ Chapter ◆

XV

In the morning she read her book, and King disappeared. When he came back, he was wearing only his pants, his hair wet and his shoulders blotchy with sunburn. She turned her eyes away from his bare chest, the old fear rising again about him, that if she trusted him he would take advantage of her.

She wanted to get him talking; she always felt safest with him when he was talking to her. She said, "Is Ireland like this?"

He dropped down on the sand, stretching out, his arms behind his head. "Like this? Faith, no. Nowhere near."

He fell still, seeming very content, almost sleepy. Not particularly dangerous. He smelled like salt and she thought maybe he had been swimming in the ocean.

"Well," she said, "what is it like, then?"

He stirred, drawing his arms down. His eyes looked off into the sky. "Ireland is green. It rains, and when it doesn't rain, there's a silver mist falls on it all, so the grass is always green, and the oak trees, and all."

Some difference in his voice caught at her, tantalizing. The fine sarcasm gone that veiled most of what he said. She said, "How old were you when you left?"

"Eleven," he said.

She wondered how old he was now. About her father's

age, maybe: Jewell had been thirty-seven. Then King had been here most of his life. "Do you miss it?"

"Well, hell, darlin'," he said. "I've got rocks, and sand, and vultures and rattlers and the sun so hot in the summer it can cook an egg at two in the afternoon. Why should I miss Ireland?"

"Does that mean you do?" she asked.

He sat up. He took a stick from the heap by the fire pit and began to dig up the sand with it. After a while, when she had decided he wasn't going to say any more, he nodded.

"Yes, I do. It's utterly different than here. It's much older than here. And it's holy. It's sacred. The land is deep and rich, the woods are dark even at noon, the rocks are gray and worn like old bones. There were standing stones near where we lived, me father said they were made five thousand years ago. And the old folk say that the ancient people are still there. You could hear voices in the water, and in the wind. See lights dancing at night on the hilltops. Every evening the church bells rang, all together, every village in time. Everybody knew you, knew your dad, knew everything. There was a story about everything, about everybody. Everything had always been as it was."

She drew her knees to her chest, her curiosity boiling at this rush of words from him, the longing in his voice. "Why did you leave? Can you go back?"

"I can never go back." He stabbed the wood hard into the sand. "They stole it."

"Who stole it?"

"The damned English. Being English in Ireland makes you a damned god. But being Irish in Ireland is a kind of crime, you see. And the punishment is sufferin', and pain, and death."

His voice grated, like stones striking together. Alarmed, she tried to be funny, to make this light again. "So to get away you jumped into the water and swam over here."

"Actually, I came on a boat." He was furrowing up the sand with the stick, his arm jerking back and forth.

"Did you really come all by yourself?"

His voice was perfectly even. "Yes, by myself."

She did not know how she knew he was lying. She could tell he had come to the end of talking about this. She wanted to go there, to the place he had talked into being in her mind, a dark green misty place of ancient voices and people dancing.

They ate the last of the food he had brought, and he went off again, in the afternoon, with his rifle. She walked down to the beach and waded in the waves, lay on the sunlit dune and read her book. When King came back he had half a dozen little birds, plump in their patterned brown feathers.

She helped him gut them and pluck them; losing their feathers, heads, and feet, they went from big handfuls to tiny naked lumps of meat. "Did you shoot these?"

"No. I set some snares yesterday," he said.

"Oh. I want to do that. Will you show me how?"

"Sure," he said. "Let's cook this up."

"I'll do it," she said. Her father had made her cook most of the time; she knew how to do this, at least.

While she was spitting the little birds he went off into the meadow where the horses were; he came back with a handful of long red tail hairs. While she turned the birds over the fire, he showed her how to braid the hair into strings and coil the strings into the snares, the hair strong, resilient, and smooth so that it slid tight at the first jerk of the poor victim's foot in the loop. They ate the birds.

"What's in that book you're reading?" he asked. He nodded at the novel lying on its open face on the sand.

She told him about Pip, who helped the desperate criminal Magwitch escape and later got mysteriously rich, and then found out the money came from Magwitch and had to give it all back. King listened attentively, but all he said in the end was, "Damned English." In the distance there was a long low wail, sad as loss. King's head came around, alert. "There's Phineas Banning's iron horse." He reached into his pocket for his watch.

Lily remembered the people at the watering hole, how they had spoken of what he did. She blurted out, "I want to help you beat the Railroad."

"There's no way to beat the Railroad."

"You did," she said.

He shook his head at her. "I didn't do anything. How could a little smoke hurt them? They've got all the money in the world. All the power."

"But that's why we have to fight them, isn't it?" she cried. "They steal from everybody. We have to fight back!"

King stuck his watch back into his pocket. "I don't know where you got this new Battle Hymn of the Republic, darlin', but I ain't no revolutionist. I'm a robber. I rob the Railroad because they have a lot of money and I like to have money without working for it. But you're not going to live like that."

This struck her like a whiplash. She felt him closing in on her. "You can't tell me what to do. You aren't my father!"

"I want you to have an decent life. I want you to be able to tell people your right name. Walk in any door you want, up front. And not run all the time."

"I'll do what I want with my life!" Her fists were clenched on her thighs; she was so angry her throat was closing up. "You talk out of both sides of your mouth: one thing for you, something else for me. Why can't you be honest with me?"

"Look, Lily. You want things simple, bad and good, honest and dishonest, but the world don't work like that. Bad people get by, and good people die, simply because they're good and won't see people suffer. My mother was good as an angel, and she died."

He stopped abruptly. He swiveled away from her, staring off across the lagoon. Lily said, "When did your mother die?"

"On the boat," he said, still staring away.

"You said you were alone."

"I was. Oh, I was, in the end."

Silence. Steadily he stared away across the lagoon. His face looked peeled, his eyes shining, his skin sleek, the insulating surface sloughed away. She could see how he was struggling to pull himself back inside again.

He whispered, "It was hell, that boat."

She said nothing, full of a bad feeling. She should have left this alone. She had heard this before, felt this way before, and hurt at the end. She watched the reeds beyond the lagoon, gray when they bent, green when they stood upright, so that the wind running through them left tracks. Abruptly she felt heavy, leaden, useless, dirty. She got up and went down around the dune to be by herself for a while.

In the morning, when she woke up, there was a tall blue-gray bird in the lagoon; she watched it fish for a while, stabbing with its beak into the water at its feet. The sun brightened. The bird unfolded the great ragged gray scarves of its wings and flew away. She and King went off and set the snares they had made. He showed her the animal trails in the grass and the reeds, and where to put the traps. Coming back along the beach, he found a piece of driftwood and put white shells along it for targets and let her shoot his guns.

"I'm going to get you a better horse," he said as they rode to their camp.

"I have Jane!"

"Jane's lovely, darlin', but she's a little long in the tooth. We'll turn her out in the tules, she'll have a grand old time."

She bent down and patted Jane's neck. The idea was beginning to intrigue her.

"I'd like a pinto horse. Like Raul's."

"No. No white horses. They're too easy to remember.

Get a bay or a chestnut." They rode around into their camp and turned their horses out. The tide was out, shrinking the lagoon down to a puddle, and barefoot they went out on the flat muddy bottom and dug up clams, round white ones and long blue-black ones.

"How are we going to cook them?" she said, following him back to the shore. He was hauling the clams in his shirt slung over his shoulder.

"Don't cook 'em," he said. "Eat 'em raw." He dropped the shirt on the sand next to the stream and knelt down to wash the clams, piling them up next to him.

"Raw!" she cried. "I'm not eating those things." She watched him pry open a shell with his knife. "Yuk!"

He washed the open clam again, cut the horrible moist gray lump out of the shell, popped it in his mouth, and swallowed. "The best way"—he was prying open another shell—"is with some real hot sarsa, like Serafa's green stuff." He rinsed out the the open shell and held it up to her. "Unfortunately I didn't bring any. Eat it."

"Eeeeyyyuuuu." She shrank away.

"This is dinner, darlin'. You don't eat this, you don't eat." He left the shell at her feet and opened another. She watched him narrowly. He seemed to be enjoying the clams well enough. Cautiously she lifted the shell, smelled the slimy mess inside, and poked it with her finger. He held out his knife.

"You got to cut it loose. Right there, see? Good. Eat it."

She ate it. It tasted odd, salty, but not as bad as she expected, and the smoothness was interesting.

"Watch out for the sand," he said, and gave her another.

"Yes," she said. "We need some sarsa."

"Next time," he said.

Sand crunched in her teeth, which sent a shiver through her. She swallowed hastily and then spat, working her tongue around on her gums. He laughed and held out the water jug to her. Their eyes met. He said, "Did I lie?"

"No," she said.

"Lily," he said, "I'll never lie to you."

"You already have," she said.

He plunked the water jug down on the sand. "I have not. When?"

"You said you swam here," she said. "Remember? That was a lie."

He rocked back, his arms resting on his thighs, his gaze steady on her. "Well," he said, "I didn't want to think about it. I hadn't thought about it for years."

"You mean about your mother? What was she like? What was her name?"

He reached out for another of the clams, worked his knife into a corner of the shell, and sliced it open. "You really want to know this?"

"You said you wouldn't lie to me," she said.

"All right, then." He nodded, almost to himself. Letting himself remember. "Me mother was beautiful. Me father told me once she was like a sheaf of wheat bending in the wind. Her hair was red as maple leaves in the autumn. . . ."

His voice trailed off. He held out the clam to her on his knife like a sickening fleshy gray fruit. She leaned forward, her mouth open, and he fed her.

"The reason we left was the potatoes," he said. "We had nothing to eat but the potatoes, which there was usually plenty of, except in the spring. But then the potatoes went bad."

"Bad," she said. She swallowed the long slippery mouthful. "In what way?"

"Well, it was strange, you know, they were fine while they were growing, or it seemed so, and when we dug them they seemed fine big potatoes, but when you cooked them, it was like a charm, the way a beautiful good potato would turn to black muck when you tried to eat it. Anyway there were no potatoes, and there never had been anything else.

"My father tried to catch us hares to eat. That's why they hanged him. Not for being a whiteboy and talkin' rebellion, see, but for tryin' to feed us. When they hanged him they threw us out of our place, and we were living in the ditch on the side of the road, eating in the damned soup kitchens where they tried to make you turn proddy. A cup of hot water with some barley in it and a carrot once a day. Sermon before and after. The English said if they gave us food, we'd get lazy, see, and not work. But there was no work, either.

"We were even lower than the shanty Irish, we didn't even have a shanty, see, but my mother had a lace curtain cousin. My mother went and begged and begged, and finally the cousin gave her enough to buy passage for her and me on a ship going to America. It was three pounds six, I think. We took everything we owned, wrapped in her shawl. We walked to the ship and on the way she sold everything we had, everything but the shawl, to get food: the cups, the knives, the blanket, my father's pipe. She kept the shawl.

"But there wasn't any food. I was so hungry all the time, all I thought of was eating, and I asked my mother for something to eat and she slapped me. We saw dead people in the ditch. That's when I realized that everybody was dying, all the Irish. The English had plenty to eat, but the Irish were all going to starve to death. It got where you just turned away, there wasn't anything to do, it wasn't even terrible anymore, see, just dead bodies here and there. You didn't dare think about it because you'd be thinking about your own body, see, that felt so close to dyin'.

"We got to the ship, and there were dozens of people who had paid for passage on this ship, far more than they had room for. They jammed us all on board anyway. At first everybody was laughing and dancing, happy because we were leaving. We were going to a better place, we were going to America. My mother hid my sister in her shawl—"

He stopped. Lily turned and stared at him, astonished. "Your sister? You had a sister? What happened to her?"

He got up and walked away. When he came back she was afraid to ask him any more questions.

But he was talking. He did not look at her; his voice went on, low and even.

"These Indians, you know, they're gone entirely. Nobody even remembers the name of their tribe. The Spanish got here, and the Indians just were gone, like there was only room for one kind of people. The Spanish took away their land, their home, and made them slaves, and they just quit. Wouldn't live like that. And I'll be damned if I know how the Irish did, for so long."

She said nothing. He had said he would not lie; now she would see what the lies covered. His hands were working, the fingers flexing in and out. He sat heavily down by the fire pit, his back slightly to her.

"My sister's name was Maire. She was three or four, a little girl." He paused. Lily waited, her shoulders stiff.

"We had no money for Maire's passage, so my mother hid her in her shawl and we got her on board that way. It didn't matter much because there were so many people you could of brought six little kids on board; other people probably did too.

"So we were all on the deck singin' and hollerin' and dancin' for joy, as the ship set sail. But then the sailors drove us down into the holds and slammed the hatches down on us, and after that we were in the holds like rats in the dark. They fed us once a day, like the soup kitchens, a cup of water with some beans in it. It was like being underground, except underground at least wouldn't have moved, and the ship rolled and heaved all the time. It was hell down there. It was full of fleas and rats, there were kids crying, and people fighting and crying and screaming, people pissed and shit right where they were and didn't bother even getting up, still less cleaning up. There was no air and no water, people died down there and lay there dead for the whole trip. It was pure hell.

"My mother hoarded all the food. She gave us little bits to eat, moldy bread, dry beans, and these broken bits of cracker I think she begged from the sailors, and just sips of water. I hunted the ship rats, like poaching the rabbits. She wouldn't eat those, either, but Maire and I did, I cut them up and we ate them raw, because if we tried to cook them the other people would know we had food and steal it from us.

"After a couple of weeks I'd got all the rats. I was hungry all the time, so hungry, you just don't know how bad it is to be so hungry. All the while we crossed, I and my sister kept at me mother to give us more food, and she'd whack us and cry and feed us one scrap at a time.

"I thought she was trying to kill us. I told her so after a while and she hit me, but it didn't hurt, it was so soft a blow.

"Then we got to the Saint Lawrence River and she was too weak to get off the ship. All that time she'd been feeding us she hadn't eaten anything herself. She hadn't eaten anything in weeks. She was light as air. I carried her up onto the deck and she died. She died in the sun, at least. She died breathing free. But she died."

Lily bit her lips; she saw his mother's body, lying there before her, on a table in a saloon, the shirt all covered with blood, the face turned away. Tears stung her eyes. Something inside her split open into a gaping wound. She should not have done this. Married their griefs. She was afraid she would cry in front of him and she swallowed down the mass in her throat.

She thought, He did it long before. He did it in Virginia City.

He said, "That's when I knew it was all a big joke, see, just a nasty wicked huge joke, and the joke's on us."

"What happened to your sister?" she cried. "Where is your sister now?"

He turned jerkily toward her, his eyes shining. "I don't know. I lost her."

Lily's hands went to her face. "Oh, no."

"Me mother died at a place called Grass Hill, which wasn't, it was an island all covered with trees. Then we went on to Montreal. I couldn't keep hold of Maire, she was always runnin' off. We tied up alongside a wharf by the city there, and they were checkin' us all at the top of the ramp to see who was healthy and who not. She kept getting away from me and taking off down the ramp toward the shore. Then they were checkin' me and she ran, and they wouldn't let me—"

He stopped. His face shone glossy in the firelight, his eyes wide. He was not looking at her, but past her. After a moment he began to speak again.

"They wouldn't let me go after her, not for a long time, and then she was gone. I looked all over. There were so many people, it was a big town, Montreal. I looked for days, but I never found her."

"Oh, no," Lily said. "Oh, no, the poor baby, oh, no."

Maybe someone had found her, some kind and good person. Monstrous possibilities rose up in her imagination and she thrust them away, she could not think of that. She was rocking back and forth, her hands pressed to her face. King was staring away into the indefinite sky. He had thought of it all.

"You couldn't have done anything," she said helplessly.

"I lost her," he said. "The last thing my mother said to me was, 'Take care of my baby,' and I couldn't even do that."

"It wasn't your fault." She put out her hands to him, and as soon as she touched him, he reached out and gripped her. His arm went around her. She stiffened, her blood hammering in her ears. He was clutching her hard; she felt the heat of his breath on her cheek.

She said, "Let go of me."

He let go at once, moved away, out of arm's reach of her. He turned his head away from her. She sat there trying to breathe right. He swung his gaze toward her.

"What's the matter? What do you think I'm going to do to you? What do I have to do for you to trust me?"

"I'm not your sister," she said between her teeth. "And you're not my father."

Tears welled irresistibly from her eyes. She wasn't sure why she was crying. The space between them was stuffed with ghosts, dead people, blood, fear, loss.

He said, "I want to take care of you."

Her heart churned in her chest, yearning and sore. She ground the heels of her hands into her eyes. "I can take care of myself."

"You can't. I can."

"I don't owe you anything."

"No," he said. He looked away from her. "You owe me nothing. That's the idea. I'm the one who owes."

She hunched her shoulders, thinking of the little girl Maire. Who else but him had known all this, who but him, for so long? She wondered if he had told her all this so there would be a girl to grieve. "Then what happened?" she said. She struggled herself down to a measure of calm. "You came out here and started robbing people?"

"No," he said, and looked at her again. His face relaxed suddenly. His eyes were narrow, calculating; the smile turned his lips. Seeing the joke. "I started robbing people right away. While I was looking for my sister I stole a hot meat pie off a windowsill. It was the best meal I've ever had. You oughta consider becomin' a preacher, as you seem to have the way of going down pretty well. I sure hope you're being as holy as that, too. What-all's goin' on between you and that Rosas boy?"

She folded her arms around her knees, startled. "Nothing's going on. Why do you think so?"

" 'Cause I see him giving you calf-eyes all the time. You giving him anything back?"

She felt hot all over. "Why should I tell you anything like that? Even if I was."

"That boy is worthless, you're wasting your time. You have more balls than he does."

"Shut up!" She swung her arm at him; he fended her off.

"I'm just telling you. Don't get stuck with somebody who's not worth your time. And if you get in trouble with him, he won't be worth any time at all, because I'll shoot him."

"Damn you!" She leaped at him, trying seriously to hurt him, her temper blown. He wrapped his arms around her and held her fast, helpless.

"See, you ain't as on top of this as you think. Use your elbows. Ouch, yes, like that. Ouch!" He let her go. She moved quickly away from him, panting, and he settled down again, his back against the sand bank. "Sit down. You know I'm not going to hurt you."

She sat. "If you touch Raul, I'll kill you."

"It's amazing to me how you ain't willing to kill anybody else in the world but me."

"That's because you're the worst person in the world."

"I won't have to touch Raul. You'll wise up to him on a little more acquaintance."

She decided she would love Raul forever. King was cynical and old and knew nothing. She fumbled for her book, thinking of the little girl Maire running away into a strange new world. She would take Raul and run away, and they would become new people somewhere else: the idea tantalized her, a whole new life, fresh and clean.

Away across the marsh sounded the long moan of the distant train.

King's head came up. He reached around to his saddlebag on the ground behind him and took out his watch. "Right on time," he said.

"Why are you doing that?" she said.

"Just curious." He wound the watch and put it back in the saddlebag.

"You're planning something."

"Frankly, right now I'm just scouting. Probably won't come to anything at all. You stay out of it."

"I can help you."

He lifted his eyes to stare at her. The smile vanished. "You're a kid and you don't know what you're talking about."

"I do too! I've been around, you know—I've seen a lot!"

"And you've read a lot of books. You're still a kid." He nodded toward the book lying beside her. "Maybe you ought to listen to your book a little more. That Magwitch fella." Getting up, he took the empty clam shells away to the lagoon. A few moments later she saw him hunkered down by the stream of fresh water, washing out his shirt. She picked up *Great Expectations* and read the last few pages.

In the night, King woke. Over him the sky arched in a blaze of stars. He thought about the time in Ireland when they were living in the ditch, and his uncle Paddy was still alive and still had his fiddle, and how one day a great coach came down the road and Paddy caught up the fiddle and cried, "Colum! Maire! Into the road, now, dance, and God love us these kind folk will throw us a penny!"

He had held back, unwilling, knowing these kind folk for the same or as good as the same as those who hanged his father. His sister scurried into the road. Small and nimble, she danced like one of the Good People at their merrymaking. The coach stopped. The curtain drew back a little, and after a moment coins showered over Maire, half a dozen coppers.

The child crowed and gathered the money up;

thereafter, whenever a coach came by she would run into the street and dance.

Paddy sold the fiddle, though, for something to eat, and not much later he died, the fiddle having been his sole joy. And soon after that, King's mother said, "We are going to America."

His life had broken when his mother died and his sister disappeared; since then it had all been random shooting in the dark, getting him nowhere. He never had anything or anybody that belonged to him alone. Until Lily.

He could hear Lily breathing in her sleep. He wanted to go over there and pick her up and hold her in his arms. He couldn't do that; she was too scared. Probably she would always be too scared. That didn't matter. All that mattered was taking care of her, and not losing her again: his luck charm, his fate. He looked up into the sky, ashy with stars, and thought about his little sister, dancing in the dust.

◆ Chapter ◆

XVI

Spitting and fuming, Joseph Hyde finally left. The smoke had ruined the fittings of the private car and it was rolled onto a spur at the Wilmington factory and forgotten. Brand went to the icehouse in Los Angeles, where the foreman remembered that somebody had asked how the ice was getting to Hyde's car, although the foreman remembered nothing at all about the somebody who asked. Brand went to the Giant Powder Company, where nobody could tell him anything.

"We sell a lot of powder," said the man in the office.

"This had some kind of phosphorus trigger."

"We sell a lot of phosphorus."

Brand went the rounds of the saloons, talking to the bartenders, who heard everything; nobody had heard anything. The story of the smoke bomb was spreading and the people Brand talked to all thought it was terribly funny.

"The Railroad always gets its own way," Harris Newmark told him. The merchant wanted the Railroad. He was working tirelessly to see that the subsidy passed in the upcoming election, he had raised the cash to open the new office and advanced Brand money out of his own pocket, but he had learned to hate Joseph Hyde and he had bridled at the demand for the car in the first place.

He flicked the tip of his cigar over the sardine tin that served on Brand's desk for an ashtray. "Forget it. You'll never find who did it."

"I'll find out," Brand said. "I always find out."

Elmo said, "I'd say, look down in Sonoratown. Except those greasers don't know for shit about gunpowder."

He and Elmo and Elmo's boys went to Sonoratown. The old pueblo lay just off the plaza, a few winding streets studded with laurel trees. It seemed removed from the rest of the city, older and smaller, with its back turned to the big new houses, the factories and stores. The laurel trees stank. The surface of the street was pounded into three inches of dust. One of the yards they passed was neatly bordered in bleached cow skulls. The houses were too close together, little adobes, their roofs covered with tar. Strings of dried chiles hung from the eaves. When he went to the door of the first house and knocked, the man who answered couldn't understand him, answered in Spanish, and shook his head finally and shut the door.

He went on from house to house. Here and there he found someone who spoke English, but nobody knew anything about the Railroad, much less the smoke bomb.

In one house, as the man shut the door, the woman leaned past him and whispered, "Serafa's." The man pushed her and slammed the door, and Brand heard his voice behind it, sharp and angry.

At the next house, they knew nothing. He said, "Where is Serafa's?"

A pointing finger directed him across the street, toward a rambling building with a porch running the whole length of the front. Along the porch half a dozen men leaned against the wall smoking cigarillos, passing them back and forth. When Brand came up, with Elmo and his friends on his heels, the smokers stopped passing their cigarillos and watched him out of the corners of their eyes.

Brand went in the door, into a warm and well-lit room

full of people, talking and eating and drinking. At once
the rumble of talk and movement stopped cold. In a
complete silence everybody in the room turned toward
him and stared.

In this well of attention, he stood in the middle of the
room and swung around, looking at every table, into
every corner. These were peons, some even barefoot,
who watched him with wide cowlike eyes. He recognized none of them. He knew Elmo and the others behind him were waiting for orders. Waiting for him to
take charge. Brand felt naked, out here in front of all
these people with no real power. He pulled the cuff of
his shirt down over his stump.

He said, "I work for the Railroad. Yesterday somebody let a bomb off in one of our passenger cars. I'll
pay a reward to anybody who can tell me who did it and
where to find him."

For a moment there was silence. The scores of pairs
of wide dark eyes watched him without understanding.
Then among them someone whispered, and another
whispered elsewhere, saying what he had said in Spanish, and the taut brown faces cleared, some of them even
smiled.

But nobody spoke up; nobody came forward. A big-
boned dark girl stood in the back doorway, a tray of
cups and pitchers in her hands. He beckoned to her. His
voice rang out, whining with frustration.

"Who are you? Hah? Do you work here? Does anybody here speak English?"

The girl moved toward him, holding the tray between
them. "I speak English, sir."

"Are you Serafa?"

"No, sir." She swallowed, her mouth trembling. Then
through the door behind her came an older woman
wrapped in a dark shawl.

As soon as she appeared, everybody in the room was
watching her. She spoke Spanish in a harsh voice, and

Brand turned to face her: he knew the boss when he saw her. He said, "You're Serafa?"

The girl said, "My mother does not speak English."

"Is she Serafa?" he demanded. He went closer to the older woman, who lifted her head, her eyes flashing. She spoke again to the girl, in a voice that snapped.

"My mother is Serafa Vargas Olvera," said the girl.

Brand was studying this woman. She was nigger-dark, but she had a lot of Indian in her too. Tall and angular for a *chica,* her look hard and strong. When he stared at her she stared back, and her wide brows drew together and her mouth tightened. She came forward into the room, saying something.

The daughter said, "My mother wants to know what she can do to help you, sir."

"She can tell me anything she knows about the bombing of the railroad car," he said. He never looked away from Serafa. This woman got his back up; she thought she was somebody, this nigger Indian.

She listened to her daughter and shook her head and spoke, still shaking her head. Brand took another step toward her.

"Tell her somebody told me she does know."

The girl spoke and the woman shrugged and shook her head again and smiled; but as she smiled, her bold black eyes met Brand's, and he knew, he knew that she lied.

He gathered a deep breath. There had to be some way to force her to talk. He said, "I want to take a look around."

"You may look all you want, sir."

With Elmo and the others he went out into the back, where three other buildings framed a dusty little yard. One of the buildings was a little two-room adobe where the mother obviously lived with her daughter—with two daughters, he guessed, counting the beds. He could tell right away that no man lived there: nothing but women's things. Next to that, the kitchen, low-roofed and dark and smelling so deliciously that his stomach growled and he had to swallow the sudden water in his mouth. The last building was an old adobe with the plaster peeling off the walls. He went inside.

A blanket hanging from the ceiling divided the room into two. There were piles of boards against the walls, kegs stacked in the middle of the room. It didn't look lived-in, with all this lumber around, but it didn't really look like a storeroom, either. There was something the matter with this. Puzzled, he went around behind the blanket, finding more piles of lumber, a couple of bales of hay, a stack of newspapers, neatly folded. Against one wall was a shelf of books.

He went over there and picked up one of the books and opened it. The title was in English—*The Governess.* Bells went off in his head. He turned and looked around again, trying to figure out what was wrong here. He could not get his mind around it; he could not make out what he was looking at.

"Do you want to see anything else, sir?" The girl from the cantina had come after him into the adobe.

He swung around. "Whose books are those?"

The girl's face was stupid, or blank, or laughing at him behind its careful stupid blankness. She said, "They are my books, sir. But I don't read them anymore, so I put them in here."

His temper swelled. She was lying. They were all lying. He pushed by her into the yard, feeling like an idiot. They knew something; they were laughing at him, snickering behind their hands. He could not look at Elmo. Trailing Elmo and the other men, he went back through the cantina.

The dark woman, Serafa, still stood in the middle of it, her black unblinking eyes following every move he made. He glanced over his shoulder, to see that the girl who spoke English had come in, and then faced the mother.

"I don't believe you. You know something. If I ever

find out what it is, if I ever find out what's going on here, I'll be down here before the spit dries and I'll take this little place of yours apart. Just remember that." While the daughter rattled out the Spanish for that, he went out to the street, gathering up Elmo and the boys, and went back to Los Angeles.

Serafa watched the door for a long moment after the railroad man left. Her heart was thrashing in her chest. She turned to her customers, who were standing around the cantina with rapt concentration on her, and said, "Please, go on eating. There is no trouble here. Luz! Bring everyone another beer." Head high, she walked out of the cantina and across the yard to her room.

She sat on the bed, her fists clenched. All she had was her cantina. She belonged here, as nowhere else, and she had power here. Now some one-handed Anglo who didn't even really have a badge could come in and throw everything on its head and threaten her and probably do as he had threatened, and she could not stop it.

She hung her head and wept. Irresistibly the image rose before her eyes, her husband Tiburcio hanging from the gallows in the plaza. She tried to escape it, but the image followed her.

She had stood in the front of the crowd, smelling the dry dust, holding her daughters by their hands, when they brought Tiburcio out to the gallows. His hands were bound. She had thought it would not happen, she had dreamed someone would rescue him, but Callahan was far away and no one else would try. He spoke to her, telling her that he loved her, that he loved their children, and her heart cracked. Surely they would not hang such a one, she thought, and then saw the hangman put the noose around his neck.

She screamed. The whole force of what was about to happen fell upon her all at once. She started forward and the people around her caught her and held her. Tiburcio called to her. She struggled in her family's arms. She did not see him plunge.

She saw him hanging.

Sitting on her bed now, she sobbed for a while, rocking back and forth. Gradually her grief choked off. She began to be angry, first at the arrogant one-handed Anglo who could come in and stir up her life like this, and then at King, who had brought the one-handed Anglo down on her.

He had known. Her fists clenched; she realized that he had known this would happen. That was why he had gotten himself and Lily out of the way.

If he had been here, could he not have stopped it? Drawn his guns and forced the Anglos to leave, stood on the threshold like a man and defended her and her children and her place?

If he had been here they might have hanged him. And someday they would come. And they would hang him.

A knock on the door brought her out of this vortex. She said, "Who is it?"

Luz came in. "Mama. What is wrong?" She sat down on the bed next to Serafa.

Serafa rubbed her fingers over her eyes. "Nothing. I'm tired." She turned away from her daughter, unwilling to be seen in such a state. "What an annoyance. Has everybody left?"

"No," Luz said. "They're all talking about it still. This smoke bomb—King did that!"

"Yes," Serafa said, her throat clamping shut. "King did that." Startled, she saw that to her daughter he had done something fine. Luz did not see that for the sake of mere impudence he had put them all in danger. She gathered herself, storing her temper away; she had to go and see to her cantina. "Damn that man," she said, getting up.

"Mama, I was so afraid of him, but you weren't afraid at all, were you?"

Serafa said nothing. She had not meant that railroad

man. Serafa doubted if Luz could understand how afraid she had been. She lifted her shawl up and laid it over her head, settled her face, straightened her shoulders, but in her heart the anger still burned, a fiery ember.

King and Lily came back in the morning, after breakfast had been served and eaten and the place cleaned up. Hiding shyly in the alleys and down in the ditches of the *zanja* they came in around the back of Serafa's place; they put their horses into the little corral and King got hay for them. Quietly Lily went around to the door into the bunkhouse.

The room was as King had made it just before they left, piled up with junk. Lily went behind her blanket wall and began to move boards out of the way so that she could reach her bed. As she was doing this, Luz came in the door.

"Who's there?"

Lily went around the blanket. "It's just me, Luz. I—"

"Lily!" Luz flew across the room and swept her up in an embrace. "Lily, I missed you so much. Lily, the Anglos came. Oh, you are safe and you are back!" She swung Lily around as if in a dance, laughing. "Josefa!" Setting Lily down on her feet, Luz dashed off through the door into the yard. "Josefa! Mama!"

King came in carrying his bedroll. Lily turned, going back to the work of fixing her room again, and the two girls burst in through the door, shrieking.

"Lily!" Josefa's face was bright. "Where did you go? Did you know what King did? Everybody thinks he is a hero. Did you hear that the Anglos came here looking for you?"

"Looking for us?" King said, straightening, and in through the door came Serafa.

She was wrapped up in her shawl; coming in, she darkened and quieted the whole space. Her girls drew back, their arms around Lily, watching their mother. She went straight up to King and said, "Get out."

"Now, darlin'." He turned toward her.

"Get out of my place! Get out of Los Angeles!" She swung her open hand at him. He dodged back, his arm raised between them, and she wheeled and stalked out of the bunkhouse.

The girls all looked at each other; Lily's stomach coiled into a knot.

King strode out the door after Serafa. "Serafa. Wait. Serafa."

Lily looked down at the blankets in her hands. "I guess I better just pack," she said. Her voice shook.

Luz's arm went around her. "No. You can't go. Oh, look, Josefa, how sunburned she is."

Josefa said, "Very likely she's hungry too, aren't you, Lily?"

"Yes," she said, around the lump in her throat. She loved the feel of Luz's arm around her. She loved being wanted. But now it was over: Serafa would send them away. She wrapped her arm around Luz's waist, laid her head on the girl's strong warm shoulder, and closed her eyes.

Serafa walked straight away across the yard; King followed her, saying, "Now, listen to me, damn it, you have to listen to me."

"I don't have to do anything," Serafa said. "You have to do something. You have to go and leave me alone!" They were coming to the kitchen door and she went into the darkness, rich with the smells of sarsa and chicken.

King went after her. "I'm not leavin', darlin', not until you listen to me."

In the middle of the kitchen, Serafa whirled around; a long knife gleamed in her hand. "Get out," she said, "or I'll kill you." The light gleamed on her face as well, on the long tracks of tears.

He stood his ground, cautious, judging the tears as well as the knife. But mainly he watched the tip of the knife. He said, "Now, Serafa . . ."

"They came here," she said, "and they went through my place, and insulted me, and insulted my children, and it was your fault they did that, King, your fault! And I won't have it again! Now, get out."

He did not move. Her face clenched with a wild fury and she rushed at him, the knife cocked in her hand.

This was the second time in a couple of days that women had jumped him. He met her charge, as he had Lily's: he grabbed her by the right arm and turned her around on her own momentum and wrapped her up tight in his arms, her back against his chest. She sobbed. In his fist her arm with the knife jerked and twisted, trying to break free and stab him. She kicked backward and he lifted her off the ground a little. She was an armful, and strong; he could not keep her like this for long.

He talked fast. "Serafa, everything you're sayin', it's all true. I know it's true. But I want to change it. I want to make you happy." As he spoke, he gathered her tighter, holding her knife hand out stiffly away from them.

"You lie! I'll kill you, King—" She thrashed in his grip.

He played his hole card. He said, "I want to go straight and marry you."

Her muscles slackened. He let her put her feet on the ground. She moved, a little, leaning against him, and her head tipped back. She said, "You talk as sweet as the devil, King."

"I mean it," he said. Carefully he let go of her with one hand and got the knife out of her grip. He kissed the side of her throat. "I love you, Serafa." She softened in his embrace, and her face turned toward him. He kissed her mouth. "I love you," he said again, and let her put her arms around him.

It was his arms around her that had weakened her, his arms around her, his body against her, his heat on her skin. She knew he was lying. Tiburcio had lied, time after time, always one more job, my dear one, my heart's own, see how I cannot let them get away with that, I must be a man.

She lay beside him in the night; he was sleeping, his head turned away from her, a stripe of moonlight across his body. She had always defended Tiburcio to everybody. That didn't mean she would do it again.

But she wanted King, his touch, his attention, his love. When she thought of him leaving she stirred toward him, her whole body moving toward him across the bed, and she put her hand on his waist.

He woke up. Turned toward her, and smiled in the dark, and reached out for her and kissed her.

"I have to go, darlin'."

"Ah," she said, twitching away. "Go, then. You crowd the bed anyway." She turned her back on him.

He bent over her, his mouth on her skin, one hand stroking her belly. He said, "I will dream of you, Serafa." He moved away, put on some clothes, and left.

What am I going to do? she thought. What am I going to do?

◆ Chapter ◆

XVII

Lily and Luz brought out the buckets of hot water. The chicken squawked; Serafa swung it up under her arm and carried it toward the kitchen stoop. Lily stood watching. The chicken's head bobbed with each of Serafa's strides, the brilliant red eye gleaming. In the dusty space in front of the pot of water Serafa gathered the chicken a little tighter under her arm, gripped its head in her free fist, and gave a single, furious twist. The chicken made no sound. Serafa let it dangle by its long scaly feet and the chicken's wings extended, it gave a shiver, and its neck pumped up and down once. Its head hung like an apple on the limb of a tree. Serafa tossed the chicken into the pot.

Luz said, "That's four." With the long fork she poked the chicken down into the hot water. Serafa went off toward the henhouse again. Luz forked the chicken up out of the water, its sodden feathers streaming. "Lily, you take this one."

Lily sat down on the stoop, spreading her apron out on her lap, and laid the hot steaming chicken on her knees, a mess of wet feathers, its head hanging down by her shin. It had been alive only a minute before. There was a great mystery at the center of this, but she could not quite fit her mind around it: it seemed to pulse back and forth between obvious and extraordinary. She pulled off clumps of feathers and stuffed them into the sack beside her.

From the henhouse came a strong high voice. Josefa said, "Mama is singing."

Luz said, "It's because King is back. He makes her happy."

Lily ran one finger over the white plucked skin of the chicken. Although they were here at Serafa's again and everything seemed right again, she could not shake the tiny cold fear that at any moment they would have to leave. She said, "Do you want to read, later?" She wanted to be certain about something, at least.

"At siesta," Luz said. She took the chicken and went inside for a knife. Josefa sat down where she had been; Serafa was coming with another chicken.

Josefa said, "We read a little more while you were gone. It was hard. Perhaps you should begin again where you left off."

"Really?" Lily said, pleased. "Just you and Luz?"

"All of us, Andres and Raul also. But nobody reads as well as you do. And it is so strange, you know, that place in the book." Serafa delivered her a chicken carcass and Josefa tossed it into the hot water and thrust it down with the fork. "They have a big fight, and she screams and sobs and yells, and then, the next day, she has a baby! Nobody ever said she was with child."

"That's, you know, kind of delicate," Lily said. She wasn't exactly sure why, since the whole matter had always seemed the opposite of delicate to her.

"It makes it all different to think of her fighting with Heathcliff while she was big with child. It isn't even his child."

Lily could not remember ever having seen a pregnant woman. She felt that Luz and Josefa must know far more than she did about all these things. She said, "I don't think it matters. She loves Heathcliff, not Edgar."

Josefa grunted, amused. "She loves nobody, that girl."

She took the chicken from the pot and began to grab off huge handfuls of wet feathers. "Love is not raging and screaming. Love is keeping house."

Luz came back, her hands bloody. "I think he's awful, anyway, he's so cruel."

Lily said, "They were cruel to him. He doesn't know any better. He does love her."

"Is that enough? He's a monster." Josefa accepted the next carcass from Serafa and dunked it. The mother stood watching them a moment, her brow bent. Lily knew that all these English words flying by meant nothing to her.

"Enough for what?" Lily said.

Luz said, "He's a savage." She wrapped her arms around her raised knees, hugging herself, her gaze distant. "Why is it that good people seem so boring and ordinary, and bad people always seem so much more interesting?"

Serafa said, "What are you talking about?"

Lily looked up at her, startled; although Serafa had spoken Spanish, Lily had understood her. She did not understand Josefa's long rushed answer. She reached into the pot and took out the dripping chicken.

"Is this the last one, *señora*?" she said in Spanish, stumbling over the words.

Serafa smiled at her. "One more." But she did not go on about the work. Still looking down at Lily, she said, "What is it about, this book?"

Luz giggled. "People who love and fight all the time."

Josefa stood back, her hands on her hips, watching her mother.

Serafa's face smoothed out; she lifted her brilliant gaze to her daughters. "Why do you need a book to get that? You can merely watch around you." She went off toward the henhouse again and gave a toss of her hips; her voice rose again in its tuneful chant.

Luz nudged her sister with her toe. "See?"

"See what?" Josefa said. "Take Lily inside and show

her how to gut this one. We're nearly done with this and now we have to make supper."

"Well," Luz said, "Mama's very happy, whatever it is."

Lily said nothing. She choked down her doubts and worries. Everything was good now. She would just be happy, like Serafa, and not think about what might happen next. Quickly she got up and went with Luz into the kitchen.

In the morning, after breakfast, she went out to sweep the wooden porch and Pigeye came around the corner.

"Lily. Hey, Lily Viner!" He called her in a loud whisper.

She frowned at him. "What do you want? King's not here."

"I know that." He came up onto the porch, his hands in his pockets, his head ducked a little, as if he were coming up from somewhere lower. "I seen him ride out. I want to talk to you."

"Really," she said. She leaned on the broom. She had always disliked him. He wore a pair of greasy serge trousers, a vest with fob pockets, a striped shirt with no collar, and a derby hat; he had not shaved in days. "What do you want, Pigeye?"

"I want you to do me a favor," he said. He sidled up to her, his voice dropping down into his chest. "I'm in a real bind, Lily, King wants me to do somepin' I can't do. But you could do it." His face brightened with hope; he peered up at her from under his brows. "You could do it, and then I make out, and King does too. Right?"

"Pigeye," she said. "What are you talking about?"

"King wants me to scout the new railroad office." He squirmed as he stood there, his body twisting. "Only I'm real leery of Brand. But you could go up there, you see. Look around, and then come down and tell me, and then everything's fine." He spread his hands to show how fine everything would be. "Right? What d'you think?"

She gave a quick look around them. Nobody was watching. She was tempted to tell him that King wouldn't care now, that King was going straight.

On the other hand, she was mildly flattered that he had asked her. At least he didn't think she was a green girl.

He said, "Please, Lily. Help me out. I tried to help you out, that time. Got my tail beat for it too."

That was true enough. She owed him something; she imagined herself someone who paid her debts. Besides, it might be exciting. She was getting bored plucking chickens and sweeping up dust. And Brand intrigued her. She said, "When do you want to do this?"

"You'll do it?" He grinned at her, eager. "You're a champ, Lily, you're a real oner. All right. All right. You come down to—you know where the office is? Corner of Hill Street and First?—tomorrow morning. All right? Tomorrow morning this time. The alley across from the office. All right?"

"All right," she said.

"Good," he said. He scuttled away down the street, reached the lane, and disappeared.

She began to move the broom back and forth again, excited. She would prove to King that she could do risky things. She hoped Brand would be there. She'd have to get a hat to hide her face. And boy's clothes, pants and a shirt. She knew how to do this. Her father had sent her ahead to scout places all the time. She'd show King. Quickly, impatiently, she flogged the dust off the porch and then dashed inside to look for the necessary clothes.

The Southern Pacific's office was on Hill Street in a new wooden building with a big false front and a porch. Sauntering down the boardwalk, Lily saw Pigeye lurking in the alley opposite, and didn't even go over there. She went in through the crowd of loiterers on the porch, pulled her hat brim down, and followed somebody else in through the door.

This room was even more crowded than the porch. All along the walls men sat reading newspapers and smoking; more men stood in the middle of the floor. Everybody seemed to be talking at once. She stood behind a tall man who was saying, "I'll do anything for money," over and over. There was no sign of Brand. The floor of the building was littered with sawdust and dirt. The walls were raw pine wood, still oozing sap. On a big piece of paper stapled to one wall there was a crude map. She wondered if it represented Los Angeles. From where she stood it looked like chicken scratches. She moved slowly around the outside of the room looking for Brand, wondering what there was of interest here to anybody.

Then a door opened in the back wall, and through it she caught a glimpse of the room beyond and realized that was the real office; this was just a waiting room. The door swung closed again. She sidled over in that direction.

Just before she reached it, the door flew open again and Brand came out.

She shrank back, dipping her head so her hat brim covered her face, but he never saw her. He stood just outside the door, his hand on it holding it open, and called out, "Who's here looking for work?"

The whole mob swung around toward him, falling into a charged silence. He glared at them. "No jobs today! I only want the people who are working on the election."

A general groan went up, and at once people began shuffling toward the street door. A man in red suspenders stepped forward and shouted, "What does it pay to work on the election?"

"If I haven't hired you already, I'm not hiring you now," Brand said.

His left arm hung down along his side; she caught herself staring at the empty cuff of his sleeve. She pulled her gaze away, looking around the room, which people were leaving now in swarms, all save half a dozen who were drifting up toward Brand.

She gave a start. The big, hairy man coming up first was somebody she knew. She scrambled through her memory. Dark, it had been. Outside, in the street. In her mind she heard him yell, she felt him grab at her and pull her off her horse. Elmo, they had called him.

For a moment she could not move, remembering that; she wanted suddenly to follow the crowd pushing out of the room. Brand went back into the office and hairy Elmo and several others trailed after him. Lily gathered herself and followed.

The room they went into was smaller than the waiting room and full of furniture, three desks, six or eight chairs, two big cabinets against facing walls. A railing separated the back third of the room from the front. Brand stood in front of the railing, saying, "Now, sit down, this is complicated." Chairs scraped on the floor. The men milled around getting settled. Lily dropped down behind a desk next to the wall.

The men were sitting down. She peeked cautiously around the edge of the desk and saw Brand half sitting on the railing, looking bored.

"Now, listen up. The election is the day after tomorrow. It's pretty much a sure thing, but I hate leavin' anything to chance, so we won't. I got lists of voters here." He waved his arm at the desk in front of him, piled up with long sheets of newsprint. "You take a list of voters and go find each one, ask him whether or not he favors the railroad. Then on election day make sure the ones who favor the railroad get to the polls."

"What about the ones 'at don't?" That was the hairy man.

Brand said, "We're hoping you can change their minds." He slid off the railing, opened a drawer of the desk, and took out a sack, which he dropped onto the desk. The sack clinked. The men before him all let out a low whoop.

Brand hitched himself back up onto the railing. Lily saw he was keeping his missing hand out of sight. She wondered what difference being crippled had made in him—what he would have been if he had had two hands. She raised her gaze to his face and suddenly felt as if she saw him for the first time, that always before she had seen only the stumpy arm.

He was younger than she had believed, younger than her father or King. His brown hair shagged over his collar.

He said, "Don't go threatening people. Just let a man know, he votes our way, you'll stand him a couple drinks. A man gets belligerent with you, just walk away."

"Yeah," said the hairy man. "We'll take care of him later." The men around him laughed.

Brand said, "After the election it won't matter. All right. Come up here, get your lists of voters, get some money, get going." He slid off the railing again and went to the desk, and the men rose from their chairs and crowded up before him, eager. Lily crept from behind the desk and slipped out the door. She was out of the office and on the street before it came to her that she had not looked around much.

Pigeye was waiting for her in the alley, leaning up against the wall of the boardinghouse there. As she walked up he pushed away from the wall and said eagerly, "Well?"

"Oh, yeah," she said. "It's an office."

"Whadya see?"

She told him about the waiting room, the back room, the desks, the railing, the windows in the back wall, all she could really remember. He said, "Is there a safe?"

"Unh—"

His little eyes blinked, reproachful. "Things like this he's gonna ask me."

"Yeah, I think so." It didn't matter, since King was going straight and would never use the information. "I think behind the railing, I think there was a big cabinet, maybe that was a safe."

"God, girl. Big black thing? Gold letters on it?"

"I don't remember." Brand had been giving out money, she remembered, but it had already been on his desk. That reminded her of what she had witnessed; she turned indignantly to Pigeye and said, "They're going to buy votes!"

Pigeye was still blinking. He said crossly, "Well, what do you think they're gonna do, girl? People don't vote for nothin'. You shoulda looked for the safe. Well, hell, ain't nothing for it now." He put out his hand to her. "Thank you kindly."

She shook his hand; suddenly she liked him a lot better than she ever had before. "You're welcome, Pigeye." She turned and went off down the alley, feeling pleased with herself.

King said, "Well, you took your time about it." He glanced at the door into the back of the cantina and put his money pouch on the table. "All right, tell me."

Pigeye screwed up his face in thought, trying to act as if he were remembering his own observations. "Well, it's on the corner of Hill Street. There's a warehouse on the Hill Street side and a barbershop on the First Street side."

"I know that." King shook the money out in a heap, dollars and half dollars and fives.

"You go in the front door there's a big room, a waiting room. Then in the back there's the real office. It's got more stuff in it, desks and chairs."

"Yeah, yeah," King said. "Get to the important parts. Is there a back door?"

"I—" Pigeye ran out of breath; he had forgotten to

ask her that. He said hastily, "There's windows in the back wall. No door."

"Is there a safe?"

"Big old safe in the back behind the railing," he said, smooth as cream.

"What kind?"

"You know I can't read," Pigeye said. "Was some writing on it. Big thing, black, two doors opening out front." That was easy, describing every safe he had ever seen.

King said, "Lock on the door between the office and the waiting room?"

"Unh—"

"You know, you should stick to cheating at cards, you're real bad at this. All right, go on." He pushed the money toward Pigeye.

Pigeye counted it into his hand, disappointed. " 'Sonly eighteen dollars."

"And overpaid at that," King said. Uneasy, Pigeye saw he was not smiling. He guessed something. He knew something. Pigeye hurried to his feet.

"Well, see ya," he said.

"No," King said. "You won't." Pigeye bolted out of the cantina.

◆ Chapter ◆

XVIII

Serafa said, "The Old Man, Mariano Rosas, maybe you could get work with him."

King was stowing away bottles for her on a high shelf. Rosas had a big rancho outside the village, one of the last spreads still in Californio hands. "Doin' what, shootin' rattlesnakes?"

"You can ride. You know horses."

"Not like a Californio," he said.

He had to get a job. He felt that dragging on him like a great weight; he had given the last of his money to Pigeye. He stooped and took up bottles, two in each hand, and lifted them up to the shelf. Serafa was behind him; she laid her hand on his back, soft, not as if she were pushing him, but close.

She said, "Rosas can't pay much. Nonetheless . . ."

He turned toward her, irritated. "Don't hound me, *se-ñora.*"

She was frowning, and her eyes searched over his face. "What's wrong?" she said.

He grunted at her. Went back out the door, into the yard, looking for something else to do. He kept thinking of Pigeye: he was fairly convinced Pigeye was holding back on something. He wondered if Pigeye had sold him out to Brand, if this safe in the railroad office was the bait in a trap.

Serafa came after him, another bait in another trap.

As soon as he thought that he was sorry. He turned to her, put his arm around her, and kissed the top of her head. "I'm not good company, am I?"

She leaned on him, her hand on his chest. "Something is worrying you. Come into the kitchen and drink a cup of coffee." Her hand stroked his chest. "You will get a good job when Rosas knows what kind of man you are."

King said, "Oh, will I?" He followed her toward the kitchen. He wasn't sure anymore what kind of man he was. The black mood closed down over him again like a hood. He felt wrapped around and around with constraints. He wished he had made sure Pigeye got out of town. Serafa led him into the dark warmth of the kitchen, where the coffee steamed; he went after her, to kiss her, to hold her, to remember what he was doing all this for.

Lily said, "So, you see, you were wrong. I can do a lot of things you think I can't."

King was sitting on his cot, staring at her; even in the dark, she could tell that he was getting angry. She said, "It was easy. Brand was there and he never even noticed me. What's the matter?"

He said nothing, but he got up and reached for his gunbelt hanging on the wall.

"What are you doing?" she cried.

"I'm going to find Pigeye," he said. He slung the belt around his hips, buckled it, and looped his arms through the straps of the shoulder holster.

Lily leaped toward him, her hands out. "What are you going to do?" She put her hands on his chest, holding him there.

He took her by the wrists. "I told you to stay out of my business."

"What are you going to do to him?"

"I should kill him. He lied to me. He double-crossed me. So did you, and as usual I ain't layin' a damn finger on you, Lily."

A wild panic fluttered her stomach. "Don't hurt him. Please don't hurt him." She had to stop him; if he killed Pigeye it would be her fault.

Still holding her by the arms, he thrust his face into her face. "You think he's an angel? You saw him in the street that night last summer."

"He tried to help me!"

"He was roughing some poor bastard up! He's in with Brand's hardcase bunch, he'll sell me to Brand for a beer as soon as he's thirsty." He moved her to one side and got his coat down from the hook. "Get out of my way, Lily."

She got back in front of him. "Please don't hurt him. I'm sorry. I won't do it again. Why do you want to know about Brand's office? I thought you were going straight."

"That isn't the point," he said. He thrust his arms into the coat and settled it on his shoulders, hiding his guns. "I asked Pigeye to check that office a long time ago. The point is he double-crossed me. He knew damn well I didn't want you involved." He leaned over her again and spoke harshly into her face. "I asked you to do one little thing, Lily, just to stay out of this. I love you, I take care of you, I give up half my life for you, and all I ask is one little thing, and you don't do it." He brushed past her and went out.

Lily sat down on his cot. She knew he was right. She had seen nothing in this but her own will; bitterly she wished she had not done it. She was not as good a person as she had thought.

She got up, went out into the cool darkness of the yard and around the shed to the corral. Jane stood against the rail, her head and her back end drooping down, but the sorrel gelding was gone. Lily leaned on the rail and put her head down on the wood. She was not a good person at all. She had always somehow just assumed she

was, but she lied, she stole, she was mean to people all
the time. She felt everything around her wrenched violently into some new configuration. She wished she were
dead. That would solve everything. She shut her eyes.

King left his horse outside the Bella Union, at the hitch
rail with a dozen others, and went inside and looked
around for Pigeye in the places Pigeye preferred to be:
dark corners and the backsides of tables. Pigeye was not
there. The hotel's great public room blazed with lights.
Around the faro tables the men stood three deep. King
went on down the street a couple of doors to Macdougal's, and after that to the place opposite, the Crystal
Palace.

There he found Pigeye, near the end of the bar playing
three-card monte with some sucker. King went out again
to the dark and waited. A steady flow of people rushed
up and down the boardwalk past him. Three men walked
by, arm in arm, singing and laughing. In the Crystal
Palace a piano began to jangle. The front door squealed
as it swung, and now it was squealing constantly. Two
men raced their horses down the street and up to the
hitch rail opposite him. A drunk teetered down the
boardwalk, stopping every so often to lean up against a
wall.

Just behind him came a scrawny ragged boy, who
stopped when the drunk stopped, his eyes hungry, waiting. King watched him out of sight. He had been that
boy once, stalking drunks.

After a few moments Pigeye came out of the Crystal
Palace and walked right past him, headed across the
street. He was counting a sheaf of greenbacks. King slid
his hand under his coat to the butt of his underarm gun,
wanting to shoot him, to get rid of him for good. The
gun filled his hand. He thought he could probably get
away with it here if he was careful.

Instead he followed about ten paces back as Pigeye went on into Macdougal's.

Macdougal's was a workman's saloon, dark and loud and always crowded. Pigeye went up through the pack toward the bar and King went after him, timing his move to get to Pigeye just as the other reached the bar.

As he went, under the cover of the coat, he drew his underarm gun; reaching the bar, he moved up close and stuck the gun through the coat into Pigeye's back.

Pigeye had his hands on the bar. At the prod of the gun he jerked up onto his toes, going rigid. Before he could even turn, King spoke into his ear.

"I ain't here to shoot you, Pigeye. You can thank my little girl for that. You get out of Los Angeles, though, because the next time I see you, I will, no second thoughts." He wheeled away, back into the crowd. Someone charged into the space he left, not that Pigeye was about to come after him, and almost at once they were separated by a wall of other bodies. King went out through the side door and down the alley to the street.

He knew he was making a mistake. Not killing Pigeye was going to get him in trouble. This going straight business was beginning to sour on him. He had to defend himself. And somehow he had to get some money. He went to the Bella Union, backed his sorrel out of the line along the hitch rail, and rode back down toward Sonoratown.

∽

Lily lay in her bed, waiting; she was ready to wait all night, but he came back sooner than she had expected. She heard him shut the door and move across his side of the divided room to his bed, just the other side of the blanket from hers. He sat on the bed. She heard him taking his boots off.

She said, "What did you do?"

His bed creaked. He was standing up; she guessed he

was taking his clothes off. After a moment the cot squealed and sighed again.

He said, "I didn't kill him. I told him to leave town."

"Good." She rolled onto her side. She could tell by where his voice was coming from that he was lying on his back on his bed. "I don't see what you got all fired up about. You let me do much more in the Virginia City robbery."

"That was Jewell," he said. "Jewell did that."

"What? How can you say that? The whole plan was your idea."

"But Jewell let me do it. He shouldn't have. And now that I'm in his place, I'm not goin' to." His voice was husky with intensity. "You know how risky that was for you? Brand could have killed you in the stage! You got between him and me once and nearly got us into a gunfight. No. It was stupid. I shouldn'ta done it. And I'm not doin' it again."

She was still a moment, considering that. Her father had never minded using her. She said, "Well, you're going straight anyway. Aren't you?"

"I'm tryin', damn it. It ain't easy. I haven't got any more money and living in town costs money."

"Then we're going to go on living here?"

"I don't know. I don't like it all that much, beyond Serafa. I'm not living in a shack the rest of my life, talking to a kid through a blanket."

She wondered if she should take that for a hint. She decided to ignore it. "We could go to San Francisco. I've never been there. Jewell said it was evil. Is it evil?"

"Oh, absolutely. And a hell of a town for an Irishman." His voice changed, pensive. "We can't go to San Francisco, though, not and take Serafa."

"Why not?"

"Well, it costs a lot of money, for one thing. Lots of money. And I have . . . There's people there."

"People you know? Don't you think Serafa

would . . ." In her mind something slipped into place. "Oh. You have another woman there."

"Well, not really. I don't have her anymore, at least. She's with some big-time gambler now, I heard. She always wanted somebody would take her out to the opera. But we burned up a lot of hot times, for a while."

She mulled this over, that he had a woman besides Serafa. Probably more than one. She realized how two-faced he was, King, double-tongued, his life a braid of truth and lies. She felt older suddenly, not in a good way. She thought she should have known this already. She wondered how he kept track of it all.

She wondered if there were another girl like her, somewhere, and knew at once there was not. He was honest with her, maybe with her alone in all the world; he wanted nothing from her; he used no guile with her. Because of his mother, because of his sister. For the sake of those two twenty years gone, he loved her perfectly. She saw herself a single flame, between his two cupped hands.

Pensively, she said, "Serafa wouldn't like San Francisco anyway, probably."

"No," he said. "Probably not."

"You and I could still go."

He broke out laughing, but he didn't answer. He was silent awhile. Then he said, "We could get a ranch some-place."

"A ranch," she said, dismayed. "You mean way out in the country?"

"Build a little house and chase down a couple of mares and go find a blood stallion. Raise fast horses and win money racing them."

Some of this she found interesting. "Could Raul come work for us?"

"Raul?" he said.

"He's a ranchero," she said. "How far away from here?"

"Never mind," he said. "I was just thinking."

"I want to stay here," she said. "Why can't we just stay here?"

"I thought you wanted to go to San Francisco."

"If we have to get away for a while. Like the other time, when we went to the beach. Not to live. I like living here." Suddenly she felt everything she cared about sliding away around her. She had no hope anything she said would change his mind. He didn't say anything, which meant she hadn't changed his mind. She thought, Why should it be up to him? She rolled over, her head on her crooked arm. Why should King decide everything? she thought. She shut her eyes. In her mind she saw the flame between his two hands growing stronger and stronger.

Pigeye kept trying to think how he would say it, maybe get Brand off by himself, what words he would use, but when he went in the door of the office and saw how crowded the place was, all these plans flew out of his mind. He went in a little way; there was a big paper sign hung across the room, which he could not read, so he knew all this was part of the election, the piles of papers, the people rushing here and there carrying piles of papers. Then abruptly he was in front of a desk and the man behind it lifted his head, and he looked into Brand's eyes.

"George," Brand said, and leaned back. "What the hell do you want?"

"Nothin'," Pigeye said, backing away. "I see you're busy, and, unh, I—" Brand's dark eyes were sharp and smart and Pigeye whirled and ran from them, out the office door and down the stairs to his horse, and galloped out of Los Angeles.

◆ Chapter ◆

XIX

Brand propped his elbows on the desk. He had always thought he had seen George before, and now it came back to him. He remembered the road going up Six Mile Canyon to Virginia City, and the man on top of the stagecoach, not finding what they were there to steal.

He even had a better name for George, a piece of information he had picked up later in Virginia City: Pigeye Reilly, who was, of course, a known henchman of King Callahan.

He caught himself rubbing the callus on his stump. His skin tingled. He told himself to get a rein on himself, he really had no proof, he was jumping to conclusions, but too much of this clicked. He knew King Callahan was in Los Angeles.

He knew King Callahan was in that cantina down in Sonoratown.

Somebody waved a piece of paper under his nose and he read it and signed it. He shook himself back to the here-and-now. The election was almost over and it looked like it was going all the Railroad's way.

When that was done, he could go after King. He even had an idea how.

◇

King usually spent the afternoon in the cantina reading the newspaper while everybody else was at siesta, but on Election Day there was no siesta. After the noon meal the men all stayed on, sitting at the tables, talking, sending the girls for beer and brandy. King grumbled awhile and then took his horse and left.

Lily was waiting on the customers. They did not leave, which amazed her, because always before the place had been empty by early afternoon. While she was putting glasses of beer on her tray, she asked Josefa, "What is all this?"

"The election," Josefa said. "This happened the last time, too. Watch. It's very interesting. And we make a lot of money." She gave Lily the last two filled glasses and she went off to serve them. As she was crossing the room, three Anglos came in the front door. One of them was carrying a black box.

All the men in the cantina stood up. The frontmost of the Anglos said, "Any of you *muchachos* not voted yet?" The man behind him, not the one carrying the box, took a fat wallet from his coat.

All through the room men started forward. The Anglos went to the nearest table and set the box down there. The leader sat down, putting a stack of paper in front of him. One by one the local men marked ballots and dropped them into the box. The man with the wallet gave each man a coin.

"Have a snort. On the Southern Pacific."

Lily raced into the back of the cantina, where Luz and Josefa were sitting on the back step drinking a glass of beer. "They're buying votes! This must be illegal." She bounced up and down, furious. "We have to tell somebody."

Luz passed the beer to Josefa. "What does it matter? The Railroad is going to win anyway."

Lily paced around the yard. "Right in front of everybody," she said. "In front of everybody!" She wondered suddenly if this was the way all elections were. If it was all a cheat. She dashed back into the cantina again, back to the front room.

The Anglos had gone. Most of the men had gone, but some remained, and when she came in, a chorus of voices rose, clamoring for beer. She went back to the taps and filled glasses and took them out on the tray.

While she was giving out these beers, piling up little coins on the tray as she did so, the door swung open again; she looked over her shoulder and saw Brand coming in.

Her skin went cold. She put all her glasses down at one table and ran from the room. Luz was putting on her apron again; she looked up as Lily came in.

"Is it still busy out there?"

"Yes—please, I can't go out there." Lily put her tray down. "You have to do it."

Luz goggled at her. "What's the matter? Are you sick?"

"No," Lily said. "Just, please, just do it." She went on out the back door and crossed the yard to her room.

There she paced up and down, too excited to read or even sit down. The Railroad was buying the election. And worse: the Southern Pacific would profit none of these Sonoratown men; the SP was bribing these people to vote to hurt themselves. King was right and the world was a joke. She dropped down on his cot, trying to think about what she should do about Brand.

She wondered if he had seen her. If he had, she shouldn't be sitting here. She went to the door, looked cautiously out to make sure she was unobserved, and went around the bunkhouse to the corral.

The boy's clothes she had worn to the Railroad office were hidden under the hay in the shed. She changed, saddled Jane, and rode out along the *zanja* until she reached the street.

She rode around for a while, looking at the buildings. She rode past the Railroad office, strung with election banners, the street clogged with traffic. There was a party going on inside; she could hear people singing. After a while, bored, she wandered away down the street. Where the street crossed the *zanja* she cut off across a broad grassy meadow and let the mare amble down to the *zanja* and drink. Dismounting, Lily sat on the bank of the ditch, her mind raging against the Railroad again.

Before her, the mare suddenly jerked up her head, snorted, and looked toward the meadow. Lily spun up onto her feet.

Brand was walking toward her across the grass. His horse waited off by the street.

She started violently; she nearly turned and ran, but she knew it was too late for that. She stood where she was, and he walked over to her and said, "Sit down, Lily, I want to talk to you."

She stood still, silent, considering this, and he said, "What are you afraid of? I'm not going to hurt you. You saved my life, back on the Virginia City road. King would have killed me." He sat down on the grass. His voice was light and easy, as if they talked like this all the time.

She dropped down next to him. Her heart was pounding; she had to be careful now, she had to say the right things. She said, "Then what do you want from me?"

"I want King," he said.

"I haven't seen King since Virginia City," she said.

He was watching her steadily, his brown eyes unblinking. His face was thin and light-boned, boyish, so that the faint shadow of his beard seemed odd and out of place. He said, "How'd you get down here?"

"I came with a mule train from Cerro Gordo."

"But you're working in that cantina down in Sonoratown."

"I am," she said. She turned her head to stare at the ditch full of water, the mare cropping the grass along it. "Is that a crime?"

"You're a decent white girl. You shouldn't be living in a slum."

She swung toward him, furious. "It's not a slum! It was the first city here, and they're wonderful, I love them. I love living there. I want to live there the rest of my life!"

He cocked up one eyebrow. "With King?"

She said nothing. She felt handled: he had made her angry on purpose, trying to shake something loose.

Brand said, "I don't have anything against you. Nobody ever has to know about what you did that time on the road to Virginia City. But King's a rat. The longer you stick with him, the worse things are going to get for you. You think slaving in a greaser cantina is bad—"

Lily said, "No, I don't. You work for the Railroad. That, I think, is bad."

To her surprise she had struck; she saw how his head jerked up, his face flushed suddenly with anger. He leaned toward her, fierce.

"Listen to me, girl. You don't know what you're talking about. There's a new world coming, and the Southern Pacific is carrying the freight. And you can't stop us. You can hate the Railroad, but you can't stand in our way. You either get on and ride or stand back and eat smoke. That scares some people. Does it scare you?" His face blazed. "Does this scare you?" Lifting his left arm, he stuck the stump up in front of her nose.

She said, "No," reached out, gripped the end of his arm, and pushed it aside.

He jerked back away from her, his eyes popping wide, and gave her a wild look. He got up, and she leaped to her feet, seeing a warning in the way he looked at her. He stood there glaring at her, all the sweet friendliness gone.

"Give me King Callahan," he said. "I'll forget what happened on the road to Virginia City."

"No, Brand," she said. She backed up a few steps; quickly looking around, she saw Jane only a little way away and went to her and picked up her reins. "You'll never forget that as long as you live." She swung into her saddle and galloped off across the meadow.

Brand let his breath out in a long sigh. He thought of going after her, but he didn't trust himself. He had just now nearly grabbed her and kissed her, and if he chased after her, he might not be able to stop again.

She hadn't given him even a hint about King. She had changed. On the stagecoach to Virginia City, she had seemed such a little girl, so shy and meek, with her book. She wasn't a little girl anymore. Remembering how she had looked, talking straight back to him, the feel of her hand on his arm, he went hot again all over. King did that to her, he thought, and his temper seethed. That was how King worked; he took an innocent little girl and made a bitch out of her. He walked across the meadow to his horse and mounted.

He had followed her from the cantina, patient, until the chance came to catch her alone. He had expected that she would be tired of slaving away in a bean kitchen, tired of King doing whatever he was doing to her. Brand could rescue her; she'd be grateful and tell him everything. Instead she'd blown up in his face like fireworks.

He knew where he could find her. And already he was itching to go down there.

Doubt swept him. Maybe he was wrong. Maybe King wasn't here at all. Maybe she had come down alone from the silver country with a mule train, wandered into Serafa's cantina, started handing out beans and beers, just like she said.

In any case, he couldn't lead a charge down into Sonoratown looking for King. He had made that move already and gotten nowhere. King had some witch sense, he knew when people were hunting him, and he always had twenty boltways out. Brand had to set up a trap for him, lure him within reach, point so many guns at him he couldn't escape.

He could go down to Sonoratown again, though, and see Lily. Lily, he thought, liking the name. Lily Viner. He had to get King first. But then, after, he would see about Lily Viner. He turned his horse into the street in front of the Railroad office, where already people were celebrating the passing of the subsidy and the coming of the Railroad to Los Angeles.

Lily went back to the cantina and swept her room and did some washing. She wondered if she should tell King about Brand.

If she told him, he would run. He would leave Los Angeles. And then what would she do?

She strung a rope across the sunny side of the yard and hung up her clothes to dry. Luz came over and helped her.

"Where did you go?"

"Just out," Lily said.

"Because of the one-handed Anglo?"

"Yes." Lily gave her a quick look. "Did you see him?"

"He didn't stay very long," Luz said. She made a little sign with her fingers, something Serafa did, too, now and then, when she didn't like somebody. "He's evil, that one."

"I don't think he is," Lily blurted. Luz looked roundly at her, surprised, and she said, "Well, he's crippled. I think you have to make allowances." She put the last of her underwear on the line, picked up the empty washtub, and went into the bunkhouse.

Luz followed her. "Then why did you run away? If you aren't afraid of him. I don't understand you, Lily."

"I just didn't want him to see me here," Lily said.

She looked around for something else to do, to keep her hands busy while her mind worked. King's part of the room was already clean. He always kept his things put away, making his cot up every morning, wiping out his tracks. She took the broom and swished at the floor; Luz went out and came back with another broom and helped her. Lily pulled the cot away from the wall and swept behind it.

If she told him about Brand, they would have to leave Los Angeles. If she did not tell him, Brand might get a jump on him.

Brand was the enemy. But she liked him, which startled her.

Maybe he would do nothing. Maybe nothing would happen. When she saw the need, she could tell King about talking to him. She slid the cot back into place. "That's good enough," she said.

Luz was looking out the door. "There's Mama, going into the kitchen. We have to go start supper." She brushed a wisp of long black hair out of her face and smiled; when she smiled, her whole face turned round and sunny. Lily went to her and hugged her.

Luz hugged her back. "Oh, Lily. What's the matter?"

"Nothing," she said, and laid her head a moment on Luz's shoulder. "Let's go help Serafa."

King came back very late; she was in bed reading when she heard the door open and close. She sat up, listening. Just by the sound of his feet she knew he was tired. His bed crunched.

She said, "Where did you go?"

"Out to the river," he said. "How'd it go?"

"Everybody says the Railroad is winning the election."

"Oh, yeah," he said. He lay back. "The Railroad always wins."

"They cheat," she said. She told him about how brazenly the men had come in and bought the votes. King gave a weary laugh.

She had come to the point where she should tell him

about Brand. Instead, she said, "Do you need money?"

"Darlin', I always need money."

"I still have that money you gave me that time in Virginia City."

"What?"

"I remembered today, while I was cleaning up. I looked in my coat. It's still there. Seven double eagles. You can have it if you want."

He laughed again, not so wearily. "Lily. My angel from heaven. Well, I'll pay you back sometime."

"You don't have to," she said, and lay down again, thinking about Brand again, thinking she should tell King. Knowing she wouldn't, not now; she couldn't leave Los Angeles, not now. She wondered who this person was inside of her, who made these decisions. Then she heard his breathing change, just beyond the blanket, and knew he was asleep, and she shut her eyes, relieved.

In the morning, with the money, he took her down into the city to the general store. Newmark's was huge, a great barn piled up with goods brought in from San Francisco and Boston, Honolulu and Shanghai and Guaymas. Lily walked around the store awhile, past shelves of ready-made pants and shirts, boxes of blue willow china, pails and pots and pans, kegs of nails, crated sawblades, steel tools hanging up on racks, ax heads in baskets with the bundled ashwood handles tilted up behind. Spools of whiskery yellow rope, a sewing machine, butter churns, barbed wire.

She stood admiring the sewing machine, with its treadle board of scrolled ironwork and its wooden cabinet, its graceful black metal body trimmed with gold paint, whose shape reminded her of a woman in corsets. King came up to her, smiling, his hands in the pockets of his coat. "Do you want that?"

"What?"

"I'll get it for you if you want it."

She stared at him a moment. "No wonder you never have any money."

"When you have it, spend it," he said. "That's my motto. There's the cloth."

In the front of the store on four tables there were bolts of calico and canvas and wool. She got some white cotton for underwear and a piece of dark blue silk and a bigger piece of red silk and four yards of sprig muslin with little red and pink roses on the creamy ground. When the man at the counter totaled everything up it came to more than fifteen dollars.

"That's too much," she said, disappointed. "We have to put some back."

"Hell, no," King said. He put some coins on the counter. "I'm sayin' you go get the rest of that muslin."

"No," she said. "It's too much as it is. Aren't you getting anything for yourself?"

The man behind the counter was wrapping the cloth in brown paper, paying less attention to that than to them. He was young, wore a brown coat and a stiff shiny collar on his shirt. He said, "You people new in Los Angeles? I thought I knew everybody here." He pulled twine from a fat roll on the wall behind him.

"We're just passin' through," King said.

"Might think about staying." Deftly the counterman wrapped twine once, twice around the parcel and knotted it. He cut the twine on a razor-edge attached to the spool. "Los Angeles is booming. Especially now, with the Railroad on its way."

She saw King stiffen at that; his head jerked around. She was afraid he was angry, but all he said was, "Gonna take the Railroad some time to get over the Tehachapis." He laid down another gold coin beside the others. "Break that up for me, will you?"

"Certainly." The counterman took the coins and went to the cash drawer; he brought back a scatter of silver and gold. "Thank you very much. Come back to New-mark's, we have everything."

"So I see," King said. He took the parcel and led her out of the store.

Outside, she said, "What's the matter?"

"Nothin'. People like that make me edgy. Butting in like that." She swung up onto Jane's back and he held the parcel up to her. "You gonna have this dress ready to wear to the Rosas' merienda?

"I don't know," she said happily. She cradled the cloth like a baby. Luz and Serafa had promised to help her make it up. But the Rosas' party was in two days. "I hope so."

"Good," he said. "Although in rags you'd be the prettiest girl there."

She murmured a small modest denial, pleased. She had a lot of wonderful ideas for her dress. At a trot she led the way back down to Sonoratown.

◆ Chapter ◆

XX

"You must go," Serafa said. "The Rosas are expecting you."

He put on the shirt she had made for him, with all the stitching. This going to the Rosas' party was some deep plan of hers to make her friends like him. She had been talking about it for days, getting ready, which he had no interest in: the village had bored him even when Tiburcio was alive. She wanted him to go, so he was going.

"We're staying overnight?"

"Yes. And coming back in the morning." She came up to him and straightened the shoulders of the shirt, trimming him up. For a moment she looked him over as if he were meat that could not look back; then her gaze met his, she smiled, and she kissed him.

"I will never ask this of you again," she said. "I know how you feel about crowds."

He said, "I hate crowds." He reached for the gun belt hanging over the foot of the bed.

"No," she said; she put her hand out.

"Serafa." He twisted away from her. "What are you doing to me?"

"Please," she said. "Nobody there has any guns. There's no need."

"All right." He put his hands up. "But I come back tonight."

She lifted her shawl onto her shoulders, her long eyes thoughtful; he knew she was calculating how much more she could wring out of him. She said, "If you wish. But make up your mind tonight, when you have seen how fine it is, and not now." She smiled. "I will make you want to stay."

He doubted that. It annoyed him that she thought it within her power to make him want to do anything. He missed the weight of his guns. When they were married he would take her out of Los Angeles. In the meantime, make her happy. He went to the door, eager to get this over with.

Everybody in Sonoratown was going to the Rosas' party, including Serafa, who for the first time in Lily's experience closed the cantina. In the morning after breakfast had been cleared off they all went out into the country. Serafa rode behind King on the sorrel gelding with her arms around his waist; Josefa's betrothed, Andrés, took her on the back of his horse, and Luz rode double with Lily on Jane.

Lily wore her new dress, fit very tight down to the waist and then billowing out in layers of different-colored skirts. Luz had helped her make it and given her a silk petticoat to wear with it. She wore a pair of old pantaloons underneath everything else, so she could ride astride.

They crossed the *zanja* and went out through the orange orchards, followed the river awhile, and at last went down a lane beaten through the grass to a sprawl of honey-colored adobes.

The ranch house was a square of buildings, linked by porches and covered walks. The courtyard was already flooded with people, all dressed in their brightest and most expensive clothes. Looking at them, Lily thought her dress was fine enough, but she wished she had done something better with her hair. Most of the girls had their hair all done up in buns and coils on their heads, threaded with ribbon and stuck with combs. They had prettier shoes too, embroidered slippers, soft laced boots. She decided to ask King to buy her some shoes; since he would spend the money anyway, he might as well spend it on her.

Raul met them in the courtyard, wearing a brilliant red shirt with gold on it. When he smiled at Lily he looked so handsome that she couldn't take her eyes from him. *Señora* Rosas in a torrent of other women came bustling out to welcome Serafa, who gave them the same grave unruffled greeting she would have given them had they come into the cantina, and then turned and introduced them one by one to King. King nodded and smiled. Lily could see by the set of his shoulders that he hated this.

Luz and Josefa were hugging everybody. Lily caught Raul watching her and, giving him the faintest nod, she edged away and got out of sight around the corner, into the shade of a lemon tree. In this hideout she turned, and his arms closed around her. She lifted her face to be kissed. For a long time they clung to one another, their mouths firmly pressed together. When they separated, her heart was galloping and she thought she was sweating.

He whispered, "*Querida*. My dearest one. Oh, I have missed you so much." His arms gathered her in again. It had only been a few days since she had seen him, and she hadn't thought of him at all, but that he missed her was gratifying, and she loved kissing him. They did it again.

Holding her against him, his lips against her temple, he said, "We must be careful. If they even guess, they'll keep us apart." His hands slid down her back and pressed briefly on her hips. She laid herself against him, wanting something more, but not knowing what it was.

"My father says if we—" She stopped, rethinking the wisdom of telling him what King had said.

He stepped back, his hands falling to his sides. "I'm not afraid of him," he said in a ringing voice.

"Sshh," she said. She was afraid of King; she knew him better than Raul did. She turned once, holding out her skirts. "Do you like my dress?"

"It's beautiful." He gripped her hands, his face intense. "You are the most beautiful girl in the world."

She thought that might mean more if he didn't set everything in superlatives. Yet that was part of his allure. She leaned toward him again for another kiss, and then, around the corner, someone called, "Lily?"

"Quickly," he said, letting her go, and raced away in the other direction. She sauntered back into the courtyard. The secrecy of this was half the fun. Luz came rushing up to her, her face shining.

"Lily! There's ice cream. Come on, it's so good!"

Serafa had no shame, all the women agreed. They gathered in the courtyard, to gossip, to share the news, to drink coffee laced with *aguardiente* and eat ice cream, the only good thing the Anglos had brought with them to California, rich with cinnamon and Mexican chocolate. Serafa sat in their midst, her head high, just as if she had never done anything wrong.

Nobody cared to say anything to her face. For all her airs, Serafa was one of them, always would be; they loved her. They needed her. So everybody had smiled and nodded when she appeared with her Anglo lover. Whom she now said she was going to marry, which was almost as big a scandal as living openly with him in a state of sin.

The priest said, "A widow may remarry, it is not adultery."

The women of the village said, "Maybe to you it is not."

"Better to marry than to burn," the priest said.

"Maybe to you."

She had presented him to Aurelia Rosas as her old friend. Her husband Tiburcio's old friend. She must have talked to Aurelia first, in private, probably long ago; Aurelia must have promised her to accept him. And so she had, looking up and nodding and putting her hand out to him. "Welcome to my house, *Señor* Callahan."

He spoke Californio, at least, although with a strange drawling accent. He said, "I am very honored to be here, *madama*." With a little bow, like the honeyed cat he was.

Serafa introduced him to others, too, as many as she could. With Aurelia and old Rosas accepting him, who could refuse? And he was a good-looking man, with his strange fiery hair, his smile, his glib tongue. He seemed pleasant enough, easy enough. Only his eyes gave him away, his cold, hard, watchful, colorless eyes, and as much as Serafa tried to keep him there with the rest of them eating ice cream and drinking coffee, they all soon saw that he disappeared into the shadows.

King drifted away to the stables; he could hear music starting up behind him, and shouts and laughter. They would dance all day in the courtyard, while the meat turned on its spits, and then they would eat all night.

He wished he had not come. He felt Serafa's engineering like a web around him. She was always making all sorts of plans for him. Like finding a job for him. Like this new thing of his going to Mass.

He had gone to Mass, a little boy, in a church with a stone floor worn ragged with the standing and kneeling on it. Where early on he had thought God spoke on the altar. Later on he realized it was only the priest, who got drunk every evening and chased the housemaid around the table. It was all like that, he thought: a lot of big talk that wore in the end down to a scruffy little lie.

Behind the ranch house was a honeycomb of pole corrals and sheds and hayricks. He felt easier here, where there were no people, only horses. He leaned up against the rail of a corral and looked over the dozen colts inside.

The colts bunched up at the far side of the corral from him and watched him back. They were two- and three-year-olds, still a little gawky, with small soft mouths, their manes and tails long and tangled, and the wild look still in their eyes. Lily needed another horse. He wondered what he might offer Rosas for one of these colts.

It had to be a fair price. He wouldn't steal anything, not from these people.

Sorting through the colts with his eyes, he culled out the two pintos, a lunky-looking gelding with a hammerhead and two colts that kept their ears pinned flat. That left two or three likely ones: he needed a horse gentle enough for her to handle, but with speed and bottom.

It came to him that he was planning, in the back of his mind, for the time when he would have to run and she would have to keep up with him.

In a sudden flash of foresight he saw himself dragging her from place to place, sometimes hungry and dirty and cold, sometimes getting shot at, always on the run. He thought of her here, in the midst of these other girls, with her beautiful new dress, other new dresses to come, a place to live forever if she wanted. Safe, and loved, and happy.

"*Señor* Callahan?"

He spun around, startled. The old man smiled at him, unruffled. Came slowly down the lane between the corrals, leaning on his cane. His white hair hung to his shoulders. He came up to the fence beside King and stood looking at the colts.

"A fair crop of young horses, don't you think?"

King saw this was a test. He said, "I like the dark bay there. Nice mover."

"Eh," the old man said, "I like a horse with more muscle. The red roan, for instance."

"Muscle," King said. The roan was the lunkhead. He saw what this was a test of. "You can ride what you

like, Don Bernardo. I think it'll be a bad day in Los
Angeles before you ride a horse that low."

The old man laughed. "Well, maybe you are right.
You were Tiburcio's friend."

"Yes."

"And Serafa's friend also. She says you are looking
for work."

"Yes," he said. That was somehow harder to say than
that he was Tiburcio's friend.

"I have need of a man who speaks English and can
read and write. A man I can trust." The old man smiled.
"But as I remember, Tiburcio was a troublemaker. I have
no need of that."

King said slowly, "Tiburcio said out loud what he
thought. If that's a troublemaker I may be one of the
same."

"Tiburcio did more than talk," said Rosas calmly. He
nodded. "I think we will both consider this, and speak
again later." He turned and went away through the corrals. King watched him go. He liked the old man, but
this job was getting real, now, and felt like a whirlpool,
sucking him down.

Raul was trying to catch Lily's eye. She pretended she
didn't see him and went over to the split log table where
the lemonade waited in a great silver bowl. While she
was dipping up a cupful, Luz came up beside her, putting cakes and biscuits on a dish to take back across the
room to Josefa. Josefa did not dance at all; she merely
sat beside her betrothed and let everybody come and pay
court to her.

"Are you having fun?" Luz asked. "You look so good
when you turn in the dance, the different colors of the
skirts."

Lily sipped the delicious sweet lemonade. "Actually,
I was thinking I might go read." She smiled at Luz.

The other girl chirruped with amusement. "Raul is trying to get you to go off with him again."

"I know," Lily said. "I think so does everybody else.
He's so obvious." She kept her back to Raul. The older
women were sitting in a cluster at the narrow end of the
courtyard, talking busily; Serafa was not one of them.
Then she saw Serafa come in from the house and walk
across the courtyard, and all the women stopped talking
and smiled and nodded at her, and she knew they had
been talking about no one else.

"Gossip, gossip, gossip," she said. "All you people
talk about is each other."

Luz put her head to one side. "What else is interesting?" She glanced toward Serafa, now seating herself
calmly among the other women. "Mama would die if
people didn't talk about her."

"What?" Lily said, startled.

Luz shrugged one shoulder; the servant was coming
out with another tray of sweets, which was what she had
been waiting for, and she began to put them on her dish.
The sweet warm aroma steamed up from the tray, al-
monds and lemons and chocolate. "Mama loves to make
everybody talk. It's her power. Good or bad, as long as
they're talking, Mama is happy. Come over and sit with
us, we'll protect you from Raul."

"I think I'll go read," Lily said.

But she stayed where she was as Luz went off across
the courtyard with her dish of sweets, and watched Serafa. She could not hear what the women were saying,
but she could see how Serafa moved her head, and the
way the people around her stirred and looked when she
spoke. Serafa pretended to go her own way, not to care
what people thought. But of course she cared; what they
thought was all that mattered.

She remembered how Serafa had raged at them when
King played his joke on the Railroad. Serafa was as
double-hearted as King. Lily drank more lemonade; she
decided she would never be so dishonest.

Suddenly Raul was beside her, saying, "Why are you ignoring me?"

She said, "I didn't see you. I'm going inside for a while. Is there a place I can read?"

He swung around in front of her. To her surprise his face was dark with anger. He said, "No! Come sit with me!"

She recoiled, her temper catching fire from his; she was suddenly aware that everyone in the courtyard was watching them. Her neck prickled. She glared at him for bringing this on her. "No," she said. "Get away from me." Turning on her heel, she walked across the courtyard.

"I want you to go to Mass," Serafa said. "Just once."

They were walking down through the orchard behind the Rosas' house. The trees were bare, the ground beneath them raked and neat; the sun shone through the branches in sheets and bars. Everybody else had gone inside for the siesta. King said, "I haven't been in a church for thirty years."

"God will not mind."

King said nothing; thirty years was a long time, even for God. She was fussing with the tails of her shawl. Her hair shone warmly in the sun and he wanted to lay his hand along her hair and take up that warmth.

"I talked to *Señor* Rosas."

"Good. What did he say?"

"He didn't offer me a job."

"He will. He must see the kind of man you are." She smiled at him. "You will be happy to know that Lily has lost her interest in Raul."

"That strutting pigeon."

"She set him down very neatly in front of everybody. She has been a great success; everybody likes her."

"They damned well better."

Serafa laughed. The ground curved away gently before them; they were coming to the end of the orchard. The gray winter grass stretched away from them, feathery clumps and bunches against the dry crusted sandy soil. Clouds like dark boulders piled up along the southern third of the sky. It was going to rain, maybe during the night, the air already heavy, charged, stirring. Serafa brushed against him, as if by accident, and he slid his arm around her.

Off to the west, below the ominous sky, a dark line streamed across the flat. The train's long hollow wail sounded.

He reached for his pocket watch. Serafa said, "Why are you doing that?"

"Just a habit," he said. "You got a thousand men in this country, they hear a train whistle, reach for their watches. Maybe a hundred thousand."

He felt the train calling him. He thought about what Pigeye had told him about the railroad office: of course, Pigeye had gotten that secondhand, and likely it was all wrong. Still, it was tempting. He needed money; he was down to nothing.

He couldn't very well go straight and plot robberies, too. He made himself stop thinking about it. He made himself think about getting a job. About convincing Rosas to give him a job. He stuck the watch back into his pocket, tightened his arm around his woman, and turned back to the ranch house.

After supper the old man invited him to join the men for brandy. They sat around Rosas' study and saluted each other with their glasses and drank the belly-searing liquor. King sat off by the door nursing his drink and listened to them talk, and soon enough their talk turned to the Railroad.

"They will never make it over the mountains."

"I have heard that the Big Men have lost all their

money and the Railroad will go bankrupt anyway. All this fuss is for nothing."

"I have never seen any advantage to it. A lot of smoke and noise."

"There are advantages," the old man said, "and disadvantages, as with everything. I am not sure myself how much importance to place on the Railroad."

"None," said one man.

"They will trample on everything we love," said Raul hotly. "We have to fight them, before they grow too great to fight. All the Anglos."

"Of that I am less than sure. The Anglos I have met are reasonable men, more like me than unlike; if we are honest and fair we shall do well enough together. *Señor* Callahan?"

King thought Raul was right, for once: the Railroad would blast away all their lives, make nothing of them here as they had made nothing of the Indians. Instead of saying that, he said, "I have no place here, I shouldn't talk."

Raul wheeled on him, his eyes glinting, quick-tongued in the midst of so many of his own. "Then why are you here at all?"

The old man said sharply, "He is our guest."

King gave a lick of a glance at Raul; he wanted to pull a gun and shoot Raul through the head, but his guns were in Los Angeles. He eased away from the wall toward the door.

"I'll go."

He went out into the cool night air. The storm was cruising in from the Pacific and the trees stirred in their dense masses; he thought they played, in the wind, joyous, their tremendous voices gathering up into oceans of sound. He thought the wind freed them; bound so tight, in their bark and roots and weight, how could they dance without the storm?

He had to get out of here. He wasn't a man here,

cutting everything to trim. The door behind him opened, and the old man came out.

"*Señor* Callahan."

"Yes, *señor*."

"I apologize for my son. He is a hothead."

"Your son," King said, "is a complete fool."

The old man bridled at that, and his voice was curt. "He is young. Not an incurable problem."

"I don't think I can work for you."

"He is the hothead. You seemed cool enough to me in there. Wiser than I expected. I need, as I said, a man I can trust who speaks English."

"You don't need me." King turned to face him, angry. "I'd have to fight half your crew, and then I'd wind up fightin' the Anglos. Is that what you want?"

"I am a peaceable man."

"I'm not." King slid his hand down his thigh where his gun usually hung. He shook his head, saying, "I can't work for you, *Señor* Rosas."

"Perhaps you are right," the old man said stiffly. "Ah, well. I had hoped to do something for Serafa, whom I hold in high regard. Good evening." He went stiffly away, back into the study. King lifted his face. The first fat grapeshot of the rain struck him, like a heavy-handed blessing. He went out into the darkness, toward the storm.

◆ Chapter ◆

XXI

Brand said, *"Whatever happened to* George, anyway?"

Elmo shrugged. He was standing in front of Brand's desk, his hands at his sides; he shifted his weight from foot to foot. Above the thicket of his beard his eyes were red; maybe he was hungover. He said, " 'Zat why you sent for me, just to ask about George?"

"Well, George is pretty interesting," Brand said. "Shut the door."

Elmo stared at him a moment, turned, and went to the office door. It was after five and everybody else who worked there had gone home for the night. Brand propped his elbows on the desk and folded his hand over the blunt end of his arm. Elmo came back toward him, his eyes intent.

"You got some more work for us, maybe?"

"Maybe. You told me once George had a partner."

"Yeah." Elmo grunted, dismissive. "Washed out. Nothing doing. *Nada.*"

"Where's George now?"

"He done took off. Ain't seen him in a while."

"I think his partner's still here."

"His partner." Elmo was having trouble negotiating the difficult shift of interest; he frowned, his lips pursed. "His partner was a washout."

Brand laid his arms down flat on the desk. "His partner is King Callahan. Have you ever heard of him?"

"Unh—" Elmo blinked at him. "The Virginia City gunfighter?"

"You remember that cantina down in Sonoratown?"

Elmo said, "He's there?"

Brand smiled at him. Sometimes Elmo surprised him; he started off slow, but when he got going he could think as well as anybody. "I want you to go down there and see if you can turn him up. You and your boys."

"And what? Bring him back here?"

Brand snorted. "I wish I thought you could. No. Find him. See if he'll talk to you. And then just tell him what I'm about to tell you."

Serafa said, "Why did you get into a fight with Raul? You could have done nothing worse! The old man dotes on the boys. He was old when they were born."

"I didn't get into a fight with Raul." Lately he always felt as if he were backing up from her; he went over to the kitchen door and looked out across the yard to the cantina. The girls had taken the dinner off the tables in there and the evening crowd was starting to drift out. "Actually, Raul tried to get into a fight with me, which is goin' to happen, you know, anywhere."

"Don Bernardo needs you. You need him. There must be a way."

"God, stay out of it, will you?" He stared across the yard. "Serafa, leave me alone."

She was still, sitting there behind him, watching him; he could feel her eyes on him. Waiting.

He said, "I'm goin' out for a while pretty soon, run down some horses, try to get up a string."

"You could do that for Rosas," she said.

He gave a little shake of his head. This was going nowhere. Then the back door of the cantina opened and Luz came hurrying out.

She saw King and ran toward him, her face urgent. "Someone is bothering Lily."

He crossed the yard at a jog, went up the steps, and opened the door. The big lanterns were all lit, the room still half full. At the far end of the back wall from the door where he stood, he saw Lily trapped behind the bar fending off a big black-bearded white man who leaned across the counter to grab at her.

King stopped cold. He knew that man: Elmo, one of Brand's bullies.

All his nerves jumped. His hand dropped to the gun on his hip, and he looked quickly around the room. Behind Elmo stood three other Anglos, calling advice and laughing. They were also Brand's men, but Brand himself was nowhere. King took his hand off the gun butt, went down behind the counter, and got between the big man and Lily; pawing at her, Elmo didn't see him coming and his hand struck King's chest and King knocked his arm away.

"Keep your hands up, boyo!"

The big man rocked a step backward, his eyes wide. Behind him, the other three fell abruptly silent. Below the level of the bar, King had his hand on his gun; if Elmo moved wrong, he meant to shoot him through the front of the bar.

"I seen you before," said the big man. He held his hands up in the air, fingers spread. His friends shifted behind him, but nobody reached for a gun.

"You jumped my girl before," King said. He leaned back; he brought his hands up, wide, palms out, and put them down on the bar. "I didn't shoot you then, and luckily for you I ain't shooting you now." He turned to Lily, standing just behind him. "Go do something else."

She stood still, her face red; she had been fighting Elmo off, and the fire was still high in her. "Throw him out! He was—"

He said, "Lily, do what I tell you."

She gave Elmo a stab of a look and went away down

the counter, her head slightly turned to watch what he did. Elmo's hands had dropped. He was mulling this over. "Sure. You know, it fits now. You're George's partner. Yeah, it all makes sense now. When he saw you in the street that night, he went dead yellow."

King said, "I don't know any Georges." He glanced toward the front door again. Still no Brand; this was an opening move, not a showdown. He felt a slow visceral coiling of anticipation. He said, "You got any reason to be here besides bother the girls?"

Elmo chewed on that. His wiry black beard grew practically up to his eyes; his lips made a red wet pucker in the middle. He said, "I ain't seen George. You know where he is?"

"I just told you, boyo," King said, "I don't know anybody named George. You work for Brand, don't you?" Behind Elmo somebody moved, and King swiveled his stare to that man. "Stand still."

The man froze. Elmo said plaintively, "You ain't too friendly."

King grunted at him. "Why should I be friendly to you?"

"Because we got a deal for you."

"You do? Or Brand does?"

Elmo glanced at the men behind him, and his voice dropped to a mutter. "You know, I'm gettin' sick of Brand."

"Are you?" King said.

"Someplace we can talk?"

"Talk about what?"

Elmo and his friends stirred again, restless, glancing around them. Elmo's tongue licked around the corners of his lips.

He blurted out, "They're bringing in a lot of money, some kind of payroll or something, on this little train. Twenty thousand dollars."

"Really. So?"

Elmo looked around at his cronies again and then

faced King, his forehead furrowed. He lowered his voice to a near whisper. "Well, you know, maybe we could steal it."

King stood back, one hand on the bar. He shot another quick look toward the front door and looked Elmo over a moment. "You know, seems to me you got all the pieces to that yourselves. Why do you need me?"

"We ain't never done nothing like this before," Elmo said, and now the man behind him, who favored Elmo around the narrow stupid eyes, said, "George said you were real good."

King let them stand there a moment, as if he had to make up his mind, and then lifted one shoulder and let it drop. "Come down here."

He led them over the corner table where he usually sat. As he went by the door he looked out and saw that the kitchen was dark. Serafa would be back in her room, getting ready for bed. Josefa came by him with a tray of empty glasses and gave him a sharp look. He began preparing a good lie in case the girls told Serafa he was talking to these people. The customers were steadily drifting out, and now Lily went down the room and snuffed the farthest lantern. King sat down at the table with his back to the corner and pointed Elmo to the chair opposite.

The others moved toward the remaining chairs. He said, "You boys stand. Where I can see your hands." He nodded to Elmo. "Keep your hands on the table."

They all showed him their hands. Lily went past them toward the door. The last few customers were leaving. Elmo planted his elbows on the table and started to say something, and King interrupted him. "You and Brand must think I'm a moron. I know he sent you down here to set me up."

Elmo said loudly, "No, we ain't." The other men all murmured, taking cover behind him.

King said, "No. Shut up. It makes me angry when people lie to me. When I get angry, you know, I'm liable to do things." He pulled his hip gun out and laid it on the table, not even very fast, and all the men jumped, their eyes big as eggs.

King took his hand off the gun, leaned back, and went on, "But listen to yourself, now. You said yourself this is a big job. Twenty thousand is a lot of money. I'm thinkin' you don't like Brand any more than I do. I'm thinkin' he's payin' you small cash, when there's all this big cash around, and you're too savvy not to notice."

Elmo rubbed his hands together. "Yeah." The other men pressed closer.

King smiled at him. "I'm thinkin' we can do some business together."

Elmo said, "Yeah."

"But I'm warning you, if you double-cross me, I'll kill you. Got that?"

Elmo licked his lips again. He glanced up at his friends and then faced King. "Brand ain't so tough. How tough can he be with one hand?"

King brushed that off. He knew how tough Brand was. He said, "I get half."

"Half!" Elmo squawked. "There's four of us. One of you."

"Half," King said. "Or I don't dance."

Elmo grumbled. Scrubbing his hands together, he glanced at his friends and then leaned forward again. "We got to talk it over, my boys and me."

King said, "No. Tell me right now, in or out. Now." He flicked a look up at the other three men. "They'll do what you say."

Elmo's tongue flickered out again. His eyes had a glassy look; as if he had a window in his forehead and little gears in there turning, King could see him thinking. After a moment Elmo said, "We're in."

The others murmured, excited, and the one who looked like Elmo leaned forward and clapped him on the shoulder. King said, "Good. When exactly is that money's going to be on the train?"

Elmo tipped forward in his chair, his eyes blazing. "Day after tomorrah, four o'clock out of Wilmington. They're putting a caboose on the end, with a safe in it."

"All right," King said. "Then the train won't get into Los Angeles until after dark. Now, listen. You go back to Brand and tell him this. We ain't takin' the train on at all. We'll rob the shipment between the train yard and the Railroad office. Got that? Between the yard and the office, in the city."

Elmo was frowning. Slowly he said, "You sure you want to do that?"

"That's what you're telling Brand," King said. "What we're really going to do is bust the train halfway between Wilmington and Los Angeles. I'll get on board, unlink the caboose from the rest of the train, get inside, and take care of the brakeman. When the caboose stops, you boys come in with the horses and the powder so we can blow the safe and get the money out. Got that?"

"Ah." Elmo sat back, smiling. "So Brand's stuck waiting for us in Los Angeles, only we never get there."

"Right," King said. "You got that? Come back here tomorrow, early afternoon, we'll go over the details."

"Right," Elmo said. He rose; for a moment he hesitated, maybe expecting something else, a round of drinks or a battle cry, but when King only stared at him in silence he turned and led his men out of the cantina.

Lily rushed in from the back. "What are you doing? That was Elmo!"

"Never mind," King said. "Just don't tell Serafa."

"They're Brand's men," she said. She followed him out to the yard, grabbed his arm, and pulled; he let her turn him around to face her. "What makes you think they aren't going to turn you in to Brand?"

"It doesn't matter what they do." He beamed at her, laughing at the thunderous frown on her face, and planted a kiss on her forehead. "Don't worry about it, darlin', I've got it under control." Light and easy, he crossed the yard toward Serafa's house.

He had been fretting for so long, worrying about money, about Lily, about getting a job; everything had weighed down on him like a lead jacket. Now suddenly the whole problem was solving itself. And Brand was handing it to him. That made it all the better. It didn't matter if Elmo was double-crossing him or double-crossing Brand, it didn't matter at all.

All that mattered was Serafa. She wouldn't take to this. But he could talk her around; he had always been able to talk her around. He didn't see how she could blame him much, anyway, when Brand was making it so easy, practically tossing it into his lap. And it was just this one time. This one last time. And then they would be fixed up for life. He reached her doorway and knocked, as he always did, and without waiting for an answer he opened the door. She was sitting on the bed, her hair down around her shoulders; she turned and smiled at him, beautiful in the webs of her hair, and eagerly he went in and shut the door.

"He ain't so tough." Elmo grunted. "He just got the jump on me, comin' in from behind me like that." They were riding on up the street toward the plaza.

"No, he don't look all that much," Roy said. "But George was plenty scared of him."

"Twenty thousand bucks," Cale was saying, over and over. "Twenty thousand bucks! What's that apiece, El, hunh?"

"Unh . . ." Elmo hated numbers.

"Twenty-five hundred each," said Elijah quietly. He shook his head. "I wish I knew what happened to George."

"Twenty five hundred?" Cale said, startled. "Naw. 'Zmore 'an that. Twenty thousand dollars, man!"

"Yeah," said Roy, "but this whatsisname gets half. And we get only the other half for all of us."

"Hey," Cale said, wounded. "That's not fair."

"I been thinkin', anyway," Elijah said, "we ought to stick with Brand. That's not bad money, couple hundred so far, more comin', and it's legal."

Elmo reined his horse over, crowding the rest of them toward the long side of the plaza, down by the water tank, where there were no people to overhear. He lowered his voice. "What I been thinkin' is, why do we go with either of them?"

Cale blinked. Roy said, "What do you mean?"

"I mean," Elmo said, "I don't see why we should have to give Callahan anything. Let him cut the caboose off the train and blow the safe open, and then"—he made a gun out of one hand and shot—"we get away, let everybody blame it on him."

Elijah said, "Elmo, now you're getting tricky."

Elmo said, "Ain't nobody gonna mind if we kill him, is there? Might even be a reward."

"Don't get too tricky. Can't collect a reward," Elijah said, "and steal the money."

Elmo grunted at him. "Shut up."

They were coming to the end of the plaza, where the streetlamps began. Elmo reined up. He was supposed to meet Brand sometime soon over at the Crystal Palace. He said, "Just don't talk to anybody about it. Don't say Callahan's name. Just keep tight and leave it all to me."

"Sure, Elmo." One by one they shook hands with him, even Elijah. Cale and Elijah rode off, and Elmo and his brother went toward the Crystal Palace.

Roy said, "I heard of this fella Callahan before."

"He's just some hardcase."

"George was plenty scared of him."

"He's just a big noise," Elmo said. The more he thought about it, the more he saw how he should have talked to Callahan, set him back on his heels, kept him thinking. But maybe it was better if Callahan didn't know how smart Elmo really was. Not until it was too late, anyway.

"Elmo," Roy said.

"Yeah, what?"

Roy turned toward him, worried. "You think he killed George?"

Elmo snorted; the idea had never occurred to him. "Naw." George had just gone somewhere. People went somewhere all the time. "Naw," he said again, louder, a little uneasy.

Brand said, "He bit, did he?" They were sitting in the upstairs room of the Crystal Palace; the roar of the barroom below came up through the floor.

"Whole hog," said Elmo. "He says we can steal the money, you know, here in Los Angeles. After you take it off the train, while you're taking it over to the office." He rubbed busily at his mouth with his fingers. "From the train to the office," he said again.

"Well," Brand said, "that makes it easier. When are you meeting him next?"

"Tomorrah."

"Good. See if there's anybody else involved besides you and him." He pulled his money pouch out of his jacket and dumped coins onto the table. "Good job, Elmo. I knew you could do it."

"Sure," Elmo said. "Nothin' to it. Well, that's all, I guess." Rising to his feet, he gathered up the money. "G'night."

"Night," Brand said. Elmo swaggered off to the door and let himself out and was gone.

Brand sat back in his chair. He knew Elmo was playing him false, but he would deal with that when he came to it. Flushing King out was the main thing. King would figure this for a trap, but twenty thousand dollars would surely lure him out of hiding. He knew now about the money on the train. Somewhere he would intercept its course. This idea of robbing it in the city street was an obvious ruse. That in itself meant King was moving. All

Brand had to do was stay with the money, and he would get his chance.

He didn't let himself celebrate. He had missed King before. But he had a gut feeling about this time. This time he was going to see King Callahan hang. He wished he had one of Joseph Hyde's cigars left to reward himself with. Furiously his hand scrubbed over the stump of his arm, rubbing and rubbing until his skin burned.

◆ Chapter ◆

XXII

King took the morning train down to Wilmington so that he could watch them make up the four o'clock train. It was an overcast day, cold and foggy by the coast, the ocean iron-gray, the sheds and squat low buildings of Wilmington gray and black. King had brought a news-paper along from Los Angeles and he pretended to be reading it while the train rolled up before the station platform.

Behind the gold-trimmed locomotive with its flaring balloon stack the yard crew hooked on three freight cars and two passenger cars. When the tender rolled the ca-boose up, King folded his paper, stuck it under his arm, and ambled down the platform toward the end of the train.

The brakeman crouched beside the back side of the last passenger car, the long iron coupling pin in his left hand, and his right hand on the foot-long oval link stick-ing out of the coupling box. As the draw bar of the caboose glided up, the brakeman all in one motion fit the link like a tongue into the oncoming iron mouth and dropped the pin through. An instant after he got his hand out of the way the coupling boxes kissed with a ringing clang. The brakeman went off toward the front of the train, waving his arms.

Passing him in the opposite direction, King sauntered by the coupling and looked it over. The pins looked an easy fit, and there was a lot of play between the edges of the two coupling boxes. He had a chance at this. He glanced at the back of the passenger car, once he was past it, and in through the curtained window in the door saw the conductor in his French military cap just going out the far end.

The train would not leave for another two hours. King circled around behind the caboose and went off to the back of the switching yard, where he had already found a place he could hole up and watch without being seen.

From here nearly all of Wilmington was visible. There was no real town, only the factory and the warehouses on his side of the tracks, and far off in the distance, Phineas Banning's mansion looming all alone in the high grass. Wilmington was where it was because here the coast arched out into the Pacific and heaped up into lumpy cypress-crowded heights, sheltering a shallow stretch of water where the steamer from San Francisco was now anchored. A half-finished breakwater led out toward the square-headed island just beyond the tip of the wharf.

The crates of goods and sacks of mail off the steamer were already piled up on the station platform. He watched the work gangs loading them into the boxcars. Halfway through the afternoon a clot of men came out of the station house, one in a brown coat leading the way and the others carrying something heavy. The man in the brown coat carried a long gun, maybe a shotgun. They disappeared into the caboose. A few moments later all the men but the brown coat reappeared, without the heavy thing, and went back through the station. Presently the last man followed, no longer carrying the shotgun.

King settled down where he was, in one corner of a storage shed; he had brought some tortillas and a canteen of water flavored with a little *aguardiente*. The work gangs loaded the cars, and passengers came out of the station house, walked up and down the platform, got onto the train. Nobody went near the caboose, not even the brakeman, until just before four o'clock.

Then the man in the brown coat came quickly from the side of the station house, climbed the two steps to the caboose platform, and went inside and shut the door. King couldn't see if this man had a left hand, but he was willing to wager a lot that he didn't.

He wondered if Elmo had lined up with Brand after all, in the end, and told him the whole plan. More likely Brand was working on his own, although what he did best was not planning but sheer bulldog tenacity: he never gave up.

He made mistakes, though, sometimes. Like now.

The train let out its long bull-roar of warning. Smoke billowed up out of the stack and the brightly colored wheels began to turn. King went at a jog across the yard.

The track leaving the yard led immediately onto the trestle that crossed the broad marsh that lay just behind the beach. King met the train at the head of the trestle, while the cars were chugging along at a walking pace. The locomotive rolled past him, the engineer leaning on his window and the fireman shoveling furiously, and then the three freight cars; the brakeman was sitting comfortably on the back platform of the last freight car, taking a pull on a jug. As the first of the passenger cars rumbled by, King reached out and caught hold of the railing and climbed up the steps.

He had bought a ticket in Los Angeles, and he thumbed it out of his coat pocket and went into the car. It was only about half full: a family of excited people speaking some other language was plastered up against the windows on the right, all chattering and screaming over every blade of grass. King went down the swaying car past them, past a fat woman who had already fallen asleep in her seat and two men reading newspapers, and went through the door and across to the next car.

The conductor was there, collecting tickets from a dozen passengers. King gave him his ticket and waited for it to be punched. He thought about the brakeman, up in the freight car; he would be no trouble if he stayed there. Probably Brand had taken care of him.

"Are we going to be on time?" he asked the conductor.

The man handed him back the punched ticket. "We're always on time," he said. "Comptonville next. Pull the signal cord if you want to get off there." He went on up the car toward the front of the train. King drifted toward the back of the car.

He leaned up against the side of the door out to the platform, taking out his newspaper again. Through the window he could see the caboose. It had no observation deck on top, and the blinds were pulled down over the windows: Brand would preserve the advantage of surprise as long as he could. King faced his newspaper.

The late sun was shining on the window, not particularly bothering him, but he made a face anyway and pulled the blind down. The conductor had gone out the front of the car. King slouched against the wall, watching the other passengers. All but one faced away from him, and that one was nodding, his head dipping toward his chest. The train had left the marsh behind and was rolling through high stalky brush that bent away as the train rolled by.

The train whistle cried again. They were coming to the first of the whistle stops. He had a while yet to wait, and he folded his arms and yielded to the rocking of the train. His nose stung a little from the smoke. He thought this engineer burned a lot of coal.

He thought about Serafa, what he would say to her, how he could convince her that he was doing the best thing. In the end, though, she'd have to go along with it. It would be done, he'd have the money, what could she do?

He'd have the money, he'd have her, he'd have Lily.

His life would be perfect. He shut down the one tiny part of his mind that knew it would be harder than this.

The train did not stop at Comptonville, but rolled with blasts of its whistle past the tiny train station platform and the crowd of children gathered to wave and scream. The passenger facing the back of the car jerked awake, looked brightly and intensely all around, squirmed, settled down, and dozed off again.

King stuck his hand into his pocket, found the opening of the heavy glove he had brought, and worked his fingers into it. The glove was stiff and he had trouble getting his hand inside it. The train whistled. They were coming to a crossroads; he had to hurry now. He opened the door onto the platform and slipped out, crouching down. His hand was still in his pocket, half in and half out of the glove; he struggled with the glove, forced his fingers into it, and then nearly pulled the whole glove off again getting it and his hand together out of his pocket.

He squatted down on the platform as low as he could and leaned out through the opening under the bottom railing. The caboose was three feet away from him, swaying along at the tail of the train. In the gathering dusk the blank window looked like a blind eye. He stretched out his gloved hand toward the coupling between the two cars, got hold of the link pin, and pulled.

Nothing yielded. The pin felt solid as part of a mountain. He inched himself farther out over the coupling and took a better grip. He watched the gap between the two halves of the coupling box. The train whistled again, warning the crossroads ahead; eight minutes past that crossroads, he knew, was the last whistle stop. He had to hurry. The train was still rocketing along, but now he felt its weight shift, slowing for the crossroads. He watched the coupling between his car and the caboose; as the train slowed, the caboose ran up a little on his car and the gap between the coupling boxes closed, and he pushed the pin forward and then backward, left and then right, and pulled straight up.

The pin came out like the sword out of the stone. He flung it out into the brush and rolled backwards onto the platform of the passenger car. The train whistled again; the locomotive had cleared the crossing and he felt its power surge as it gathered speed. The caboose was falling back. Empty track flew by between him and it. King on the platform clattered through the deserted crossroads. Back there a hundred yards up the track, the caboose still rolled along, but falling farther and farther behind. The brush no longer bent away from it but stood up around it. The track curved, and the caboose vanished into the wild mustard.

King let himself relax; he sat up, one arm hanging over the railing. The hardest part of this was over. He could forget all the swarms of extra plans he had made, in case he could not uncouple the caboose, in case he got trapped on the train with Brand. The rest of this should be just a job of work. He got to his feet, taking off the big glove, and straightened his coat and put the glove in his pocket and went back into the car.

Brand had been half asleep, tucked into a corner in the back of the caboose; the change in the sound of the train woke him up. He lifted his head, hearing the rumble of the locomotive fading away into the distance, the *tick-tick-tick* of the caboose wheels sounding steadily louder and slower. He had been cut off from the rest of the train.

The hair on the back of his neck stood up. He eased the shotgun into his arms, the barrels across his short arm, the triggers under his finger. The caboose was barely moving now. He got his feet under him, moving an inch at a time.

The caboose stopped. In the utter silence he thought

he could hear the blood pulsing through his veins. He held his breath, watching the door.

Out of the stillness grew another sound, the rumble of horses' hooves. He gathered himself. His chest hurt; he wasn't breathing. He drew a long slow breath, puzzled, and tired of waiting. Where was King? Then heavy feet tramped on the caboose platform and the door burst open, and a bulky form crowded into the oblong of pale light. Brand's finger closed on the shotgun's front trigger.

Just as he fired, something in his mind clicked. He jerked the shotgun barrels up. The gun bellowed into the ceiling of the caboose. The big man yelled and ran out again through a rain of dirt and wood splinters. Brand swore. He bounded to his feet and charged to the door and out, into the gloom of evening, and swung the shotgun to cover the four men by the caboose's tail.

"Stick your hands up!"

"Hey," Elmo shouted. He staggered back, tripped over the tracks, and sat down hard. He pointed his hands at the sky. "Hey, boss, it's us!"

Brand swung the shotgun around; there was nobody in front of him but Elmo and his three toadies. Just behind them were five horses, although there were only four men. His temper seethed. He swiveled the shotgun to aim at Elmo's belly and almost pulled the trigger.

"Where is he?"

Elmo gawked at him. The others were shuffling their feet, looking as if they wanted to be gone. It was nearly dark; Brand could not see their faces. He leaped down off the caboose, rushed over to Elmo, and rammed the shotgun into his chest.

"Where the hell is he?"

Elmo said, "Boss—boss—" He waggled his hands in the air. "We ain't done nothin'—we was—" His eyes popped with the effort of thinking quickly. "We was gonna catch 'im! We knowed he was here—"

"Well, he isn't here," Brand roared. He broke the shotgun over his short arm and scrabbled in his pocket for another shell. "Where the hell is he?"

One of the others said, "He was supposed to be here. He told us—" The man beside him grabbed his arm and silenced him.

Brand swore again. "You stupid bastards. You can't do anything right." He strode toward the horses. The men held back, and he wheeled toward them. "Come on!"

They were hanging back around the caboose. Elmo got to his feet. He said, "Boss—what about the money? You gonna just leave all that money out here in the middle of nowhere?"

Brand snarled at him. "There isn't any money, Elmo. It was just bait, damn it." His nerves were singing, a wild urgency fluttering along every nerve. "There's money in Los Angeles. That's where he is, the son of a bitch. Let's go. We can still get him. He's moving, but he's not gone yet. Come on." He swung onto the nearest horse. The other men were standing there watching him, bewildered. He roared, "Come on, you stupid bastards!" He reined the horse around and spurred hard up toward the road back to the city.

In Florence, the last of the little whistle stop stations before Los Angeles, the train stopped and the engineer and conductor and brakeman talked over the missing caboose. King got off and paced around on the platform, nervous; if they decided to go collect the caboose before the train went on, he would have to call the whole job off and go back to Sonoratown. But the railroad men knew about Brand, and their schedule gripped them. They left the caboose; the train started for Los Angeles on time.

Dark was falling when the train pulled into the station at Alameda and Commercial Street. King got off, moving quickly through the crowd that had come to welcome the train, and at a jog went up to First Street and over to Hill.

He thought he had about an hour and a half, maybe two hours, before Brand caught up with him; but he had everything ready, a mallet, a chisel, a crowbar and some pipes, half a stick of dynamite, all in a canvas mail sack hidden in the alley across from the Railroad office. When he reached the building a little after five, the last of the clerks was locking the front door.

The clerk went hurrying off, and King sauntered out of the alley, the mail sack in his hand. The office stood on the corner, its front door opening on Hill Street. On First Street on the left stood a wood frame building that housed a barbershop and a doctor's, both shut down for the night. He thought the dry goods store to the right of the railroad office had a night watchman, and as he went down the alley between the office and the store he kept an eye out, but didn't see anybody; the store was silent and lightless. At the back of the railroad office, he jimmied up one of the windows and climbed in.

The room inside was dark. He struck a lucifer and looked around. Pigeye had pictured it accurately, for somebody who had never been here: the desks, the railing, the big cabinets on either side. The only thing he had gotten wrong was the safe, which he had described so completely and so well, and which wasn't there.

The lucifer went out. King struck another, held it up, looked carefully to the left and to the right. There was no safe.

The match burned his fingertips. He dropped it and by memory found his way on past the railing and down a step to the main floor of the room, and then to a desk where he had seen a lamp. He lit the lamp. In its honey-colored light he surveyed the room inch by inch.

One of the two big cabinets held green buckram-bound ledgers. The other was a wardrobe. He went over the desks, opening each drawer, finding nothing.

He laughed, feeling like an idiot: all this work and there was nothing to steal.

He went around the room again, thumping his hands over the walls, looking for false doors. Opening the door into the front room, he cast a look into it, shook his head, and shut the door again.

They had to have a safe. He had never heard of an SP local office without a safe. Of course this was a temporary place. Maybe they were waiting until they built the permanent one. He walked around the room again, carrying the lamp. Then he saw the little rug in the middle of the floor behind the railing.

He pulled the rug back. A square outline showed in the raw planks of the floor. He set the lamp down, found a brass ring fit into a socket on the trapdoor, and pulled it up.

"Faith, now. Isn't that clever."

The safe was set just under the level of the floor. It was factory new, the gold paint fresh and bright, the black steel door glossy in the lamplight. The combination dial and the two steel door handles all gleamed importantly. He set the lamp down beside it and opened the canvas sack. He had wasted some time finding this thing, and getting it open was going to take more time. The benefit was that the flooring around it would muffle a lot of the sound.

With the chisel and the mallet and the crowbar he attacked the lower of the heavy knobbed hinges. The floorboards made it hard to reach, hard to get the chisel to the right angle. Patiently he banged and wrenched, first with the chisel and then the crowbar, using the pipes to get more length on the crowbar, until he had twisted the hinge up and opened a gap in the edge of the door big enough to stick his thumb into. Getting out the dynamite, he opened the end of the stick, took out the fuse and poked its end into the hole, and then poured the powder in over it and jammed as much of the paper in after it as he could. He threw the rug, the canvas sack, and a cushion from a chair on top of everything to muffle the sound, lit the fuse, then took the lamp off behind the desk and crouched down.

The boom rattled him. It sounded loud as a cannon shot. Everybody in Los Angeles must have heard it. He had to hurry now. The explosion had blown the rug and the sack off and ripped up the cushion, sending a cloud of downy feathers floating around the room; the safe door had popped up out of its frame. He used the crowbar to pry it all the way out of the opening, uncovering the inside set of doors, two panels of sheet steel, with a keyhole lock.

He was running out of time. His ears strained, expecting to hear feet running, shouts of alarm, the crackle of shots. With the mallet he hammered the chisel into the brass keyhole and broke it out of the door, reached into the ragged slot it left behind, and pushed the lock levers down. The door slid open.

He picked up the lamp and held it so that the light shone into the recesses of the safe, which was fit with wooden shelves and pigeonholes. The stacks and sheaves of paper didn't interest him; he pulled them out and flung them across the office. Out of the large lower compartment he raked a folio of blueprints. Then a big ring of flat brass keys. Beneath them was a leather sack, sealed with wax. When he gripped it, the sack clinked.

He sucked in a deep breath, triumphant. Pulling the sack up out of the hole in the floor, he broke the wax off the flap and, reaching inside, brought out a handful of coins, flashing gold in the lamplight, ten-dollar gold eagle pieces, so new their edges felt sharp.

His whole body sang. This was the best part of any robbery, having his hands on the money, knowing he was getting away with it.

He stuffed the leather sack into the mail sack. He groped around again in the safe, but there was no more. Still, this was enough—nothing like twenty thousand dollars, but enough. Now all he had to do was deal with Serafa. He swung the sack up over his shoulder, blew out the lamp, and went out the back window into the dark.

Raul said, "Lily, I think you are mad. One moment you love me more than life itself, the next moment you can't bear me. What is the matter? What did I do?"

He and his brother had come over after supper, Andrés to see Josefa, Raul to pester Lily. She turned her face away from him, fetching up a sigh. "You don't understand."

Most of the evening's gathering were leaving or already gone. Serafa had come in to stand guard over her daughters' virtue, and was sitting with Luz near the front door, drinking coffee and receiving the greetings of her customers as they passed by on their way out. In the corner Andrés and Josefa sat holding hands and talking. Lily felt a stab of envy. Now suddenly she wished she loved Raul again. She wished Raul were someone else, but she wasn't sure who.

She said, "You know, I think people live in one world and think in another."

"You're certainly mad." He grabbed her hand and tried to kiss it. She pulled away from him, angry.

"Just leave me alone, will you, Raul? I have to work." She got up, took her tray, and went around from table to table, taking the dirty crockery. The back door opened and King came in.

As soon as she saw him, a bolt of alarm went through her. Something had happened. His face was intent, and he was in a hurry; he had his coat on and both his handguns. Her insides began to flutter. She put the tray down and stood watching him cross the room to Serafa. Luz had gotten up to shut the door behind the last of the diners. King dropped down in the chair she had just left and leaned toward Serafa.

"I just robbed the Railroad office. I've got enough money out there to buy us a little ranch someplace in Mexico. You have to come with me, right now. We'll get married, we'll have everything we want."

Serafa stared at him, her mouth falling open. Suddenly she stood up, pushing back from the table. "You have done what? What are you saying?" She flung down the coffee cup in her hand. "Damn you!"

Lily went up behind King. He didn't turn toward her, but he put his hand out, holding her back. He said, "Serafa, this is the only way to do it. The boat to Guaymas sails tomorrow morning. We can be on it. It's the only way."

"The only way!" She turned on him, her face blazing with rage. "The only way for you, perhaps! What about us? How could I leave my home? How would I give up everything that I have? What about Lily? You knew I would never go along with this."

He jerked his head back as if she had struck him. "Actually," he said, "I thought you would, since you said you loved me."

"You knew I would not." She flung her arms up jerkily, like angry wings. "That's why you hid it from me."

He swung a look around at the rest of them, then faced her again. His voice was perfectly even. "Look, Serafa. I haven't got any time to argue. Either you come with me now or it's all over."

"Get out," she said. "I hate you. Get out!"

His face set hard, all angles, the muscles clenched at the corners of his jaw; but he said nothing, only stared at her. Abruptly he turned on his heel and strode toward the back door.

"No," Lily cried. She rushed forward, and Luz wrapped her arms around her; Lily wrenched at the other girl's embrace. "King! Don't go without me!"

King wheeled toward her. Raul cried, "Lily!" He sprang in front of her, his arms out, fencing her into the room. Luz clung to her with both hands. King hesitated on the threshold, almost gone. His face worked. His gaze met Lily's.

Serafa stepped forward, her voice rising. "Don't do this to her, King. Let her stay with us. She has a home here. What can you give her?"

King's hand was on the latch of the door. He never looked at Serafa; his gaze rested on Lily. His mouth twisted. Abruptly he wheeled and slammed out the back door.

Lily shouted, "King!" She tore with her fingernails at Luz's hands on her. Raul clutched at her.

"Lily. Wait. No. Lily, listen."

"Let me go!" She struck Raul, yanked her arm out of Luz's grasp, and plunged on out the door.

"Lily!"

She leaped down the steps into the yard. King was nowhere. She ran on across the yard and around the old adobe to the shed. King was standing there with his hands on the top rail of the corral, leaning on his outstretched arms, staring into nothing. She stopped.

She said, "I'm going with you."

"No, you're not," he said. He turned around, facing her. "Lily, you have to stay here."

"But I want to be with you," she said. She took a step toward him. She thought of not having him there; her belly twisted, cold. "You promised me you'd take care of me."

"I can't take care of you!" He started toward her, and she reached out to him and he caught her hands and held them away from him. He looked hard into her eyes. "Listen—you remember what I said—Life's a joke? Well, it ain't a joke, it's a test, and I failed. But I ain't lettin' that happen to you." He gave her a shake, let go of her, stepped back. "I want you to come with me more than anything in the world, Lily, but Serafa's right. I'm a rotten son of a bitch, I had my chance, and I let you down. You ought to forget about me." He went around the fence to his horse.

"Where are you going? Will I ever see you again? Are you really going to Mexico?"

"I don't know. Maybe. Maybe I'll take the steamer up to San Francisco. I'll come back. I'll send you money." But he was drawing away, disappearing into the dark.

"Please come back," she said to the empty darkness.

Her chest hurt; her eyes were bleeding. She turned woodenly back toward the cantina. Luz stood in the doorway. She went up gratefully into Luz's arms.

"This is awful," she said. "This is awful."

Luz said, "You stay here, Lily. You must stay here with us."

Raul said, "This is where you belong, lovely Lily."

She wanted to hit him. She wanted to strike out at all of them. Sinking down into a chair, she clenched her fists in her lap and stiffened herself against crying. She wasn't going to stand for this. There had to be some way to make this not happen. She fought down a great lump in her throat, struggling to swallow. They were all around her, hovering, protective, smothering.

"Leave me alone," she said, and when she saw how Luz flinched back from her, a needle of guilt stabbed her in the heart. She put her hand out. "I'm sorry, Luz. I'm sorry."

The other girl caught her hand. Josefa said, "I'll bring the brandy." She went off across the room.

Lily shut her eyes. Soon everything would stop whirling around her and settle down into place again and she would stop hurting. She heard Andrés murmur, "He robbed the Railroad office. Papa said he thought he was dangerous."

Luz said, "Not to us. To them, maybe. To the Railroad. To the Anglos."

Raul said, "He is an Anglo."

"No, he's not," Lily said. "You don't understand. You—" She stopped. Out in the street she could hear horses galloping.

A wave of foreboding washed over her. She got up. The front door crashed open and Brand strode in.

He had a shotgun in the crook of his arm. Behind him came the black-bearded bully Elmo and three other men. Lily stood where she was, her hands at her sides. Brand glared at her, scanned the room with a sweeping look, and said, "Where's the *señora*?"

Lily said, "Leave her alone. King's gone. He left." She collected herself, thrusting down her anger and her fear. She had to be careful; she had to do the right thing here.

He took two steps toward her. "Where is he?"

"I don't know."

He studied her a moment; his face was implacable. He said, "Tell me where he is, Lily. And I won't hurt anybody else."

Serafa came into the room.

As soon as she came in, she was the middle: everybody else turned and watched her. She had the black shawl wrapped around her, framing her face in its dark masses. She looked Brand over from head to toe in a single dismissive glance and turned to Lily. Her eyes were wide and sleek and steady. She said in Spanish, "What does he want?"

Lily said, "He is looking for King."

Serafa came up between the girls and the mass of men, her face turned toward Brand. She said, "Tell him that he is gone, he will never come back. Tell him they may look wherever they wish for him here."

Lily started to turn this into English, but Brand cut

her off with a jerk of his hand. He swung around toward the men. "Go around, look all over the place. If you see him, shoot him." He waved his short arm, and two of the men went out the front door, two tramped back to the rear door and out to the yard. Brand faced Serafa again.

"Tell me where he is, I'll go easy on him. I won't shoot him right off. I'll let him go to trial. Tell me where he is."

Serafa stared back at him. Lily looked at Luz and shook her head; she could not manage so much in Spanish. Taking a step closer to her mother, Luz murmured a short version of what Brand had said.

Serafa drew her head back, her chin jutting out and her mouth shut like a seam, and said nothing. Brand shifted back and forth on his feet like a reined-in horse. "I'll get him, sooner or later. When I do I'm going to hang him. If I catch him here and you haven't told me, I'll hang him from your rafter here, chile-picker."

Luz's voice abruptly stopped. Josefa moved, sidling closer to her mother and her sister. Brand's voice rose to a yell. "Tell her! Tell her that, damn it!"

Lily said, "Stop. She doesn't know where he is. You're wasting your time."

"Shut up," Brand said. He glared at her, a look like a punch. He said, "There was a man killed that night in Virginia City, girl. I've got you sixty ways on accessory to murder. Just make me angry."

Elmo and a scrawny young man tramped back into the room. "Found him yet?" The others drifted in from the back. "Anybody find him?"

"He's not here, is he?" Lily said. "We were telling you the truth."

Serafa reached out and grabbed her arm and shook her. Luz said, "Lily, be still."

Brand said, "The truth. I'll tell you the truth. Tell her, too. If I ever find out he's been here again, even for a minute, I'll tear this place down to the ground. Got that?

Tell her." His eyes blazed. "And if you see him again, I'll get you, too." He jabbed his stump at her, turned, and started toward the door.

"You bastard," she cried, furious. "You can bully women, can't you? That's easy enough."

Serafa shook Lily's arm again, harder. Brand glanced over his shoulder at her, his lip curling, and went after his men into the street.

Serafa sank down into a chair, her face haggard. Luz shut the door, her gaze shifting from Lily to Serafa and back. Her mother lifted her head.

"I should have gone with him," she said. "I should have gone with him." She pulled her shawl up over her face.

Lily twitched. She could not keep still, and she got up and went out the back door and into the cool darkness of the yard. She felt hot all over, Brand's assaults like iron rasps drawn up and down her skin. The will was rising in her, an irresistible decision coming on her like a great wave.

Raul came up beside her. "Damn the Anglos! We ought to rise up and throw them out of California!"

She said, "I know where he is. I'm going after him." She turned toward the horse shed.

Raul strode along beside her. "You can't go by yourself. I'll go too."

She said, "I'm not coming back, Raul." She circled the end of the bunkhouse and went into the corral, where Jane was dozing by the fence.

"My horse is out in the street." He reached out and clutched her arm, and when she faced him, he smiled at her. He said, "I will be worthy, Lily."

Startled, she said, "What do you mean by that?" But he was gone.

Elmo led up two more fresh horses, and he and his brother began putting their saddles on them. Brand was

sitting down with his back to the trunk of a tree. They
were waiting on a corner of the plaza; there was some
big shindig at the Pico House across the way, from
which came the sound of music and jubilant shouts, but
here it was quiet and dark, with the scrubby trees making
it darker yet.

Brand shut his eyes, trying to get some rest. He had
been up since just after dawn and no telling where this
was going to end.

Elmo said, "How much money did he get?"

Brand did not open his eyes. "Couple thousand." He
could sense the big man standing there next to him. He
decided if they ever got within reach of that money he
should keep Elmo in front of him.

"If you ask me," Elmo said, "we oughta be out scout-
in' the roads. Just sittin' here, what good is that?"

"Shut up and wait," Brand said. He folded his short
arm behind his head, his hand lying casually in his lap
near the shotgun.

Elmo shuffled around a moment. Somewhere behind
him Cale was humming off key. Over there at the Pico
House a whole lot of people whooped at once. A horse
was loping toward them.

Elmo said, "Well, I think—"

"Shut up," Brand said, and opened his eyes and stood
up. Roy trotted up to them.

"You're right. She taken off right away. One of the
greasers went with her."

Brand growled in his throat, pleased. He didn't bother
looking at Elmo. "All right. Let's ride."

King told himself he had done this all before; he had
left women before, had women throw him out, there was
always another woman, somewhere. But he could not
remember he had cared so much before.

That was because of Lily. When he thought about Lily

he hurt, deep in his chest, an old wound opening again. He was always losing somebody.

He should have seen this coming. Now he could see that, all the while, things could only have happened this way. But his idea had seemed so reasonable at the time.

He should have known she would never leave Los Angeles. And she should have known that he couldn't stay.

He followed the road down out of town, keeping the horse to an easy lope. The sorrel was fresh and fit and would get him down to the ocean before sunrise. Then he would make up his mind what to do. He had other places he could go. Other people he knew. He had a lot of things he could do. He always had another chance.

The leaden feeling dragged at him. A sense of things closing down on him. Chances fading out. He saw, suddenly, his life dwindling off before him, a succession of leavings, each time more lonely.

He struggled to push that away from him. This was just one more bad dream; in a few days he would forget it. He had already left the city behind. He moved off the road, cutting south through the fields and orchards to pick up the trail to the beach where he had stayed with Lily. The mail sack with the money hung over the front of his saddle. He reached down and patted it. At least he had the money.

He should have left some of it with Serafa. With Lily. Except Brand would have found it and used it against them.

His mood plunged again. He tainted everything he touched. He ruined everything.

He let the horse pick its way across the bed of the river, dry after the long summer, a wide stream of sand and gravel tufted with willow saplings. The moon was rising, a half-open eye. The wind harped in the long grass of the river's far bank and he gigged the horse up onto the meadowland and at a soft trot moved on south.

He dozed a few times; the sorrel carried him on. The

night lengthened. He stopped once and drank the last of his water and ate the food he had with him.

Soon after he rode down into the arroyo, he realized somebody was coming after him.

Whoever it was made no effort to be quiet. He reined the sorrel off to one side of the wash and circled back a hundred yards around a big patch of storm-drifted wood. Two horses were trotting fast down the arroyo toward him. He reached up under his arm for the .46, and then the sorrel under him swelled up with breath and gave a great blast of a whinny.

He swore; he pulled the gun out, but one of the oncoming horses answered, and he recognized the voice of Lily's mare Jane.

He leaped forward, unthinking, spurring the horse in a bound over a mass of tangled brush. Up there Lily gave a yell. They rushed together, their horses shoulder to shoulder, and he reached out and she was in his arms, laughing.

"I knew I'd find you," she said. "I knew you'd come here."

King held her, his face against her hair. "God, Lily," he said. "I missed you so much." Beyond her, waiting, was the ranchero's son Raul, looking glum.

King said, "Hello, Raul," and the boy lifted his hand in a desultory wave.

Lily drew back into her saddle, smiling at him. He could make her face out in the gloom; day was coming. He said, "What the hell are you doing?"

"I'm going with you," she said. "Raul too. We'll be good, we promise."

He gave Raul an instant's glance and forgot him. Turned his eyes on Lily again. "Does Serafa know?"

The girl shrugged. She braced her hands on her saddlebows; she looked tired, smiling, her eyes direct and sleepy. She said, "I think she wishes she'd gone with you too."

"Well," he said, "it's too late now." Then his sorrel

horse lifted its head, its ears pricked, looking back up the way they had come, and from out there the wind carried a sound into his ears, the clink of an iron shoe on a stone.

He lifted his reins. "Somebody's out there."

Lily twisted in her saddle, looking back, and Raul nudged his horse up. "I thought I heard something—before—"

"Damn," King said. Standing in his stirrups, he swept his gaze over the plain.

The sky was turning pale, but the land lay tangled in shadows. Up beyond the arroyo bank he could see something moving. "Fifty to one it's Brand."

Lily swung toward him, dismayed. "They must have followed us."

King shook his head at her. "You have a lot to learn, darlin'."

"I'm sorry," she said. "What should I do?"

He drew the .46 out of the holster under his arm. "Here. Go on ahead. Up where the arroyo gives out onto the beach there's a little rise and a clump of brush. Wait there, cover me getting across the arroyo."

She took the gun. "What are you going to do?"

"I'll slow 'em up. Do what I tell you." He reined past her, toward the shelter of the bank of the arroyo, where the night still hung like a black tent.

She and Raul galloped on, making a lot of noise. King drew his other gun. Up a hundred feet into the arroyo, the bank had caved in, half filling the wash with sand and rock, and pinching the trail down against the bank; Brand would have to come that way.

His blood sang: he had Lily back. He would make a new start after this; he would get it done right this time.

The horse sighed under him, tired. He swung his right leg across his saddlebows, slid down to the ground, and began to creep up closer toward the trail. He could shoot a couple of the horses and stop them that way, but if he killed Brand, he would stop them forever.

The daylight grew steadily stronger. Now he could hear horses moving down the arroyo, enough of them that on the narrow path they got in each other's way, their stirrups knocking, their voices in low growls warning each other off. A light wind picked up, flavored with the tangy smell of the chaparral. Somebody said, "Damn!" Then into sight through the narrow gap between the sandy bank and the tangled driftwood a horse trotted, another right behind.

That second rider was Brand.

King pulled the trigger, almost without thinking; the first horse went down like a felled tree across the trail. The second rider wheeled his horse around, but the men coming after blocked his way out. King raised the pistol and shot twice into the plunging mass of bodies.

He heard one bullet wail off a rock, but he knew he hit something with the other. They were yelling, fighting each other to get out of his way. A surge of triumph coursed through him, hot like lust, tingling in his hands and his belly. He dashed forward, ducking down behind the brush, shot once more to keep them worried, and angled over to get another try at Brand. Two of the horses were down, one thrashing. A volley of wild shots rang out, aimed at nothing. The men were scrambling and stumbling back up the arroyo and he could see two of them helping one who was hurt. They were pulling back out of reach, out of sight. He darted out across the open floor of the arroyo toward the cover on the other side, to get one more shot at Brand.

Something struck him in the back, knocked him facedown into the sand. An instant later he heard the report of a long gun. He couldn't breathe. Somebody was bellowing, somewhere. He was drilled through; there was blood all over his chest. There seemed a heavy weight on his back, a heavy spreading weight holding him down.

Lily, he thought. Lily.

He had two more shots in his gun: let them come to

him. He coughed. His mouth filled up with blood. He wasn't going to last very long. Lily, he thought. Lily.

Lily was so tired her legs shook; but now that she had found King again, everything would be all right. He would figure out what to do next. She led Raul out onto the broad white apron of sand at the mouth of the arroyo. The wind was rising strong off the land, sweeping out toward the ocean where it pounded blue and white along the beach. She saw the hillock he meant, massed with brush, and reined the mare toward it, turning to wave to Raul.

Up the arroyo, two shots rang out.

She pulled the mare to a stop; Raul rode up beside her. "There!" he cried, pointing toward the hillock. "There!"

"Wait," she said, turning to look back. Up in the arroyo there was another shot. She thought all those came from King's leg-iron. He would be coming now, he would be right now galloping down toward them, with Brand maybe on his heels. She reached around to her saddlebag, took out the .46, and shortened her grip on her reins.

More shots, from different guns. No sign of King. Something was wrong. She said, "He's trapped," and wheeled the mare and galloped back into the arroyo.

"Lily!" Raul shouted behind her. "Lily, wait!"

One-handed, she sent the mare at a dead run up across the broad flat sand, toward the high narrowing banks, where the mass of driftwood choked the ravine, in her free hand she gripped the revolver. More shots blasted, up ahead of her, and then she heard a harsh shriek of triumph that stood every nerve in her body on end.

"Got him!"

She yanked the mare to a skidding halt. There on the black bank before her a human shape suddenly rose up against the sky, the straight black line of a rifle barrel jutting from its crooked arms.

The rifle barrel jerked around, aiming down into the arroyo up ahead, and she knew it was aiming at King. She jerked the .46 up with both hands, put the front sight square on the man on the bank, and pulled the trigger. The recoil threw her fists with the gun up and back and she let her hands drop again right back into line and shot again, and the black shape toppled forward into the tangle of brush and driftwood.

She bounded down from her horse. The crash of the shots seemed to die away slowly, as if the low little wind carried them off. She dashed around the driftwood heap, watching the bank above her and also the arroyo beyond the tangle of limbs and grass and roots. The man she had shot hung suspended in the midst of the great drift, snagged on the branches; she saw he was black-bearded Elmo. Then on the ground beyond, she saw King.

He was sprawled across the blank moonlit sand, on his face; on the white sand a great black stain was spreading away from him. She sobbed. He was dead. She was too late. There was no sign of Brand, no sign of anyone but King and Elmo. She went across the sand to him and knelt down and laid one hand on his shoulder.

She almost shouted. He was alive. He stirred under her touch. She gripped his shoulders and he rolled heavily over, his head wobbling.

He said, "Careful. Somebody up there," his voice slurring.

"Elmo. I got him." She pulled his arm over her shoulders. "Come on. Hurry." His feet moved, and he dragged himself upright, leaning most of his weight on her. They staggered off down the sand. In the shelter of the driftwood heap she let him down again. His blood covered her, a slime all over her arms, her shirt soaked through. Looking back, she saw the short way they had come marked with great splatters and pools.

She straightened, looking as far as she could up the trail, and then turned and swept her gaze all around. There was no sound but the steady distant rolling of the surf, the cries of seagulls. She stooped down by King.

"I'll go get your horse."

"Don't bother," he said. He lay on his back, his head a little to one side, at an awkward angle; she saw he had no strength to straighten his body out. He said, "Take care of yourself, Lily," and smiled at her. Blood leaked out of his mouth. His eyes fluttered and he died.

"King," she said.

Silence. She turned to look up the trail again. A white rage boiled up into her skull. She had dropped the .46 back up there on the sand, and she ran over and picked it up.

She would kill Brand for this; she would shoot him a hundred times, shoot him to pieces, feed the pieces to dogs. She trotted back to the shelter of the driftwood heap. Raul was coming with King's sorrel horse and Jane, leading them by the reins. She stood beside King's body, looking up the trail. Pulling out the tail of her shirt, she found a dry place on the cloth and wiped the blood off her hand.

Brand would come here, eventually. She would be waiting.

Raul said, "Lily. Listen to me. It's him they want. We can go, we aren't important, they won't even care. Nobody will ever have to know."

"Go, if you want," she said, her gaze steady on the place where Brand must appear.

Raul lingered only a moment. She sensed him there behind her, but he said nothing more. He got on his horse and rode away out to the beach.

She sank down on her heels next to King and put her hand on him. She was frozen into this one moment. The cry of a seagull startled her, and she looked up, surprised to see the bird wheeling free through the sky, when all the world was dead.

"What do I do now?" she said.

He had to hear her. He had to answer. She could not leave him. He was still there, she could not leave him for Brand to drag him around, surely he was still in there, somewhere.

A wash of guilt broke over her. She had brought him to this. If she had let him kill Brand back on the Virginia City road he would still be alive. Looking back, she saw now how he had bent, changed his ways, all for her sake, and that had gotten him killed.

He had lived like a fox, wild and ruthless, invulnerable, until he found her. That was the real risk, loving someone.

She looked up the arroyo again. Brand was not coming. Maybe he and his crew were too shot up to fight anymore. She fingered King's shirt. "You did for him, you know. You always did win. Fox over the hound, anytime." Her eyes hurt. "King," she said. "Please don't go. Please."

Her own voice jarred her. A child's voice, crying for her father.

She had to grow up now, right now; she was alone. She had to take care of herself. Yet she could not bring herself to go.

The rising sun brightened the sand of the arroyo; she could see his tracks across it. She saw where his horse had been, in the shelter of the bank. Nothing had trapped him. He had run forward on the trail, up the arroyo, to where he had been shot. She made herself see that he had not died for her sake, but because he had wanted to shoot Brand.

Now here she was, waiting to shoot Brand.

She looked down at the gun in her hand. She had already killed one man today; she decided maybe she should find out how that fit before she did it again.

She felt the world heave forward again, grind into motion on down the track. What had he said? "Take care." Listen to him, then. She had to get out of here.

She put her hand on his body again. She could not even bury him.

This was not him, this was just another joke, a false King, to fool Brand.

She stood up, looking around her. The two horses were nibbling at stray blades of grass growing in the sand. She would take the sorrel gelding; she would need its speed and stamina, and she could learn to manage him. She went to Jane and peeled off her saddle and bridle and dumped them. Have a grand old time, Jane. The mare did not go anywhere, did not know yet she was free. Lily turned to the sorrel.

When she picked up the reins, she saw the mail sack.

That was the money.

She pulled the mail sack off and dumped it next to King's body. More of the joke. As if this mattered. Let Brand have it, who wouldn't even get to spend it. She would find some other way to live, a better way, a new way, her own way. One that wasn't King's killing and dying, or Serafa's pretending to be free and then knuckling under. Lily would have a single-hearted, honest, forthright life.

She had left her books behind, which she would miss more than the gold; but she would get other books. She would go to San Francisco, where certainly she would find books.

She kept the gun.

The sorrel shifted its feet when she mounted it. Tired as it was, it danced under her, its mouth chattering the bit; she knew the least touch on the reins, the slightest tilt of her weight, would send it bolting. She felt naked. Her life spread out before her like the white beach, which the tide had swept clean. She lifted the reins, and the sorrel burst into a gallop, carrying her away, and she let it bear her a long distance before she even tried to take control.

Brand's left arm was broken. He had strapped it to his side, but he was still bleeding; his knees wobbled when he walked. He sent Elijah, the only man of them not wounded or dead, up to Wilmington for help. Leaving Cale to nurse his bad leg, Brand circled around along the upper edge of the arroyo, fighting his way through the tarry chaparral until he could see King sprawled on the ground there, lying in a great pool of blood.

His muscles slackened; he sat down heavily on the bank of the arroyo. His strength was gone and now his will paid out also. He had wanted King alive. He had wanted to look him in the eyes and say, "I beat you. I brought you in to hang."

For a while he sat there slumped on the arroyo bank. Turning his head, he could see Elmo's body half buried in dead branches and twisted clumps of dry grass where it had plunged down into the wash. He saw that King had not shot Elmo. Nor gotten where he was now on his own. Brand recognized the old mare standing half asleep over in the sun; he could see two lines of tracks leading away over the beach.

One line went south, the other north. He wondered which was hers. Holding his throbbing arm against his side, he struggled to his feet and looked out over the land as far as he could. He thought at the edge of his vision, far to the north, he could see her, a shadow in the sunlit haze, but he wasn't sure, and he wasn't strong enough yet to follow. He sat down again, staring into the distance as far as his eyes could reach, keeping hold on her with his eyes.

Available by mail from

**TOR
FORGE**

1812 • David Nevin
The War of 1812 would either make America a global power sweeping to the pacific or break it into small pieces bound to mighty England. Only the courage of James Madison, Andrew Jackson, and their wives could determine the nation's fate.

PRIDE OF LIONS • Morgan Llywelyn
Pride of Lions, the sequel to the immensely popular *Lion of Ireland,* is a stunningly realistic novel of the dreams and bloodshed, passion and treachery, of eleventh-century Ireland and its lusty people.

WALTZING IN RAGTIME • Eileen Charbonneau
The daughter of a lumber baron is struggling to make it as a journalist in turn-of-the-century San Francisco when she meets ranger Matthew Hart, whose passion for nature challenges her deepest held beliefs.

BUFFALO SOLDIERS • Tom Willard
Former slaves had proven they could fight valiantly for their freedom, but in the West they were to fight for the freedom and security of the white settlers who often despised them.

THIN MOON AND COLD MIST • Kathleen O'Neal Gear
Robin Heatherton, a spy for the Confederacy, flees with her son to the Colorado Territory, hoping to escape from Union Army Major Corley, obsessed with her ever since her espionage work led to the death of his brother.

SEMINOLE SONG • Vella Munn
"As the U.S. Army surrounds their reservation in the Florida Everglades, a Seminole warrior chief clings to the slave girl who once saved his life after fleeing from her master, a wife-murderer who is out for blood." —*Hot Picks*

THE OVERLAND TRAIL • Wendi Lee
Based on the authentic diaries of the women who crossed the country in the late 1840s. America, a widowed pioneer, and Dancing Feather, a young Paiute, set out to recover America's kidnapped infant daughter—and to forge a bridge between their two worlds.

Available by mail from

TOR FORGE

THIN MOON AND COLD MIST • Kathleen O'Neal Gear

Robin Heatherton, a spy for the Confederacy, flees with her son to the Colorado Territory, hoping to escape from Union Army Major Corley, obsessed with her ever since her espionage work led to the death of his brother.

SOFIA • Ann Chamberlin

Sofia, the daughter of a Venetian nobleman, is kidnapped and sold into captivity of the great Ottoman Empire. Manipulative and ambitious, Sofia vows that her future will hold more than sexual slavery in the Sultan's harem. A novel rich in passion, history, humor, and human experience, *Sofia* transports the reader to sixteenth-century Turkish harem life.

MIRAGE • Soheir Khashoggi

"A riveting first novel.... Exotic settings, glamorous characters, and a fast-moving plot. Like a modern Scheherazade, Khashoggi spins an irresistible tale.... An intelligent page-turner." —*Kirkus Reviews*

DEATH COMES AS EPIPHANY • Sharan Newman

In medieval Paris, amid stolen gems, mad monks, and dead bodies, Catherine LeVendeur will strive to unlock a puzzle that threatens all she holds dear. "Breathtakingly exciting." —*Los Angeles Times*

SHARDS OF EMPIRE • Susan Shwartz

A rich tale of madness and magic—"*Shards of Empire* is a beautifully written historical.... An original and witty delight!" —*Locus*

SCANDAL • Joanna Elm

When former talk show diva Marina Dee Haley is found dead, TV tabloid reporter Kitty Fitzgerald is compelled to break open the "Murder of the Century," even if it means exposing her own dubious past.

BILLY THE KID • Elizabeth Fackler

Billy's story, epic in scope, echoes the vast grandeur of the magnificent country in which he lived. It traces the chain of events that inexorably shaped this legendary outlaw and pitted him against a treacherous society that threatened those he loved."